Having left school at 15 due to deteriorating eyesight, which was gradually corrected, Julie entered the Royal College of Music, where she gained her associateship on oboe and piano.

Julie continued as a music teacher, also gaining a London University degree in English and history. Her early life in East London has been a constant inspiration to her historical research.

To Lucy and Justin
Thank you for all
the love you spread
in the world.

Julie

I would like to dedicate this book to my long-suffering husband who patiently puts up with my many mood swings and is my constant encouragement and delight.

Julie Roxburgh

Gertie and Amos

AUSTIN MACAULEY PUBLISHERS™
LONDON * CAMBRIDGE * NEW YORK * SHARJAH

A CIP catalogue record for this title is available from the British Library.

ISBN 9781398401679 (Paperback)
ISBN 9781398401686 (ePub e-book)

www.austinmacauley.com

First Published 2022
Austin Macauley Publishers Ltd®
1 Canada Square
Canary Wharf
London
E14 5AA

Chapter One

The bell tolled to tell them it was time to rise. Gertie pushed off the filthy, ragged blanket and climbed out of the rusty metal bed which she shared with Alice and Ruth. The three little girls made their way silently to the workhouse dining hall where the matron stood with folded arms, waiting to strike anyone who had the temerity to speak.

Gertie was cold; that was nothing new. She was hungry too. That was nothing new either. She had lived all her five years in this stark comfortless building and as far as she was concerned it was home. She had been taken from her mother as soon as she was weaned and that was the last she had ever seen of her. They told her she had died.

"...and a good thing too, bringing a fatherless, little heathen into a decent, God-fearing institution, to be thrown on the goodness of the parishioners. You are beholden to your betters, the honest folk of this parish and don't you forget it!"

So they all reminded her. Gertie was never likely to forget it since it was drummed into her almost every day of life. Although she had no idea what she had done, she thought it must have been something terrible, and she lived with a sense of guilt and dread that she would go to hell and burn forever for her sins. It seemed that no matter how hard she tried to be good, there was no escape. At least, that's what Mr Pidmore, the vicar, said when he came to take the services. Twice on Sundays and every Thursday evening, they were herded into the chapel beside the ugly red brick workhouse building, and there they were warned in dreary monotony that there was no hiding from God's wrath. The vicar said that a man called Amos had told him all about what God would do when He was angry with people. He said God would 'slay with the sword; not one of them shall escape'. Even if they tried to dig a hole to hide in, or climb a mountain, God would find them and punish them and make a serpent bite them. Mr Pidmore also said that God would visit the sins of the fathers on the sons, or, Gertie supposed, in her case, the mother on the daughter. It seemed a bit unfair, as Gertie didn't know what she or her mother had done to deserve such punishment. Perhaps she could find this man Amos and ask him. She was too scared of Mr Pidmore to ask him!

Breakfast was a silent, dismal affair. Unsweetened porridge, little more than a couple of spoonfuls, and a half tankard of watered ale was the usual ration. The men sat at a long table down one side of the room and the women on the other. The children sat at either end; girls separate from the boys. A long grace was said before and after the meal and then, under the constantly baleful eye of the matron and her assistants, everyone filed out, once more in silence. Gertie and her companions all went to a long room at the end of a cold flag-stone passage, and there they sat, whispering when they dared, mending blankets and sewing patches on ancient, worn garments, while one of the 'charity' ladies read stories to them from the Bible or other improving works. Gertie would soon be going to the workhouse school and she thought this would be exciting. Apart from going to the chapel, she had hardly ever been out of the main building and its depressing acre of grass before, and she couldn't wait for the time when she and her best friends would be allowed to put on fresh, clean aprons, tie a pretty brown bonnet over her dark curls and march with the big girls out of the front door and right down to the end of the lane to the 'poor' school. She would work hard and learn many things and then she would know what to say to Amos when she found him. And perhaps one day, if she was really clever, she could go to London and ask the Queen all about God and what to do about these terrible sins of hers. After all, the Queen would know if anyone did!

It was two years since the beautiful girl in the picture that hung in the dining hall had been made Queen. Gertie vaguely remembered that day a year later when they had all been given clean clothes and there had been some rather ancient-looking flags hung about the passages and main rooms. Later on they had lined up in the street outside to watch a great procession of people waving banners and playing instruments. Everyone had cheered loudly. That evening they had all been given an extra helping of meat at supper and then they had to stand up and ask God to bless the Queen. Gertie heard whispers that things would be better now this kind lady was on the throne, but so far nothing much had changed in the workhouse. Perhaps it took a long time to put things right, even if you were Queen. Or perhaps this lady, Queen Victoria, didn't know about poor people and how they lived. After all, if you live in a palace (not that Gertie knew what a palace was like, but it sounded wonderful) with lots to eat and fires everywhere, you wouldn't want to go trudging about looking for miserable places like workhouses. Gertie decided that, when she had learned to read and write, she would send a letter to the Queen telling her all about what life was like for poor people and then she would know and be able to do something about it.

"Gertrude Thomas, you are day-dreaming again. The good people of this parish do not work hard in order to support wicked, idle little girls. Bread and water for you for the rest of the day, my girl!"

The matron's voice, loud and angry, broke into Gertie's dreams, but she was used to such scolding and only said, "Yes matron, sorry matron," and got on with her work. It was not long now. As soon as she could read and write, she would tell the Queen all about how miserable life was for people such as her. And then everyone would rise up in horror and condemn matron to bread and water as a suitable punishment for being so cruel.

But she, Gertie, would say, "No, I forgive you. I cannot see even my enemies suffer." And then they would all cheer and give her lots of sweetmeats and she would never be cold or hungry ever again.

++++++++++

Gertie started school that Autumn. On her first day, she clung tightly to Alice's hand as they tramped through a fine, cold rain to the new building, only a year old, that had been built for the poor children of the parish. It was called the National School. Gertie and her companions went in at a door marked 'Girls', and then they all had to line up in the yard until, at the ringing of a bell, a teacher ushered them into a long class-room lined all the way down with benches. The benches were tiered, the big girls sitting at the back on one side, the boys on the other. Gertie and her friends sat right in the front on the girls' side. After prayers were said, the teacher, her kind, thin face almost hidden behind thick, ugly spectacles, sat at a large wooden table and beside her was a black board on an easel. One of the big girls handed a slate and slate pencil to each child, and then all was quiet while the little ones copied their letters from the top of the board and the older children practised their neatest writing. The big girls and boys took it in turns to read from a book and this seemed to be all about the different countries of the world. Gertie learnt later that this was called a geography lesson.

At midday, a bell went, and it was time for the children to go back to the workhouse. Miss Tiffen, the teacher, had praised Gertie's work, had not raised her voice once, and had even handed out biscuits to everyone during the mid-morning break. Gertie knew that she was going to love school.

++++++++++

By the time she was eight, Gertie could read and write very well. She was one of the star pupils at the school and had moved back on to the middle benches. Now she was learning how to do sums as well as proper needlework, not just sewing on patches as she had to do at the workhouse. But the more she was praised at school, the more she seemed to be scolded and disliked by the matron. She was often put on bread and water and sometimes even made to sit in a dark, little room all by herself for hours on end. At these times, Gertie realised that she could day-dream as much as she liked, and she began to imagine a world where no one went cold or hungry. It must be possible to make sure that there was enough food for everyone. But she couldn't do this all by herself! She needed help, and a grown-up who knew how to set about making the world a more comfortable place to live in. She determined that now was the time to write to the Queen. But then she realised with a terrible shock that she had no paper and no pen or ink. How could she get these things? Perhaps Miss Tiffen would know.

The day after one of her lonely vigils in the little cell, she went to school full of excitement. She would speak to Miss Tiffin during the play period and explain her plans. But when the children arrived at the school there was a further shock awaiting Gertie. Miss Tiffen had gone! It seemed her mother had been taken ill suddenly and the teacher had to leave immediately to look after her. Mr Pidmore stood in her place, his stern, grim features stirring fear in the hearts of even the sturdiest lads. Everyone stood in silence and Gertie could hear her heart pounding so loudly that she was sure Mr Pidmore would reprimand her. But he only said:

"Let us pray for Miss Tiffen's poor, stricken parent and for our own souls, steeped in sin and wickedness as they are."

Then he droned on about how terrible they all were and how God would punish them however hard they tried to hide. Gertie remembered Amos and wondered how she could contact him. Goodness, there were so many problems to solve and now here was Mr Pidmore commanding her to recite her times tables. She knew up to ten times quite well, but when she stumbled on eleven elevens he glared at her for a moment then told her to sit down. One of the older girls was able to finish them and after that Mr Pidmore began telling them about some people who lived in a land called Africa, which was far away. Mr Pidmore had gone all the way there to tell these people about Jesus as they had never heard of him. When he wasn't saying prayers, the vicar made his travels sound very interesting. Gertie was spellbound. She could see the sun-drenched land and hear the children laughing, warm and happy. In a hot country like that she thought that food would grow just everywhere, so no one would be cold or hungry. *At least she didn't have to worry about them*, she thought. She wondered why everyone didn't go and live there. Perhaps there wasn't enough room, although Mr Pidmore said that it was a very big country, ever so much bigger than England, it sounded.

During the short play time, Gertie always stood by the low wall that divided the girls from the boys. She thought the boys' games much jollier than the silly ones that the girls played, and she wished with all her heart that she had been born a boy. They seemed so much more carefree and laughed more than the pale, fragile little girls that she was expected to look after.

The day that Miss Tiffen left, Gertie was standing by the wall as usual when one of the big boys came over to her. He looked about eleven years old, and he was tall and strong, with dark brown eyes and hair that stood up in untidy tufts. His face was smeared with dirt from some game he had been playing, but he smiled at Gertie and said:

"Hello, little'un. You often stand here, don't you? What's your name?"

Gertie smiled back but looked round apprehensively. It would be the cane if she was seen talking to a boy.

"Gertie. What's yours?" she whispered.

"Oh, my name's Amos. Where do you live?"

Gertie's heart gave a leap. "Amos?" she almost shouted. "I've been wanting to meet you ever since Mr Pidmore told us about you, but I thought you were grown up!"

The boy looked puzzled. Then he laughed and his teeth were white and even in his grubby face.

"You're thinking of the man in the Bible. I was named after him. He died hundreds of years ago. Why do you want to meet him?"

Gertie's heart sank again. So the one person she had pinned her hopes on was dead! That only left the Queen. But perhaps this Amos could help her. He seemed kind and rather jolly, so she decided to confide in him. She looked round again. No one was watching.

"Well, you see, I was born in the workhouse and everyone there keeps telling me how wicked I am, but I don't know what I have done and so I can't repent my sins, which is what Mr Pidmore says we must do."

She went on to explain all about Amos and the Queen and how she wanted to contact them.

"But Amos is dead, and I haven't any paper or a pen and I don't know what to do." She suddenly felt that she must seem like a silly, little girl to this big boy, but Amos didn't laugh. Instead he nodded seriously and said:

"I live in the workhouse as well. I haven't been there long, which is probably why we haven't seen each other. I think your idea of writing to the Queen is a very good one. How brave are you?"

"I don't know. Why?"

"Well, I have a plan." And as he told her his idea Gertie's eyes grew round as saucers.

That night, as soon as everyone had gone to bed and all the candles were extinguished, Gertie lay listening to the footsteps of Matron dying away in the distance. Her heart was thumping again, and she felt sick with fear, but she couldn't let Amos down now. What would he think of her if she didn't follow his plan? He would probably never speak to her ever again. Alice lay breathing evenly beside her, Ruth having grown too big to share their bed, so Gertie slid silently out of bed and crept along the dormitory, feeling her way gingerly in the semi-darkness, only the light of a half-moon helping her not to bump into beds and partitions. She found the door. Suppose it was locked? But she turned the great brass doorknob and it pulled open quite silently. Amos was waiting for her outside with a lighted candle.

"Where did you get that?" she whispered loudly.

"Sh. You'll wake the dead! Just keep quiet and follow me."

They crept along the gloomy passage and down the stairs to the first floor. At the end of another passage Amos stopped at a door and listened. All was silent. He tried the door, but it was locked. Then from his pocket he produced a strange-looking key.

"My dad's." He grinned. "Part of his 'professional' equipment! He was a thief and died last year in prison." The key unlocked the door with a little click, and they slipped quickly into the room. It was the Matron's parlour. Amos went over to a desk in the corner and looked carefully in one of the drawers. It was empty except for a small bottle of gin and a dirty glass. He tried the next drawer and the next and at last there were pen, ink and paper. He picked them up and handed them to Gertie who was shaking with cold and fear. But no one came, and they crept out of the room, locked the door once more and made their way back to Gertie's dormitory. Amos gave her a hug.

"Good girl. Now the rest is up to you. See you tomorrow." And before she could say anything he was gone, only the candle casting strange shadows as he disappeared down the corridor and into the boys' wing. Gertie hid the paper, pen and ink in a little hole under the window ledge, her own special hiding place, and snuggled down beside Alice. *Well*, she thought, *she may not be able to meet the Amos from the Bible, but this one was a very good substitute.* She slept.

Chapter Two

The letter was written at last. In her very best writing, and with hardly a blot, at least none that the Queen would notice, with the pen working with very little need of mending to the end of the letter, Gertie had described what her life was like in the workhouse; how she knew she was wicked because everyone said so, although she didn't know what she had done, and how she had worked hard for three years so that she could learn to write to the Queen. Starting the letter had been the most difficult bit. What did you call the Queen? 'Dear Majesty?' 'Dear Queen?' or even 'Dear Victoria?'. In the end she had decided that 'Dear Queen Victoria' sounded best.

It had taken Gertie many days to complete the letter. Hiding pen, ink and paper in her pinafore, she was terrified that the ink would leak out and leave tell-tale marks. Goodness knew what would happen to her if she was found out for stealing! Each play time she sat by the wall in the school yard, hidden behind an old tree stump and added a few lines as carefully as she could. But at last she felt that she had told the queen everything she could think of. And then came the problem of how to end the letter. Finally, throwing all caution to the winds, she wrote:

'Love, Gertie.'

And underneath:

'GERTRUDE THOMAS, aged 8 years
Workhouse, Plumstead, in Kent'

Amos had given her lots of help and encouragement, whispering to her over the wall as she sat writing by the tree stump, and even mending her pen a couple of times. When the letter was finished, she had shown it to him. He said it was 'first rate' and that he was proud of her.

"One day you'll show us all, Gertie Thomas," he had said. She glowed with pleasure and determined to live up to his praise no matter what she had to endure in the process. *Let them torture me, or throw me in the deepest dungeon, with Amos' help I will change the world*, she decided.

Then they both realized that there was another problem. How were they to get the letter to the Queen? Gertie would just have to hold on to it until they thought of something. They managed to return the pen and paper to matron's study without being caught and surprisingly she seemed not to have noticed that anything had gone missing. Gertie supposed that matron didn't write many letters!

After a few weeks a new teacher was appointed to the school. She was young and pretty and Mr Pidmore was very nice to her, introducing her to the class in a voice that made Gertie shiver for some reason. Amos managed to catch her eye and he grinned at her. She turned away quickly; girls and boys weren't even allowed to look at each other without being punished. She supposed vaguely that that was why she hadn't noticed him before their first meeting.

Miss Rosemead proved to be just as kind and understanding as Miss Tiffen had been. She praised good work, smiled when she said, 'good morning', and seldom used the cane and even then didn't really hurt anyone. Mornings once more became Gertie's happiest times. She decided that Miss Rosemead would be just the person to help her to carry out the plan, so, on a warm spring day, the little girl carefully hid her precious letter in the pocket of her pinafore and walked excitedly to school with her friends. She knew exactly what she would say to Miss Rosemead and couldn't wait for play time.

The morning seemed to go very slowly, but at last, at ten thirty, they put down their slates and began filing out of the two doors into separate playgrounds. Gertie waited until everyone had gone, and then, her mouth dry and her legs shaking, she walked bravely up to the teacher. Miss Rosemead looked surprised, but said in a kind enough voice,

"Yes, Gertrude, what do you want?"

"Please, Miss," said Gertie, curtsying nervously, "I need to send a letter and I don't know how…"

The young teacher smiled and said,

"Well, first of all, you must seal the letter and write the directions on the outside. Then you must either get someone to frank it for you, or you must go to the post yourself. You will have to pay a penny to send it."

Gertie was dismayed. She had never owned a penny in her life! But she wasn't going to be stopped by such a minor consideration, so she went on boldly.

"Can you frank it for me, Miss Rosemead?"

"Oh, no." Laughed the teacher. "Only people of rank can do that. But if you give it to me I can post it for you. May I ask who you are writing to?"

Gertie handed the precious letter over to Miss Rosemead and watched anxiously as the teacher read it through. Would she laugh at her or be angry? But the young woman did neither of those things. Instead she produced a small kerchief from her reticule and blew her nose rather firmly. Then she took Gertie's hand very gently and said in a rather husky voice,

"And are all these things that you have written true?"

Gertie swallowed. She hoped that she hadn't made any of it up. She didn't think she had.

"Yes, Miss. I have told the Queen everything as best I can. You see, there are still lots of things I don't understand, but I don't think I have lied. We are cold and hungry most of the time and everyone is always cross with us, although we don't know why. Alice and Ruth say the same and so do the other girls I have spoken to." She didn't mention Amos, as even this kind lady might not be too please if she knew that Gertie talked to boys!

"And so, you see, I thought that if the Queen knew what it was like to be poor, then she could make a law to say that everyone must be warm and have enough to eat. She can't do anything if nobody tells her about it!"

And then, to Gertie's surprise and no small embarrassment, Miss Rosemead hugged the child, stroking her hair and crooning over her. Gertie didn't dare move in case the teacher's mood altered and she turned cross. In her experience, grown-ups tended to change from kindness to anger in a moment. But just as she thought she was going to suffocate, the teacher unclasped her and said,

"I will post your letter for you, Gertrude. It will be our secret; between just you and me! How exciting it will be to await an answer. Only think, if Her Majesty were to reply in person! Now go and sit down dear, as it is time to continue lessons."

Gertie returned to her bench as the other children began to file in. Her mind was in a turmoil. She wasn't sure that she really wanted all this hugging and nose-blowing over her letter, nor did she want it to be Miss Rosemead's special secret. It belonged to her – her and Amos. Were grown-ups always like this, taking over and making such a fuss over everything? She sighed. Well, it was done now and there was no going back. She would just have to see what happened when the Queen replied.

++++++++++

Amos was really pleased when Gertie told him about how Miss Rosemead had promised to send the letter. Gertie didn't tell him about the 'huggy' bits or that it was to be a special secret between her and the teacher. She thought it best just to tell him that the letter was to be sent.

The waiting seemed like years. Days passed and then weeks; one week, two, until Gertie began to wonder whether Miss Rosemead had really sent the letter. And then, one day, about a month after Miss Rosemead had made her promise, there was a great to-do in the workhouse. Gertie was just about to set out for the schoolhouse when matron burst into the hall shouting Gertie's name and brandishing a piece of paper.

"Gertrude! Gertrude Thomas, what is the meaning of this?" she thundered.

Gertrude froze. In all the time she had been waiting and during all the excitement of writing the letter and posting it, it had never occurred to her that, of course, a reply would be directed to her personally, at the workhouse. But it was unheard of for the inmates to receive correspondence, and matron opened everything. *What had she been thinking of, and why hadn't she directed it to the school?* She stood trembling as everyone waited in breathless silence while the Matron descended on her like a great fiery dragon.

"You wicked, wicked girl, what stories have you been telling and who gave you permission to write letters? And letters to her most gracious Majesty! How dare you waste the time of such great and important people with your lies, you silly, insignificant, little orphan girl. You shall be whipped and locked away. You should be sent to an asylum; you must be a lunatic!"

The matron's eyes were almost popping out of their sockets and her voice had risen to screaming pitch as her face turned from red to purple. Gertie thought with alarm that she was going to have a fit, but then came the awful words:

"COME WITH ME!"

Gertie was dragged out of the line of gaping girls and almost thrown into matron's office. The door slammed shut and there they were alone together and facing one another, the ogre and the little girl. Fear, hatred and fury gripped Gertie as she stared at this dreadful woman, but in spite of being almost overwhelmed by her situation, she stood her ground. *After all*, said a still small voice trying to make itself heard through her fear, *hadn't she only written the truth*? And since matron knew all about it, the Queen must have replied. No one had the right to pry into her private affairs, not even matron. So, to the amazement and consternation of both of them, she whispered in a tiny voice:

"It's mine! The letter is mine! You had no right to read it; it was directed to me. Please give it to me!"

As Gertie, trembling with fear, put out her hand to take the letter, the matron sat plump down on a chair and began fanning her face with a kerchief, blessing herself and asking what she had done to deserve such an ungrateful wretch to be put in her charge. But it was clear that the truth was beginning to dawn on her. The letter was indeed directed to Gertrude. By punishing the child, she would only seem to prove what Gertrude had apparently stated in her letter. Lies, of course, all lies, but the people loved a scandal and if all this should become public knowledge... She glared malevolently at Gertrude, but then her face broke into a horrible smile and she spoke in soft, silky tones:

"You must, of course, be given your property. But when you have read it, I hope you will write back to the Queen explaining that you are a wicked girl who makes up stories just to cause trouble to those who care for you and who have given the best years of their lives for your welfare. You will sit by me and I will tell you what you are to write. Then we will forget this whole sorry incident. You will, of course, say that you are very, very sorry for wasting Her Majesty's time, and to me for causing me so much distress. Your apology will be addressed to the assembled inmates at breakfast in the morning."

Although Gertie was not quite nine years old, she became aware that matron seemed afraid. Why? Was there something in the letter to make her fear Gertie, or was it the fact that Gertie had received a reply? Was the matron really not supposed to pry into the inmates' private belongings after all? She had thought that they weren't supposed to own anything. She stood in silence, staring at the older woman and saying nothing, frightened and bewildered. But she managed to speak at last, her mouth dry and her voice sounding strange in her ears.

"I have committed one wicked deed. I stole pen, ink and paper from your desk. But if I had asked you for those things you would have punished me. I only wrote to the Queen what is true. I just thought she would want to know what it is like to be an orphan. I only told the truth, which is what Mr Pidmore said we should do. We are cold and hungry, and I don't know if that is because there is not enough money to give you to feed us or what, but I don't think she is hungry and she looked like a kind lady and I just thought she wouldn't want us to be neither. Perhaps you could explain that that is all I meant."

"Very well, Gertrude. I will not press you for an apology, but there is no place here for children who show so little gratitude to those who care for them and who work to support their very existence. I will see to it that you are found a situation as soon as one becomes available. You may go."

Gertrude, the unread letter clutched in her grubby hand, turned and pulled open the heavy, oak door. Once outside, she thought for a moment that she was going to faint. But then excitement and curiosity overcame the dizziness and she hurried up to her dormitory, where enough light from a window allowed her to be able to read the letter. The paper was thick and of a beautiful creamy colour and on the top, under a coat of arms, were the magic words, 'Windsor Castle' printed in flowing letter. She began to read:

My dear Miss Thomas,

Her Majesty has asked me to answer your letter to her, for which she sends you her sincere thanks.

She is most concerned that children like yourself are cold and hungry and wishes me to assure you that all the ministers in her government are working very hard to make sure that everyone has enough to eat and a warm home. The problem is that there are so many people living in England that it is not possible to see to everybody and all their needs very quickly. I am sure that once the messenger of this letter has been shown around your workhouse, he will be able to suggest some simple improvements that will make your lot a little less irksome. Please believe me that her most gracious Majesty cares about all the children of her lands.

I remain your obedient servant,
John Smith, Secretary.

Gertie read the letter several times. Although she was disappointed that the Queen herself had not answered, at least everybody at Windsor Castle and all the 'ministers of her government', whoever they were, would now know about the plight of the poor people. But where was this messenger that Mr Smith mentioned? Had he been too frightened of matron to say anything, or had he been shown around and gone before anyone knew he was there? If that was the case, then Gertie was sure that the master and matron would have told him lies and only shown him the best bits of the workhouse. She felt a sudden despair and sitting down on her bed, she allowed the enormity of what she had done to flow over her. She had no friend except Amos and no one who could help her. She would be punished while she was here and then sent off to some horrible situation without any chance of furthering her education. Oh, why had she acted with such haste? She was, after all, just a silly, ignorant, little girl. Gertie lay down on the bed and sobbed.

But during the next few weeks, no more mention was made of the letter. Life went on much as usual, with school in the mornings and work on sewing or learning to clean vegetables in the afternoons. To her surprise, Gertie was moved to another dormitory with the bigger girls, where she had a bed all of her very own. The food seemed to be a little better as well; there was more of it and it was not burnt quite so often! Had the messenger said something, or was the improvement simply the result of a little more money from a kindly benefactor? Gertie didn't care. The weather was warm, she was not so hungry, and she had Amos to whisper to whenever she could at play time. Amos told her that he was soon to be apprenticed to the arsenal and then they wouldn't be able to see each other until she was found a situation.

"As soon as I am twelve years old I am to go and work in the rocket sheds in the arsenal. The work is very dangerous, but I am not afraid. I will get my wages and be found a lodging in town, and then, as soon as you are free, we will be able to see each other on your day off."

Gertie had shown the letter from Windsor Castle to Miss Rosemead, of course, but apart from saying 'well done, dear', in a rather absent-minded sort of way, she had not seemed to be interested in it. Disappointed, Gertie had tucked it away in a new hiding place, along with her few precious possessions and decided that there was no more she could do at present. Now she would have to wait until she was sent out into the world, where she would be free to speak to other people and to find out who were the best ones to tell about how miserable it was for the poor workhouse people.

At last the day of Amos' twelfth birthday arrived. He had whispered his goodbyes to Gertie the day before and they had held hands for a moment over the wall.

"As soon as I have lodgings, I will write to you, care of the school," he had said. "And when you are free you can tell me where you are staying and then we can meet. Don't cry, Gertie, remember that we are going to change the world, you and me!"

Gertie sniffed and wiped her nose on her sleeve, managing a watery smile. She promised to write as soon as she had been found a position, and then he was gone. She wondered miserably if she would ever see him again. Life wasn't really like that.

The days after Amos had left seemed dreary and endless. Lessons were still interesting, but the sparkle had gone out of learning. The Queen's letter had been sent and replied to, Amos had left, and she was soon to be sent away to some situation where she was sure she would be treated like the most menial of creatures. And although the weather was still warm, the food at the workhouse seemed to be creeping back to what it had been before the messenger came; meagre, tasteless and horrible. Gertie supposed that at least things couldn't be worse than they were now, wherever she was sent.

Her birthday was in July. On the day that she was nine years old, she was once again called into the matron's office. There was a strange lady sitting in one of the chairs and she looked plump and motherly. The matron was all sugary sweetness and Gertie wasn't sure that she didn't prefer her in her angry mood.

"Gertrude, this lady is Mrs Mabbett. You are to go with her, and she will care for you from now on. You are to work in the cartridge factory at the arsenal and you should be very grateful to Mrs Mabbett for her kindness in taking on a workhouse orphan. Say what's proper, like you've been taught to do."

Gertie curtsied to the woman and held out her hand.

"It is very kind of you, ma'am," she said shyly.

Mrs Mabbett stood up and took her hand, smiling kindly at her.

"Well, you're a skinny, little thing and could do with a good scrub, but I can tell you've got spirit and that's what my girls need. Spirit and good health! She's not sickly, is she, Mrs Pritchett?"

"Bless you, no! Fit as a flea." Then her voice turned into a whine as she went on. "But what can we do, with the little we are given to buy food for these poor wretches? Why, it's as much as I can do to feed myself, and if I don't keep well, who is to look after these poor, motherless little mites?"

Mrs Mabbett stared hard at the matron, who was of decidedly broad proportions, but she merely replied,

"Yes, well, we will have to put some flesh on these bones before Gertrude can cope with a full day's work."

Then, turning to Gertie and smiling, she said,

"Go and collect your things dear and we will leave at once."

In a dream and not quite believing what was happening to her, Gertie went up to her dormitory and collected her few possessions; a small brooch that had belonged to her mother, the queen's letter (she always thought of it as that) and the pair of woolly gloves that had certainly seen better days. As it was Saturday the school was closed, so she hurried down to the kitchens to say goodbye to her friends, who were all preparing some sad-looking vegetables at long wooden tables, and then returned to matron's office as fast as she could run. She knocked on the door and a voice called, "Enter." The two women were sitting in polite and icy silence, drinking tea from the prettiest cups that Gertie had ever seen. She stood in the doorway trying to catch her breath while Mrs Mabbett rose, put her cup and saucer carefully on the desk and said,

"Thank you for the tea, Mrs Pritchett. Gertrude and I will leave now and not take up any more of your valuable time."

With that she took hold of Gertie's free hand and said,

"Come along, child," and sailed out of the office, dragging Gertie in her wake. The door closed and that was the last Gertie ever saw of Mrs Pritchett. Not matter what the future held in store, she could only feel elation at leaving the workhouse and its matron far behind her.

Chapter Three

A carriage and horses stood outside the workhouse and Gertie, her heart thumping with excitement, was lifted into it by a man wearing a black coat, a very tall black hat and carrying a horsewhip. Mrs Mabbett climbed in and sat beside Gertie, her plump cheeks pink from the exertion and her merry blue eyes sparkling.

"Well, Gertrude, I am sure you have never travelled in such style before," she said, smiling kindly.

"No, ma'am," Gertie managed to stutter, her thoughts racing and her mind in a turmoil. Everything had happened so suddenly! One minute she was a little workhouse orphan and now, here she was bowling down into the town in a grand carriage, with a kind lady who was about to give her an important position in the arsenal, and wages as well! Two whole shillings a week was the sum mentioned and to Gertie, who had never owned any money, this seemed a fortune. As they rode along, Mrs Mabbett explained what she expected of her.

"You will lodge with two other little girls in my house until you are old enough to look after yourself. The other girls are from the workhouse, like you, but a little older. I always take on two or three at this time of year. The older girls tend to marry in the summer and so there is always a place vacant. Taking on you young ones means that you can learn the trade and spend a few years as experts before you run off with some poor, unsuspecting young man!

"You will work eleven hours a day, six days a week and on Sundays I insist that my girls attend the local Methodist chapel, unless, of course, they belong to some other church. We are strict Methodists ourselves and like our girls to follow in our ways. Mr Mabbett and I believe that we have the best turned-out, mildest mannered of any young ladies you'll find in this part of the world."

And so Mrs Mabbett chattered on, while Gertie tried to answer politely and at the same time look out of the carriage at the wonderful, exciting world that she was driving through in such fine style. One day she would be a great lady and have a carriage of her very own, and then she would show them!

They had raced down the lane, past the school and across the common and were now careering at great speed down a very steep hill with houses becoming ever more numerous as they journeyed on. At last the horses stopped outside a tall, narrow house in a rather mean street, noisy with carts and people selling wares from barrows. Gertie felt bewildered. She had never seen so many people or so much traffic. The workhouse might have been dirty, cold and cheerless, but at least it was quiet, and life was well ordered. Here she felt as though she had been thrown into bedlam. She was lifted from the carriage and Mrs Mabbett, alighting and thanking the man in the tall hat all at the same time, took Gertie's hand and hurried her up the steps of the narrow house.

"Here we are. That is my brother George who owns the carriage. Done very well for himself, he has; on the town council and the board of guardians, though how he manages to run a carriage and educate five children, Goodness only knows. Still, he like to show what a benevolent citizen he is and pretends never to grudge me a good turn. There! Wipe your boots on this mat and hang up your shawl on that hook. That's right, that will be your very own hook and you can write your name under it if you like, same as the others have done."

Gertie, delighted to have a hook of her very own, nodded, vowing that she would put her name there as soon as was possible, and then followed Mrs Mabbett and her chattering into a room to the left of the staircase. There were carpets on the floor, chairs with soft cushions dotted about the room and a fire burning in the grate. Everywhere was cluttered and the atmosphere stuffy, but Gertie didn't notice any of this. To her it was the most beautiful room in the world. It was bright, friendly and best of all, it was warm. Mrs Mabbett was saying:

"This is the parlour. After supper you may sit in here for an hour with Mr Mabbett and myself until bedtime, which is nine-thirty sharp. Breakfast is at six o'clock and dinner at eight in the evening. We eat in the next room. Come along and I'll show you."

She led Gertie, who seemed to be walking in a trance, into the dining room and then she was taken upstairs to the very top of the house where she was shown the room that she would share with the other two orphans.

"This is your bed, and this is your own drawer for your things. You can put your name on that as well if you like. Now, you must be tired, so I will leave you here to have a wash and a little rest, then we will have a bite to eat, and after that I'll take you to the girls' factory, where you will start work this afternoon."

Gertie mumbled her thanks and then, as Mrs Mabbett's footsteps died away, she sat sown on the bed that was now her very own. She looked round the room. A window with clean, pretty curtains, a carpet, worn but serviceable on the floor and a charming coverlet on her bed; all these she took in as if in a dream. And there, in a corner, wonder of wonders, was a marble-topped table and standing on it were a wash basin and jug in cream coloured china, painted all over with roses. Gertie buried her head in the coverlet and began to cry. But these were tears of joy and soon, fearful of incurring kind Mrs Mabbett's wrath, she went over to the little wash-stand and using the soap and towel provided – a luxury almost unknown in the workhouse, she careful washed her hands and face, remembering to include her neck and ears so as not to leave a 'tide-mark' as Miss Rosemead had called it. Then, tidying her hair as best she could, not daring to use the little hairbrush on the chest of drawers in case it was not meant for her, she placed her things in the drawer she had been shown and finally sat with her hands meekly folded in her lap, waiting for Mrs Mabbett.

After a short while Gertie heard footsteps on the stairs and Mrs Mabbett appeared in the doorway.

"That's right. Come along, child, there is a light luncheon prepared in the dining room."

Gertie followed Mrs Mabbett downstairs and into the room where what seemed to her to be a feast had been spread on the spotless white tablecloth. A little maid-servant, not much older than Gertie herself, curtsied and hurried from the room. Gertie stood and stared.

"Sit yourself down, do, and tuck in. We can't be doing with skinny Lizzies in the factory. There's bread and ham and pickle and a wedge of cheese if you'd rather."

Gertie, who had eaten nothing but some rather watery porridge all day, tucked into everything with enthusiasm, while Mrs Mabbett chatted between mouthfuls and plied her with yet more goodies. At last it was time to leave, Mrs Mabbett giving instructions to the little maid on how to wash the dishes, store the remains of the food and cook the evening meal.

They walked to the factory. The entrance to the arsenal was through a large gate facing the river, and once inside Gertie was fascinated by the number and size of the buildings which were dotted about in a vast area of land. Great tall buildings with imposing pillars and doorways, ugly-looking sheds bigger than the workhouse and small, low buildings, all separated, stretched as far as the eye could see. Everywhere there were people hurrying in and out and an acrid smell seemed to hang over everything.

"You'll soon get used to that," said Mrs Mabbett kindly, as Gertie coughed and wrinkled her nose. "That's only a mixture of saltpetre and other chemicals that go into the making of the explosives. You'll be working on making cartridges. It's not dangerous, we haven't had an accident these ten years, so don't you go getting any missish ideas! Here we are."

Since Gertie hadn't even given a thought to the idea of her work being dangerous, she felt this advice to be rather unnecessary, but she followed Mrs Mabbett meekly into the dim interior of the 'girls' factory', one of the many cartridge-making sheds. There, seated at long tables and with strange-looking frames in front of them, were some fifty girls, ranging from Gertie's age to about sixteen. Mrs Mabbett went up to an older woman who seemed to be in charge.

"Thank you, Mrs Saunders, I'll take over now. Will you get little Gertrude here seated, and show her what to do?"

Gertie was taken to a table where some little girls were sitting, busily placing the finished cartridges in boxes. Mrs Saunders, as lean as Mrs Mabbett was plump, said sharply,

"This will be your place, Gertrude, next to Rose. You will take a box from that pile in the middle of the table and Rose will show you how to pack the cartridges in the correct manner. I shall expect you to work quickly and in silence. Talking is kept to a minimum as this work requires concentration."

Gertie curtsied and smiled at Rose, sitting beside her and gratefully accepted the box which Rose had chosen for her. The older girls put the racks of filled cartridges on her table and she spent the next few hours happily placing them carefully in the boxes.

By the time seven thirty arrived, she was exhausted. Although the work was not difficult and Rose was a pleasant partner, whispering to her with questions about where she came from and how old she was when she dared, the strange smell was giving Gertie a headache, and she was not used to sitting for long hours in one place. Cleaning vegetables had involved quite a lot of walking about the kitchen and the chatter amongst the women had made the work less tedious. Even in school there had been a time for play. She suddenly began to miss the workhouse, her friends and the familiar, if dreary, routine. Gertie could never have imagined even in her wildest dreams that she would miss her life in that cheerless place, but it had been home to her all her life and it was what she knew and understood. Now here she was, suddenly thrown into an alien world, without any friends and with a whole set of new rules and new people to get to know. She felt sick and the tears welled up in her eyes. She choked back a sob, but Mrs Saunders was at her side at once, her black heady eyes staring, it seemed to Gertie, right into the child's very soul.

"Come, Gertrude, it is time to go back with Mrs Mabbett. You have done very well on your first day and I am very pleased with you. Everything will soon become familiar, and I am sure Rose will be a good friend to you."

Wiping her eyes in surprise, Gertie gave Mrs Saunders a watery smile and said,

"Yes ma'am, thank you, ma'am," and remembering to curtsy, she joined Mrs Mabbett, who was collecting the two other girls who were sharing her home with Gertie. Alice was small and fairy-like, with blue eyes and long golden locks. Lily was dark haired, with olive skin and brown eyes constantly sparkling with mischief. She linked her arm into Gertie's.

"Come along, green-un, we'll soon have you laughing, won't we, Mrs Rabbit?"

The older lady flushed with pleasure as they walked back to the house.

"None of your sauce now, Miss tiger lily," she said, and they all swung happily along the dirty street until they reached the welcome doorway, which was wide open, a tall, thin man standing in it, smoking a pipe and looking anxiously out for them.

"Good evening, Mr Mabbett. You see, we have once again brought Mrs Mabbett home to you all in one piece!" And the irrepressible Lily unhooked her arm from Gertie's and ran up the steps, pulling the man's shoulders down and kissing him on his whiskery cheek. Alice and Gertie walked up the steps after Lily, Gertie curtsying and shaking his hand as Alice introduced her, while Mrs Mabbett clucked and scolded behind.

"Really, Mr Mabbett, ten years I have worked in that factory and never a mishap. Must you be forever looking out for me? Now just you all come in, wash your hands and we'll sit down to a nice, hot supper!"

++++++++++

Life became a pleasant routine for Gertie. At the end of a week she received her first pay packet – a small brown paper bag containing four bright, shining sixpences and one extra penny.

"The penny is for your first day last week," said the lady who handed Gertie her wages. "You give one of the sixpences to Mrs Mabbett for your keep and the rest is your very own. See you don't spend it all on sweetmeats now!"

Gertie took the money home proudly, delighting in being able to give Mrs Mabbett one of her very own coins. Lily took the three of them to the corner shop where they all bought a hapoth of comfits and that evening they sat in the parlour singing songs, accompanied with more enthusiasm than accuracy at the pianoforte by Mrs Mabbett. Mr Mabbett sat in his favourite chair, his pipe smoke adding to the already stuffy atmosphere and his eyes in his thin, tired face looking with love and affection at the happy scene. Gertie had never known such contentment. Mrs Saunders, who looked after the little girls at the factory, had praised her work and said she could soon go on to the next table where the cartridges were finished off. Mrs Mabbett said she was a good, well-mannered 'little love', and Alice and Lily had soon become her close companions. Life at the workhouse, her old friends there and even Amos, were beginning to fade and become a dream. She still thought of Amos, of course, and wondered how he was doing and if they would ever meet at the arsenal, but she was so busy with her new life that she scarcely had time to miss him.

On the Sunday after her first pay-day she was taken to the chapel which was used for Sunday worship by the devout Methodist folk of the town. Although this was her second Sunday at the Mabbett's house, Mrs Mabbett thought Gertie needed time to 'sort herself out' as she put it and left her to herself for an hour or two. But now it was considered time for Gertie to pay her respects to God. The service was very unlike the ones Gertie had been used to at the workhouse, where Mr Pidmore had stood in his pulpit and droned on for hours while everyone tried to stay awake. There was no chance of dropping off to sleep under the glittering eyes of Mr Johnson, the preacher. Standing at a small table, which was covered with a green cloth and littered with books and pamphlets, he stared round at the packed congregation as silence fell and people shifted uneasily or expectantly on the hard wooden benches. Mr Johnson's sermons were anything but dull, and this Sunday's was no exception. After waiting until there was complete silence and Gertie felt an almost uncontrollable desire to giggle, he suddenly brought his fist down on the table with an almighty bang. The books all jumped, and Gertie gave a startled gasp.

"Sinners," he thundered. There was silence. Gertie clung tightly to her ancient prayer book.

"Sinners all, we are all, all sinners in the sight of the Lord." He looked round and his gaze seemed to bore right into the very soul of every member of the congregation. "And so man is brought low. Enter into the rock and hide in the dust from before the terror of the Lord and from the glory of His Majesty. The haughty looks of man shall be brought low, and the pride of men shell be humbled; and the Lord alone will be exalted in that day. For the Lord of hosts has a day.' thus spoke the Lord in a vision to Isaiah."

Silence again.

"For the Lord of hosts has a day…" Mr Johnson banged the table with the palm of his hand on every word as his voice rang round the tiny hall. Then, his voice dropping to a whisper, he repeated: "For the Lord of hosts has a day. And where will you be on that day? And you, and you?" as he pointed to various self-conscious individuals in the congregation. "Where shall we all – all of us, be on that day? Why, on our knees, praying for mercy. For we know, beyond a shadow of a doubt, that we are all sinners…" There was a long pause. Still whispering, he continued, "But there is salvation. For the Lord said unto his disciples, 'Truly, I say unto you, unless you turn and become like children, you will never enter the Kingdom of Heaven.'"

This news surprised Gertie. During all her life in the workhouse she had constantly had it drummed into her that she was a wicked girl and would go to hell and burn forever. Now here was this preacher telling everyone to be like children. Perhaps they didn't mean her? Maybe there were other, innocent children in the world, who had a father and a mother and who didn't have to work for a living. He probably meant them, for they would have no reason to be wicked. The preacher was continuing.

"Hallelujah, brothers and sisters. Let us sing our most uplifting hymn."

And they sang a rousing chorus which was unfamiliar to Gertie, but which she soon picked up and which she thoroughly enjoyed. When the service was over, they all went outside and shook hands with the preacher who seemed to be very hot, with beads of perspiration standing out on his forehead. When it was Gertie's turn to shake his hand, she smiled shyly up at him and said, "I really enjoyed your sermon, Mr Johnson, but I have lots of questions I want to ask you. May I come and visit you sometime?"

Both Mrs Mabbett and the preacher looked surprised, but just as Mrs Mabbett was in the process of clucking and blessing herself, Mr Johnson said, "Why, of course you may come and see me. I live in the house at the back of the chapel and Mrs Johnson can give you a nice cup of tea while you fire away with your questions."

He turned to Mrs Mabbett.

"Would this afternoon be too soon, ma'am?"

Mrs Mabbett was all pink with pleasure and assurances, and so, when the afternoon service was ended, Gertie joined Mr Johnson and one or two other young people who Gertie recognised from the arsenal and they all trouped down the little alleyway beside the chapel to the rather dingy house. Mrs Johnson had laid out a fine tea for everyone with the very best bone china.

At first Gertie felt awkward and clumsy, but she was soon made to feel at home by everyone and as soon as tea was over they all remained sitting round the table, plying Mr Johnson with questions. Gertie began,

"Please, sir, I have always been told, at least until I came to live with Mrs Mabbett, that I am a wicked sinner because of what my mother did. But today you said that everyone should be like children. And then there was Amos telling everybody that there was nowhere to hide, and Mr Pidmore saying that my mother's sins would be 'visited on me'. I worked hard and tried to be good, but it seemed that there was no escape. What am I to do?"

Mr Johnson smiled kindly at her.

"Why, you see," he said, "God gave us the chance to do the things that we think are right. If we know we are doing wrong, then we are sinners. But Jesus said that if we believe what we are doing is right, then we are innocent."

He went on to speak of something called 'original sin' and other things that Gertie found difficult to understand. The other children, all older than her and all seeming to follow what Mr Johnson was talking about, joined in until at last the preacher put up his hand to silence.

"I have an idea. Since you are all so interested in the scriptures and your education is being sadly neglected, I propose to open a Sunday School. Every Sunday afternoon, after the service, we will all meet here, and I will instruct you in the Bible and the teachings of Christ. In that way you will not only be helping your immortal souls, but you will also be practising your reading and writing abilities. I am afraid I am unable to help you with your arithmetic but at least we will be making a start!"

Everyone was delighted with this plan and so it was agreed that they would meet the very next Sunday. They would each donate a penny of their wages to help with the cost of the tea, and they also agreed to tell any friends who were interested to come along and join in the lessons. Gertie went home with her mind awhirl and her heart singing with joy. At last she was going to find out how she could be saved from being cast into the 'eternal fires of hell' as Mr Pidmore had put it! Although she was secretly hurt that Amos had never tried to contact her, she vowed that she would try to find him and persuade him to come along as well. Life was suddenly very good.

Chapter Four

Two years later came the terrible explosion. It happened in one of the sheds on the morning of the seventeenth of September 1845. At ten o'clock in the morning, just as the arsenal clock was chiming the hour, there was a noise as if the whole world was coming to an end. There followed a strange silence, and then shouts of 'fire!' could be heard as everyone left their tables and went rushing out into the yard, joining the throng of people hurrying in the direction of the explosion. Gertie saw several men trying to push open the door of a small building, and as it gave way under their weight, flames and acrid smoke came billowing out. Men and boys spilled out into the yard, coughing and trying to douse their burning clothes with their bare hands. Her heart gave a sudden lurch as she recognised one of the lads. It was Amos. His hair was burnt and his clothes smoking, but as soon as he could breathe, he went back into the building before she could make her way to him.

"Amos!" she shouted, frantically pushing through the crowd that had gathered at a safe distance from the building. "Amos!"

Then she saw him, helping to drag out a man who looked as though he were terribly burned. Amos laid him gently on the ground and several women rushed over to tend him as more men were brought out. There were seven in all, but although the fire itself had not taken hold, all the victims were found to have died in the blast. As soon as the last body had been laid on the cobbles Gertie rushed over to Amos, who was sitting against some railings, his pale face streaked with dirt and soot. His eyes were closed, and he was trembling. She began gently wiping his face with her linen kerchief – a present from Lily on her last birthday. She was crooning gently to him and soon he opened his eyes. He looked at her vacantly at first and then with sudden recognition.

"Why, it's Gertie, isn't it? I remember you! You wrote to the Queen when we were in the workhouse. It – it is very good to see you." Then his eyes closed again, and he slumped sideways. Gertie, upset that he hardly remembered her after all they had meant to each other, shook him hysterically, calling his name and shouting for someone to come and help. He had never been far from her thoughts and he couldn't die now; not now she had found him at last. "Amos, Amos! Someone, please help. Oh, please help me with him!"

Suddenly Mrs Mabbett was at her side with a pitcher of water.

"There, there, my love, don't take on so, he is only swooned. Here, wet his lips with water from this jug. That's right. Gently now. He'll be fine as fivepence in no time, you'll see!"

But Amos was very ill for some weeks. He had inhaled a great deal of acrid smoke and was unable to breathe properly, so Mrs Mabbett said. Lying in the infirmary, unable to earn his keep, he began worrying that he would be sent back to the workhouse.

"They'll take away my work and my lodgings and give them to someone else," he said fretfully to Gertie, on one of her many visits. She shushed him and stroked his forehead.

"No, they'll never do that. Mrs Mabbett will see to it that you have somewhere to live, and I've heard that they are keeping on all the workmen who got hurt and survived. They say you are a hero and I heard talk of compensation."

The rumour was true. Amos and the other men returned to a hero's welcome and a small sum in recognition of their bravery. The inquest had decided that the arsenal was at fault in not providing the proper tools for the work and in future it was to be policy that all shed doors must open outwards, so ensuring greater chance of escape.

During the last two years the Sunday School had been flourishing and now that Gertie had found Amos again she began the task of persuading him to come along to it.

"You need not join in if you do not wish, but Mr Johnson is so interesting, and he has taught me to write really properly and to read out loud with hardly a stumble. I am sure you can do all those things and it would be company for me. There are ten of us altogether and we all take a penny and there is a delicious tea before we begin. Do say you'll come."

Amos had grown taller than ever. His hair still stood up in tufts and his face was still streaked with dirt, but he looked down at the little girl and grinned with tender affection.

"All right, little-un, I'll come along." He tweaked her pigtails. Gertie was very proud of her long, brown hair which she brushed religiously every morning.

She and Amos were standing by the arsenal gates and she jerked her head away from him in mock anger.

"You leave my hair alone, Amos Parker. Race you to the end of the street!"

They ran, laughing and panting as they reached the corner, and then they parted, Gertie back to Mrs Mabbett's and Amos to his sparse lodgings a few streets away.

School that Sunday was a great success. Amos appeared at the door of the Chapel before afternoon service and Gertie scarcely recognised this splendid young man. He was searing a smart, almost white shirt, a jacket and black trews. His scuffed boots had been polished until they shone, his cap covered his wayward hair, and his face and hands were clean. He looked the height of respectability, or so, at least, Gertie thought. Her heart gave a little lurch as she saw him, standing so tall and handsome and with so much confidence. If she could have had a brother, she could not have wished for better. She went shyly over to him.

"Hello, Amos, thank you for coming."

He looked down at her with his laughing, brown eyes.

"Why, Gertie, how pretty you look! Pray, ma'am, may I escort you to your pew?" He offered her his arm. Giggling, her pale cheeks slightly pinker than usual, she linked her arm in his and they walked to the front row of benches, where Gertie greeted her friends, introducing Amos to them rather self-consciously. Some of the young people were already known to him and Gertie sat in a rosy glow of happiness throughout the service, wondering why she should be so blessed and worried whether it could possibly last. Surely God would visit some terrible retribution on her soon? But when tea was over and everyone crowded into Mr Johnson's little office grandly called his 'library', Amos proved to be very knowledgeable about the scriptures. A desire to 'better himself' as his foreman, Mr Langham, put it, had led him to read whatever he could lay his hands on, the Bible being the most available tome. But although he had read the Bible, he had not understood a great deal of it, and now here was Mr Johnson both ready and willing to discuss and explain it all to him for as long as he wished. In fact, by the time the preacher recollected the hour, it was past nine o'clock. Mrs Johnson had looked in on the gathering three times, and finally there was Mrs Mabbett and one or two other frantic ladies knocking at the door, convinced that their charges had been brutally murdered and their bodies hurled into the river.

"Whatever would Mr Mabbett say if his little Gertie was done for?" Gertie heard the voice of Mrs Mabbett wailing in the hallway. Everyone had been enthralled by the evening's lesson and went home full of zeal and promises of working even harder, the frantic ladies being placated by having their charges returned all safe and sound. And so that year passed. Christmas came and went, Amos being invited to the Mabbett's festivities and giving Gertie a specially fine hairbrush and comb which caused her to be speechless with delight. Her present to him, a silk cravat, had cost her nearly all her savings, but she still felt it a poor exchange for her beautiful gift; the back of the brush all covered in chased silver. But Amos was both delighted and touched by her thoughtful present, and the evening went off in the greatest merriment. Gertie was learning to play the pianoforte under Mrs Mabbett's irregular tuition, and she was able to pick her way through a few of the more familiar carols, much to Mr Mabbett's delight.

The New Year was cold and dreary, with snow flurries quickly turning to slush and most of the time a cold, sleety rain making everything feel constantly damp and uncomfortable. But spring arrived at last and although there were no trees in the mean streets surrounding the arsenal, Mr Mabbett had a tiny square of 'garden' at the back of his house which he tended with loving care, and here, in proud rows, sprang up the yellow daffodils which were such a source of delight to Gertie when she went down the yard.

Sometimes, on a Sunday between services, Mrs Mabbett would pack a picnic and they would all make their way up to the common near to where Gertie's old workhouse stood, and there, with Alice and Lily, and Amos when he could spare the time, they would play games of hide and seek and touch as touch can, Lily organising everybody, the laughter echoing across the common and annoying all those dour folk who attended the grand Parish Church, which had stood for nine hundred years and was considered the proper place of worship for all the 'respectable' folk. But Mr and Mrs Mabbett were not of the persuasion that Sunday should be a day of gloom and silence. Nor did Mr Johnson object to laughter on the Lord's day, provided it was kept within suitable bounds.

"For Jesus laughed with His disciples and did not deny them their simple pleasures," he said.

On his fifteenth birthday Amos announced that he wished to join the ministry. Mr Johnson was delighted and said he would give him all the help he could. Gertie was pleased, but she couldn't help worrying. How would he earn a living? Suppose he was sent to a church a long way away? Did preachers have a choice in such things? But when she voiced her fears to Mr Johnson he only laughed.

"Why, Amos won't be a minister straight away! He has several years of study ahead of him before he can be given a living. But it is a fine thing to have a vocation and to know what direction God has shown him to take in life. I have great hopes for your beau, Gertrude."

Gertrude started and blushed. Although Lily often teased her about her affection for Amos, she had never thought of him as more than an adored elder brother. Her 'beau'! That was a new idea entirely and she went home turning it over in her mind. She would soon be twelve years old. Was not that far too young to have a beau? She hoped that Mr Johnson would not mention such things to Amos; she knew that young men could be frightened away if they thought they were being trapped by 'some scheming female' as Mr Mabbett put.

"A pair of bright eyes and a neat figure and I was done for," he would often say, smiling lovingly at his wife, who would scold him as she turned pink with pleasure, heaving her now rather more comfortable than trim figure from the room.

"Really, Mr Mabbett, whatever will these young innocents think of us!" she would scold, all the way down to the scullery, where she could be heard noisily clearing away dishes and giving her orders to the long-suffering little maid. But he knew that his wife was always secretly delighted by his words.

But what of Amos? He would scarcely want to be chained to a little girl, a 'little-un' as he called her, and Gertie was sure he thought of her as no more than a sister to him. Still, as long as this kept him by her side she was happy for it to remain that way. And anyway, she was still young; she might meet other young men that she preferred to Amos. She tossed her head and went on her way, ignoring the small voice in her heart which was telling her what she already knew; that such an idea was inconceivable.

On her twelfth birthday Gertie was promoted to the next to top table at the factory. The work was harder and could be dangerous, but the nimble fingers of the girls under Mrs Mabbett's watchful eye managed to make the cartridges without mishap. During the summer months, Amos would sometimes meet Gertie at the arsenal gates and they would go either up to the common or back to Mrs Mabbett's where they would consume a large dinner and then pour over Amos' books and essays in the parlour. Gertie had become as absorbed as he was in the Bible and together they would often discuss and study late into the night, only stopping when the one candle afforded by the kind-hearted Mrs Mabbett had guttered and gone out. Then Amos would rise guiltily, tripping over various pieces of furniture as he tried without success to make his way silently to the front door, Gertie giggling and shushing in his wake. Sometimes Alice would join them in their studies, but Lily, two years older than Gertie and already growing into a robust young woman, scorned the idea, preferring to spend her spare time going up the hill and flirting with the young military cadets. Having the artillery situated in the town was a great temptation to any young lady with leisure on her hands and even the girls from the factory found time to saunter past the imposing gates on long summer evenings and Sunday afternoons, their hair pinned up under stunning bonnets and their waists constrained by horrendous corsets. Gertie and Alice occasionally joined Lily on one of these excursions and shy, little Alice suddenly and inexplicably found herself the sinecure of a young and dashing cadet named Percy, who, it seemed, had eyes for no one else. At thirteen Alice was still small for her age, petite and doll-like and Percy treated her as though she were a delicate piece of porcelain china. Gertie was disgusted and said so.

"How can you let yourself be treated so? He will walk all over you and make you his slave, Lal. For goodness' sake show a little assertiveness."

But Alice, who never answered back and always did as she was bid, seemed to love every moment of Percy's attentions.

"Oh, well, if that's how you feel, you have my blessing. Bear him dozens of puny offspring and die exhausted at thirty. But don't say I didn't warn you!"

Gertie had heard Mrs Mabbett speak just so of a neighbour who had died in her twelfth confinement. She vowed she would never allow herself to be treated like that by anyone, especially a man! She smiled to herself. She and Amos might have their differences, and sometimes they quarrelled like two pole-cats, but he would never treat her like a fragile, little doll. Heaven forbid!

The summer passed and autumn brought rain and great gusts of wind that blew the rubbish along the cobbles and into the running gutters of the town. Mr Mabbett, his cough troubling him more than usual, looked thin and ill and by Christmas he had taken to his bed, Mrs Mabbett and the girls taking it in turns to nurse him, running home from the factory during the short lunch break and spending every spare penny on the various linctus and potions prescribed by poor Dr Fraser, himself little more than a wraith. Christmas came and went without the usual celebrations, and Gertie thought with regret of what fun they had last year. Mr Mabbett's illness worsened, and Mrs Mabbett took the unusual step of taking some compassionate leave. But it was all to no avail, and on a dreary day in February 1847, Mr Mabbett died. Twenty years older than his grieving wife, his lungs diseased from the nature of his work, he finally gave up his soul into God's safekeeping.

The funeral service was a very moving affair, attended by most of the workers from the arsenal, for Mr Mabbett was loved by all who knew him. Amos, unable to leave his seminary, sent a card of consolation and a beautiful wreath of flowers. Mr Johnson and his wife did all they could for the widow, but it was many months before she regained even a shadow of her former merry self, and she never could find the contentment of her earlier years. Being strong herself, she had often treated her husband's ailments with scorn, telling him that he was imagining things. Now she blamed herself for not taking his illness more seriously and it took every ounce of persuasion from all who knew her to convince her that it had not been her fault.

"He was so much older than you, Edith, and his work had damaged his lungs. You gave him every care and attention and no man could have asked for more. He wanted for nothing. Hush now, calm yourself," said one kind neighbour.

"Little ones. I never gave him little ones. But did he blame me? No, not him. He was saint, that's what he was, Mabel, and I was a monster not to appreciate him more."

Life eventually returned to some sort of normality, the empty chair by the parlour fire the only constant reminder of the poor widow's loss.

Lily left to marry a young officer soon after Gertie's thirteenth birthday, and Alice went to live with an aunt in Kent who needed a live-in nursemaid.

"But what about Percy?" asked Gertie, bemused.

"Oh, he will wait until I am sixteen. He has promised me that we shall be married then. He will visit us whenever he is able."

So Mrs Mabbett and Gertie were left alone together in the silent house, with only the maid for company. Amos went away to a college to study; his fees having been offered to Mr Johnson by a kind and wealthy lady who belonged to the Methodist church. He and Gertie kept up a regular correspondence and now that Lily was gone, Gertie seldom went near the artillery. She had no interest in the officers and knew that if he would have her, then there was no man in the world she wished to marry more than Amos.

Chapter Five

On the evening of her sixteenth birthday, the twenty-fifth of July 1850, Gertie heard a knock at the front door. Sarah, the long-suffering maidservant, went to open it and voices could be heard raised excitedly in the hall. The next moment the door to the parlour had been flung open and there, framed in the doorway, was a tall and handsome young man, his brown eyes dancing and his wayward hair, brushed at last into some semblance of order, shining in the candlelight. With a cry, Gertie swiftly left the pianoforte, where she and Mrs Mabbett had been singing their favourite songs between sips of port wine, and rushed to the young man, crying,

"Amos, oh Amos!" She almost flung herself at him. He laughed and lifted her up in his strong arms.

"Steady, little-un, you'll have us both over!" He laughed again. Then he put her gently back on her feet and looked her over from head to toe. "Why, you've grown into a real lady. And a beauty, too! She's a credit to you, Mrs Mabbett, ma'am," he said, remembering his manners and shaking hands with the beaming widow and offering his condolences on her widowhood. Then he turned back to Gertie. "I wouldn't write to let you know I was coming as I wanted it to be a birthday surprise."

"Oh it is, it is. It is the best present ever! Pray come and sit down and tell us all about your studies and how was your journey and are you home for good now? Sarah shall make us some supper. Sarah!"

Breathless, Gertie was clearing a seat for Amos, plying him with questions and calling for the maid all in one go. Amos laughed his infectious laugh once more.

"Calm down and get your breath back, Gertie. I am not about to run off as soon as I have arrived here." He turned, as the maid appeared, looking rather flustered. "Sarah, will you be so good as to prepare a little supper for us? You will not object to my giving orders to your maid, ma'am?" he said, turning with his winning smile to Mrs Mabbett.

Sarah hurried off as the widow clucked and assured him she had no objections.

"Now," said Amos, patting the space beside him on the settle. "Come and sit next to me, Gertie, and I shall tell you all my news. But first I must hear how you are both doing and whether your promotion is to your liking."

The evening passed all too quickly in a glow of happy excitement. Mrs Mabbett hovered over the couple like a mother hen with her chicks, and Gertie, shy at first in front of this rather splendid young man, soon forgot her self-consciousness in the comfort of his easy manners.

"You are grown into such a gentleman, Amos. Is that what they teach you at this college of yours? I thought you went there to learn all about Jesus and how to write sermons."

"Well, we do learn all those things," said Amos, chuckling. "But we learn a lot of other things as well."

"And one of them is how to be a gentleman," said Gertie with a worried frown. "You won't consider yourself above us, now you know how to speak properly and behave in a gentlemanly way, will you?"

"Oh, come now, little-un, do I look as though I consider myself above you? I look on this house, if you will excuse the impertinence, ma'am, as my home, and you as my family. Come, Gertie, don't spoil our evening by getting into a fit of the grumps, for you must know that I am the same Amos as ever I was."

"Well, your hair certainly is," said Gertie giggling, as tufts of it began standing up again in spite of the macassar oil he had liberally applied all over it.

Sarah produced a light supper of bread and butter and cakes and then Gertie played the piano again, accompanying them as they sang from Mrs Mabbett's old song book, Amos' fine tenor voice giving confidence to Gertie's sweet soprano tones. Suddenly Gertie stopped and looked rather crestfallen.

"Oh, Amos," she said. "Should we not be singing hymns, rather than these jolly airs? Isn't that what you are supposed to do?"

Amos laughed again, showing his even white teeth. Gertie's heart turned over. Goodness, he was so handsome!

"Even preachers are allowed a little fun now and again, Gertie. We are not wholly concerned with doom and hell-fire! Why, you remember all those picnics on the common, sanctioned by Mr Johnson, while all the gloomy church folk went past us with glum faces, tutting and muttering? But who are the real Christians? Those people who wear their best clothes for their weekly visit to the church, but who themselves live in style, ignoring the poverty around them, or those of us who live and work amongst the poor and the hopeless, promising joy and resurrection by believing in the living Lord? We live by His teachings every day, not just on Sundays! And as Jesus laughed and told funny stories, we believe that laughter is part of our worship. It is certainly balm in the midst of misery. So, my dearest little-un, let us sing our hearts out while we may. The Lord knows there is enough misery to make up for one evening of jollity!"

However, it turned out not to be the only evening, but one of many, stretching into a rosy future. For Amos, his old lodgings no longer vacant, agreed to reside with the two ladies in Beresford Street, Mrs Mabbett finding herself with neither the energy nor the inclination to give a home to any more orphan girls from the factory.

"It will be good to have a man about the house again won't it Gertie? We will be able to sleep more soundly in our beds, knowing that we will be protected from burglars and all manner of shifty persons with you here."

So Amos moved in with Gertie and Mrs Mabbett. He slept in an empty room on the first floor, opposite Mrs Mabbett's bedroom, while Gertie and Sarah shared the attic room at the top of the house. Since no living had become vacant at any of the local chapels, Amos contented himself for the present with lay preaching, returning to his old post in the arsenal, welcomed with open arms by Mr Langham the foreman. He was glad to see a worker like Amos back at his old place, grumbling that so many men were of an untrustworthy nature these days and did not stay the course.

Working from seven in the morning until eight in the evening, rushing back to Mrs Mabbett's house for supper, which had been put hack half an hour for his convenience, and then helping Gertie with her studies, Amos had little time to concentrate on improving the moral standards of the local population. But improvement there needed to be! Although the chapels were full each Sunday, the majority of worshippers were women and children; the men from the arsenal were in general too tired and too disinterested to take part in any kind of service, however informal. Amos began to despair of ever reaching their immortal souls.

"How can they ever learn if they won't even listen to me or take me seriously? Oh, they are friendly enough, but they laugh at my words and would rather spend their time drinking and merrymaking than thinking about the hereafter."

Gertie tried to hush this outburst. They were sitting late one evening in the parlour, her books open with the idea of studying various texts. But Amos' mind was not on the work in hand. He had fidgeted all through dinner, and now, every few minutes, he would get up and stride irresolutely about the room, one hand running through his hair, making the tufts stand up more than ever. Gertie couldn't help giggling.

"Oh, Amos, do sit down. You look like a surprised penguin, flapping about like that!"

"It's all very well you laughing, little'un, but it is the souls of these men that are at stake. How am I to make them listen?"

"Well, I don't think I am the person to help you there. You must talk to Mr Johnson and see what he has to say. Surely he can give you some advice?"

But the minister was of little more help than Gertie when it came to saving the souls of the men in the arsenal. Instead he merely sermonised in a general sort of way.

"You see, Amos, these men already belong to a kind of brotherhood, and that is enough for them. To their minds what we have to offer them is a threat. We threaten to destroy their close comradeship and isolate them from what they know and understand. Only by gradual and gentle education can we enlarge their minds so that eventually they can learn to embrace the Lord. We have a long and arduous fight ahead of us Amos. In the old days it was the village that was the community. Now towns are rapidly growing into cities and men are no longer brothers. It is the factory that has become the community and the factory is no place for considering the needs of the soul, or so they believe!"

So poor Amos was left to fight a lonely battle, the good-natured workers treating him with a kindness and tolerance which he found more irksome than outright antagonism. In every spare moment, usually in the precious hour set aside for lunch, he talked to any men who would listen, while they munched good-naturedly on their bread and pickle and winked at one another over their mugs of ale. Amos talked of the opportunities offered by attending chapel regularly, of how they could improve their working conditions through education and knowledge.

"Don't you see, by sending your children to the Sunday School and learning to read and write yourselves, you are ensuring an education for the future workforce of this country! Only that way can we gain fair treatment for all, by meeting the bosses on their own level. Attending chapel is not only about saving our souls in the hereafter. It is also about caring for each other here, while we are alive. Although our work is arduous and even dangerous and the days are long, we are sure of work and have some security in the arsenal. But what of those poor souls who have none of these things? Are we to neglect them because we are comfortable? Will you not also give just a little of your time, say an hour on Sunday, to pray for them, brothers, and support the work our good minister does amongst the lowest and poorest in our society? We have little enough ourselves, God knows, but there are those who have far, far less."

They smoked their pipes, ate their lunches and listened kindly. But at the sound of the factory hooter they returned to their work, silent and without comment, except for the odd murmured remark that all that preaching was 'women's business'.

On one of these occasions Joe, who worked in the same shed as Amos, walked with him back to their bench. Joe's gentle, northern accent, voiced the thoughts of most of the men who suffered Amos' preaching.

"You see, lad, it's like this. Our life is here among our mates. We get on. We understand one another. We've all got the same needs, the same problems and the same way of living and thinking. You're asking us to give up what we have worked and slaved for all our lives. Security. Security and comradeship. These are good things. Once introduce religion or politics into our lives and you destroy all that. Brother will fight against brother and father against son. You know yourself that this has already been happening out in foreign places, and we want none of it here. We know as well as you do that the poor folk out there need consideration. But we are not the men to do that. No lad, leave us be. You go and preach to the wealthy and the ones with the power to change things. They're the ones that need to look to their souls. We are content as we are."

That evening Amos went back to the dilapidated, cosy house that he thought of as home and once again poured his heart out to Gertie and Mrs Mabbett. They were sitting over the remains of their dinner, a fine, tasty stew, mopped up with a slice of delicious fresh bread that Sarah, amongst all her other duties, had managed to bake without mishap that afternoon.

"Perhaps they are right," he said. "Perhaps they don't need more than their work and their comradeship!" But Mrs Mabbett bridled.

"Why, Amos Parker, how can you, a good Methodist and a preacher, say such things? Not need to consider the Lord? Not beg for forgiveness to cleanse their immortal souls? Why, I never did! You'll be telling me next that you need no more than a comfortable home and a pair of bright eyes to keep you from the fires of hell! Well, I'll tell you this; if that was all that was needed to make the world go round, then it would be a far better place than it is at present. You listen to your conscience, my lad, and never mind what the Joes of this world tell you. They've never thought beyond the needs of their stomachs, and that's their problem. But where does it leave the rest of us, I should like to know! There are those with more money than sense ruling the rest of us and telling us what for and leaving us to die of disease and starvation for want of a few pence that they could well do without."

Mrs Mabbett's homily shamed Amos into renewed zeal, and he vowed that, whatever the pitfalls and arguments he should encounter, he would never again doubt his own belief in the power of the ministry. Somehow he would go out there and Fight the Good Fight, whatever the cost!

The following Sunday Mr Johnson was summoned to a Council of Methodist Ministers, and Amos was to preach in his place. All that week Amos had wheedled and cajoled his workmates to come and support him in this, his first service at his own local chapel.

"I don't want to be preaching to a congregation made up entirely of women and children! This is my first real chance to lead a service and I need you there, all of you, to give me support, just like we do in the sheds. It's not just your women-folk that need saving; your souls are as good as theirs any day! Say you'll come along, just this once. Just to give me a hand?"

And so, much to his surprise, that Sunday the little chapel in Joseph Street was packed out, the women leading their menfolk in with determined expressions on their faces, and the men, awkward in their stiff Sunday clothes, clutching their caps and sitting self-consciously. And when they stood up to sing they stumbled over the words of the old hymns they'd not sung since they were children, dragged to the chapel by their grim-faced mothers. Now here they were being dragged there by their equally determined wives. Not much had changed it seemed in their sorry existence!

But after the first ten minutes or so of acute embarrassment and foot shuffling, they forgot themselves as they listened to Amos, whose quiet voice, the voice they had listened to for so many lunch-times, began preaching to them again. It was the same voice, certainly, but now there was a strength and confidence in it that they had never heard before, and which stirred emotions in them that they had thought long since dead and left behind with childhood.

"Friends, brothers, fellow-workers. You are welcome to our congregation. You see before you a poor and hapless sinner! I know some of my faults, and I am certain that I have many more of which I am, as yet, unaware. That is a great sadness and must be rectified before I can hope to meet my Maker in the joyous Hereafter. But there are joys here on this earth which it would be a sin to deny. The joy of a kind face and a loving hand in friendship; a warm fire and nourishing meal; of a happy home and comforting smile. These are the gifts of love that we all understand and many of us are lucky enough to know. The love of a family; our own family. But how much greater can that love – that ecstasy of happiness here on earth – flow if we embrace the whole of humanity as our family. Together, I say to you…" He looked at the faces of the congregation, upturned and expectant, and his eyes seemed to bore into each one of those men sitting still and silent, their heads bare, their hands still clutching their caps. "I say to each one of you that together we are the Lord's family, the Body of Christ, the children of the same heavenly Father. Together we can inherit the Kingdom of God. By including all those who are less fortunate than ourselves, by showing love and compassion to even the meanest of our kin, then our family, our loving, caring, family, can grow daily. We must each of us reach out our hands to our fellows and take them to our hearts and give them succour. For to reach out to them is to reach out to God Himself. I tell you, sisters, brothers, little children." Here Amos' voice began to rise and his eyes to blaze. "Only by offering our hands to those in need can our own immortal souls be saved. Then the joys of Heaven will be ours. But –" And in the silence, he looked round once again at the expectant audience. His voice dropped to a whisper. "But only neglect our neighbours and we do so at our peril." The silence in the hall was almost tangible.

"For then not all the prayers in the world can save us from damnation, from the terrible and eternal fires of hell. God is a just and merciful God, but it is in our own hears that we must search for repentance and that love which alone can save us. Ignore our innermost hearts and we ignore the eternal damnation from which there is no escape."

There was silence again as he gave the listeners a chance to digest this awesome prospect, but the sermon ended at last, and the little organ piped up with the final hymn as the congregation shuffled out into the bright winter sunshine. Many of the men stayed to speak to Amos, to congratulate him on the service and to assure him, eyes downcast, that they would certainly come again. "When you're preaching, lad," said the honest Joe. And Amos had to be content with that. The congregation dispersed and he was left, exhausted and slightly downhearted, to be chivvied and encouraged by the two women who were the only family he had ever really known.

Chapter Six

Throughout the following day Gertie thought very hard about Amos' sermon. She knew only too well the deprivation and suffering experienced by the poor. Always cold and hungry as a small child, often punished simply for being an orphan and never knowing the warmth of a mother's love, she realised that her concerns lay more with trying to help these people in a practical way rather than in dealing with their spiritual welfare. She would leave the ministration of their souls to the more idealistic Amos. But she was certain that her future lay in helping him to bring about a fairer and kinder society. How she was to do this she had not the faintest idea, but she determined that she would do whatever lay in her power to do. If she could only save one child from the torment and misery she herself had experienced, then she felt that her life would have been worthwhile. But with Amos as her guide and mentor she felt strong enough to slay dragons in her desire to give hope to the hopeless and succour to the poor. So, while her nimble fingers worked on the cartridges, her mind was planning ways in which she and Amos could begin their works of charity.

Perhaps Amos could rent a room or a hall somewhere and start up his own congregation, she thought. *Then that same room could be used as a soup kitchen and even Sunday School for the orphans and children from the workhouse.* She and Amos could arrange outings and picnics for the poor and teach them to read and write. They could gradually recruit more like-minded people and soon they would have a whole series of schools throughout London and even England!

She was so excited by her thoughts and dreams of success that her fingers became still until suddenly she realised that Mrs Mabbett was standing over her and chiding her for her idleness.

"Gertrude Thomas, whatever are you about? You have been sat there these five minutes in a trance. Thinking of fine brown eyes and a handsome face I'll be bound!"

Everyone giggled and Gertie hurriedly went back to her work, apologising, her head lowered to hide her blushes.

That evening she hurried back to Beresford Street, her mind in a whirl of excitement. She couldn't wait to tell Amos of her ideas. She rushed upstairs as soon as she reached home, washed her hands and brushed her silky brown locks, which she now wore in demure braids, and then tripped down to the dining room aglow with enthusiasm. She helped Sarah to lay the table, chatting absentmindedly to her, and then at last she heard the firm tread of her dearest Amos. Tired and covered in dust from his work, he grinned at the two girls and gave Gertie a peck on the cheek.

"Hello, little-un, how was your day? You look very well." He went up to his room to wash and tidy himself for supper, which he insisted on calling dinner. It seemed an age to Gertie before dinner was eaten, everything cleared away and she and Amos could retire to the parlour to sit over his books and papers. "For I'll have no arguing at my table," had said Mrs Mabbett in awful tones. "Religion is a very fine thing and there is no more devout believer than myself, nor Mr Mabbett, God rest his soul, but the dinner table is not the place for such discussion. Grace is said and that's an end of it. As it says in the Good Book, there is a time and place for everything," and she had folded her arms and shooshed them out of the room.

But they were alone at last. Amos turned to that place in the Bible which Mrs Mabbett had quoted, about a time for all things, but Gertie stopped him as he began to read.

"Here it is in Ecclesiastes," he said. "To everything this is a season and a time to every purpose under the heaven."

"Amos, I have been having lots of ideas on how I can help you! You must let me tell you all about them and then we can work out together how we can make them happen, please, Amos," she begged, as he seemed to be listening with only one ear to her and glancing at the text as she spoke. She gripped his arm, her eyes wide and anxious. "Please, you must listen to me and tell me whether or not I am being foolish. Oh, I do hope you think my idea a good one; I so want to help all those who are poor like we were! We have been lucky, Amos, you and me, but there are many who are not so fortunate and who are at this moment starving and living in misery. Surely now is the time to help them!"

The urgency in her voice and the hand tugging at his sleeve made Amos turn to her with a serious expression on his usually cheerful face. He placed the Bible back amongst the pile of books on the little table at his elbow and smiled gently.

"Why, whatever is it, little-un? What is this idea that has made you so excited? Calm down and we'll discuss it like two rational grown-ups."

She stopped pulling at his sleeve and composed her hands demurely in her lap. She tried to put her thoughts into some kind of order while Amos waited patiently.

"You see, Amos, the first thing is this. The men you work with, and who came to chapel yesterday, said they would only come again when you were to preach. But how often is Mr Johnson away? And they are not likely to want to go much further afield to listen to you at any other chapel where you might get the chance of preaching. It is all so unsure and…and…"

"Indefinite?" asked Amos.

"Yes, that is the word! So what I thought was this. Suppose you – we – find a hall or room somewhere near here that we can have for nothing, or at least at a very low rent. Then you could preach there every Sunday and I could run a Sunday School and perhaps we could get other people to help in the evenings, say using it as a soup kitchen and haven for the homeless. If it was a success, we could get other halls and rooms until there was a string of them everywhere. What do you think, Amos? Oh, do say you think my plan is a good one!"

She had become agitated again, grasping the lapels of his worn and grubby jacket, her face animated and her eyes wide. He gently unhooked her fingers and took her hands in his.

"What you say makes sense, but Gertie, such things cost money and there is none to spare. I am afraid this is just a dream, and you would do better to put it out of your mind, at least for the present. No, we will simply have to wait until a suitable living can be found for me and then we may think again. You must put such thoughts from your mind and concentrate on your studies, for if you are to be a true help to me you must complete your education. You are still barely more than a child as yet, and a female, scarcely able to understand the complexities of these things. Now, let us read this passage that Mrs Mabbett quoted to us."

Gertie couldn't believe what she was hearing. Amos seemed almost like a stranger to her, pontificating on like an old man. She pushed the Bible to one side and stood up, staring at him with anger and disbelief.

"Amos Parker, what have they done to you? Where is the boy who helped me to steal pen and ink from matron because we cared about being poor ourselves? Now that you are no longer hungry and homeless have you given up fighting for the rights of those less fortunate than yourself? Is that what all your fancy learning does for you? How can you talk so, to give up before you have even begun! Amos." She clutched at his coat again, shaking him in her agitation, "Listen to me. It may be a dream now, but together we can make it a reality." Her voice ended on a sob and she sat down on the settle, twisting her kerchief in her hands. But Amos was not to be spoken to so, especially by a girl whom he considered little more than an amusing sister.

"I am sorry that you should think so of me, Gertie," he said, his voice cold and angry. "But I have a great deal more experience of these things than you and I have no intention of being coerced into agreeing to such hair-brained schemes, especially by a young lady who should know better than to act like nothing more than a fishwife. NO!" Gertie began to remonstrate. "My mind is made up. There is no money for such ideas and neither of us has the time to play 'Lady Bountiful'. You need to spend more time at your books as it is, if you are truly to be of help to me, since there are still many gaps in your knowledge. Let that be an end of it, there is no more to say on the subject." And with that he walked stiffly out of the room.

Gertie remained on the settle where he had left her, waves of misery flooding over her. Not only was this the first real quarrel they had ever had, but she also knew that Amos seemed to have changed in subtle ways. Was it merely because he was grown-up and she was still only a girl, or was there something more; something that had happened to him during his years in the college? The tears ran unchecked down her cheeks until at last, the guttering candle finally flickering out, she crept up the stairs and crawled into bed, to cry into the pillow until she finally fell into an exhausted sleep.

Breakfast the next morning was a stiff and silent affair, with neither young person looking at the other and Mrs Mabbett, aware that something had happened, trying to keep up a merry stream of light-hearted gossip. But the meal ended at last, and they all made their way to the arsenal, Gertie walking with the older woman and Amos going on ahead. All through that day Gertie worked mechanically, her fingers making the cartridges, but her mind was numb. She felt exhausted and everything seemed distant and unreal. When home-time finally arrived, she knew that she couldn't go on like this. She would confront Amos; tell him he was right, and she was sorry – anything that would make things better between them. But Amos didn't appear for dinner. The meal was once again eaten in a strained silence on Gertie's part and this time Mrs Mabbett kept her conversation to no more than the odd observation on the weather or the flavour of the carrots. But just as the meal was over and Gertie had stood up to help clear the table, the front door was heard to open, and the familiar tread echoed along the passage. Before Mrs Mabbett could stop her, Gertie rushed out of the room, almost colliding with Amos as he was about to open the parlour door. They stood facing one another for a moment and then, without a word, Amos took her into his arms and kissed her, a long and passionate kiss. She melted into his arms and there they stood, oblivious of time or of Mrs Mabbett, who had glanced briefly into the parlour and quickly taken herself off, closing the door gently and retiring to the kitchen, her plump face beaming with pleasure.

Amos released Gertie at last, saying what a brute he had been, and he had no right to speak to his 'little-un' in that way. Breathless, Gertie denied any such thing and insisted she had been nothing but a silly and foolish child. They laughed and kissed again and then Amos led her to the settle, where they sat, hand in hand, desiring nothing more than to be in each other's company. But at last Amos spoke,

"What you said last night does make sense, my love, but it is also true that we have no money to finance such schemes. There are so many questions to solve before we could set your ideas in motion. But I have thought hard about them, and the first question for which I demand an answer, and which it should not be so very difficult to solve, is this: if we are to work together, my dearest little-un, then we cannot continue in our present state. Miss Thomas," he said, putting his hand on his heart and going down on one knee. "I beg that you will consent to be my wife. You cannot be so cruel as to deny me now. To say yes will make me the happiest of men!"

With his brown eyes sparkling, his hair standing on end more than ever and his infectious grin lighting up his handsome features, Gertie thought he had never looked so fine. She laughed and blushed as she almost threw herself into his arms.

"Oh yes, Amos, of course I will marry you. But only on condition that from now on you listen to all my ideas and take them seriously!"

"I would not dare to do otherwise!" said the young swain, as they waltzed about the room in each other's arms. They fell on to the settle at last, giggling and exhausted and then, after kissing once more, made their way quietly upstairs, separating on the landing, Amos to his room and Gertie going on up to her little bed in the attic, making sure not to wake Sarah in her excitement and once more scarcely sleeping, although for very different reasons. Next morning she woke with dark rings under her eyes, causing Mrs Mabbett to tut in concern.

"You two young people should not spend so much time pouring over your books," she had said, but with a twinkle in her eye. However, Gertie vowed to say nothing to her until that evening, when she and Amos could announce their momentous news together.

The day seemed to flag on endlessly, but work finished at last, and Gertie skipped home with a light step. She went upstairs and washed and then joined Mrs Mabbett in the parlour. They had chosen that room to sit in as Gertie had informed the good widow that she had something of the greatest importance to impart. Mrs Mabbett played her part, appearing mystified, blessing herself and wondering whatever could be so important that the must need assemble in there.

Amos finally arrived and before he could wash thc day's dirt from his tired limbs he was dragged into the room by an excited Gertie. Then, standing together hand in hand, the young couple told Mrs Mabbett their astounding news.

"Dearest Mrs Mabbett, Amos has asked me to marry him, and I have said 'yes'! And we are to set up a chapel of our own together and I will run a Sunday School and a soup kitchen and –"

"Whoa! Steady on, little-un. One thing at a time," Amos said, laughing, as she ran out of breath in her excitement.

Mrs Mabbett embraced each of them in turn, congratulating them and hugging them between her laughter and tears.

"But where are you to live?" she said innocently. They stared at her, crestfallen.

"Oh!" stammered Gertie. "Oh, Amos, we forgot to discuss the details. May we not stay here?" She turned to Mrs Mabbett. "Please say we may, dearest ma'am, or at least until we find a suitable lodging for a married couple. That is agreeable to you, Amos, is it not?" she asked anxiously, her dark eyes wide, not wishing to anger him. He put his arm round her waist and squeezed her tight.

"If Mrs Mabbett is agreeable, then that is exactly what we should wish to do." He flashed his most beguiling smile at the widow.

"Well, I am sure I couldn't say!" she said, pretending fluster to cover up her pleasure. "You are welcome, of course, but are any of the rooms suitable for…for a…married couple?"

Gertie flushed and giggled, but Amos, for once the practical one, said,

"Suppose Gertie and I have the attic room, which is quite large enough for our present needs (here he squeezed Gertie a little tighter) and perhaps Sarah can move into the room I occupy at present. Of course, the decision must be yours, ma'am, but this seems a suitable arrangement for the moment if you think fit."

And so it was agreed. The wedding was arranged for the first week after Christmas, Mr Johnson was to marry them and Mrs Mabbett was to be Matron of Honour, with two of Gertie's friends from the factory as bridesmaids. Mrs Mabbett, practical as ever, hunted out her own wedding dress, which she snipped and tucked and measured until it fitted Gertie's trim little figure like a glove, there being no money for such refinements as new clothes.

The wedding was a simple affair and afterwards everyone went back to the house in Beresford Street to fill up on wedding cake and ale, Joe and several of the arsenal workers joining them in the celebrations. But the day ended at last, and nothing was left to do but to kiss Mrs Mabbett a grateful goodnight and walk up the two long flights of stairs arm in arm to the little haven under the eaves, where, for once, Amos silenced Gertie's chatter.

++++++++++

Now that they were married, Gertie was able to unfold her plan to Amos in its entirety. During the last month she had thought through her ideas in the greatest detail, and now, that first Sunday after their marriage, walking home from the little chapel in Joseph Street, she broached the subject of looking for a hall or unused building to Amos once again.

"I am sure it is of no consequence what condition it is in, for we can clean and rebuild it good as new ourselves. Or, if we cannot find an old chapel, then there are many halls available at a small rent. Why, I know of three public houses that hire out their halls. The Labourer's Union sometimes meets in one!"

Amos stopped in his tracks, his face solemn as he turned to Gertie,

"My dearest love, you surely are not suggesting that we use public house property in which to preach the word of the Lord? God knows I am not against the occasional glass of port wine and do not align myself with those who advocate total abstinence, but a public house, a den of iniquity, really Gertie, I thought you would have more delicacy!"

Gertie was taken aback. Once again she saw the slight primness turn down the corners of his mouth and was in sudden fear that if he was not careful Amos might turn into a prude.

"Well, Amos, that may be so," she said sharply. "But if you want the working men of this parish to turn to God, you will have to go to them, because sure as eggs they won't come to you!"

They had reached home by this time and Amos put his arm round her and gave her a hug.

"Come, sweetheart, let us not quarrel again on our first full day as man and wife. I hear what you are saying, but I would prefer to preach the Lord's word in a consecrated house of God rather than in a heathen back room. Please say that you will support me in this Gertie, at least to begin with, for I rely on you so completely."

Gertie melted.

"Why, of course, Amos, we will first of all seek out some chapel or private room for your ministry. I only meant the other if all else fails."

The dark moment passed, and he was his usual cheerful self again, but in her heart Gertie felt that what she had said about the workmen was true. She only hoped that her belief in their fickleness was not justified. She admitted ruefully to herself that she cared little for their immortal souls but did care passionately that neither they nor their families should suffer hunger or deprivation. And even more, she cared for those in the direst poverty, without work or hope. But she also knew that for Amos the care of their souls mattered more to him than the comfort of their bodies. Well, between them, Amos looking after their eternal life and her seeing to their material needs here on earth, the poor of this Parish should be some of the best cared for in Kent, or even England!

They both agreed that the first thing to do was to approach Mr Johnson to see what advice he could offer. Gertie still helped out with the Sunday School and so, that same afternoon, once the school children had all been packed off to their homes with a tract to learn by heart for the next week, she and Amos joined Mr and Mrs Johnson for another cup of tea in rather quieter surroundings. The minister was aware of Amos' desire to set up a small congregation of working men and had therefore drawn up a list of derelict chapels, unfrequented halls and odd back rooms he knew to be dotted about the town. The list looked quite formidable. There seemed to be no end of buildings vacant or scarcely in use.

The couple thanked the minister and decided to set about inspecting those nearest to the arsenal immediately.

The first few 'halls' they inspected were discovered to be little more than tiny back rooms, hopefully offered at a nominal rent by the near destitute who had no interest in religion but who were desperately trying to keep from the workhouse. Families squashed into one room so that the other could become vacant were all too frequent. Gertie's soft heart went out to all these folk and left to her own devices would have agreed to renting half a dozen of these squalid little hovels. But her resolute husband dragged her quickly away from this possible disaster and they made their way finally to Rodney Street, where the ancient Bethel Chapel stood, near the Ship and Half-moon stairs. The derelict little chapel immediately delighted Gertie and she begged Amos to approach the owners at once. But the day had already darkened into evening and the cold air was beginning to bite through their thin clothes. Amos was firm.

"No, darling, we will return next Sunday, having first discovered the owners in order to obtain the key, and then we will see whether such a building is any longer fit to hold a congregation. We must not rush into anything but explore all possibilities before we make our decision."

The prim mouth had returned, and Gertie could hear overtones of Amos' college training in this rather pedantic speech, but, instead of allowing herself to be worried by the way her love seemed to react to any impetuosity on her part, she merely giggled and squeezed his hand.

"Yes, Amos," she said primly. "We shall do as you say, of course. You know best, my love." And Amos, unsure whether she was serious, or was laughing at him in her gentle way, walked on, puzzled and slightly hurt. Surely his wife was not turning into a skittish little creature, unconcerned with the serious aspects of life? Not his Gertie, who cared so passionately for the poor and destitute of this Parish and who had such plans for helping him in his vocation? They walked on in silence, this young couple who still had so much to learn about each other and who were going to change the world!

During the following week Amos made enquiries about Bethel Chapel. It seemed that it belonged to the Scottish Presbyterians but was no longer suitable for their needs. Amos must see a Mr Ranwell, who would be able to furnish him with its history and who was a deacon of the Church. Mr Ranwell was now residing near Plumstead Common, and so, one dark evening, Gertie and Amos walked up the long hill and across the common to the pretty little cottage which turned out to be not far from the old workhouse. They rang the bell and an elderly lady wearing an old fashioned mob-cap and spectacles answered the door. She showed the couple into the parlour, which was cluttered with an incredible number of what-nots, occasional tables and hard horse-hair chairs. Everything, even the mantel piece, seemed to be covered in draperies and the smoking fire made their eyes water. The old dame directed them to sit down on the singularly uncomfortable-looking settle and then bustled out in search of 'the master'.

Amos and Gertie sat in silence for what seemed an age, the ormolu clock on the mantel piece ticking away the minutes as the fire spluttered and crackled. At last the parlour door opened and an elderly man entered, his tall frame having to stoop low to miss the dark beam over the door. He was thin and craggy, his white eyebrows highlighting the darkness of his deep and glittering eyes. He shook hands with them both as they rose and spoke with a soft Scottish accent.

"Good evening to ye both. I understand from my good housekeeper, Mrs Peebles, that you would be wanting to hire the wee Bethel Chapel?"

"Yes, sir. I am a preacher of the Methodist Church but have not yet found a suitable venue for setting up a congregation. At present this will be of a purely voluntary nature until I can find a vacant living, but both my wife here," and he pushed Gertie forward, "and myself are particularly anxious that the men of the arsenal should have the opportunity to hear the word of the Lord and so we felt that a chapel as near as possible to their place of work was the ideal answer and Bethel Chapel seems to fulfil that ideal."

Amos was twisting his cap in his hands and to Gertie's private amusement looked quite nervous under the old man's scrutiny. So, her fearless hero could sometimes be subdued! She supposed it was the fear of losing something he wanted so desperately that made him so unsure of himself. She took pity on him at last and gave a little curtsy as she flashed her sweetest smile at the old gentleman. The stern and flashing eyes softened, and he melted visibly.

"You see, sir, my husband is concerned for the souls of these poor men who at present have so little in their lives and are therefore inclined to turn to alcoholic beverage as succour. If we could only help them to follow the word of God and turn away from their present habits, then not only would their souls be less likely to be condemned to perdition, but their situation in this life would improve; both theirs and that of their poor wives and families. My husband and I both know the misery and degradation of poverty, sir. We were raised in the workhouse just by here."

The old man turned away and stared into the fire.

"Aye, aye. Well, I wouldn't be knowing about that. I am sure the Good Lord would not be displeased if the place were to be used for His holy work once more, even if it is to you Methodists. But mind, it's no fit for human habitation as it stands! Ye'll need to spend some time on repairs and the like. It's only wood and yon roof is full of holes."

"Well, sir, that is not a problem to us. In fact, by getting men from the arsenal to help with the renovations, we will be half-way to leading them to the Lord. The main problem is rent. We can afford so little and have no guarantee of an immediate congregation, though I am sure that as word spreads, we will be able to cover expenses."

"Hmph! You're mighty confident, young sprogget! But I like that in a man. The chapel's yours, if you can make a go of it. If it's still going in six months from now, then we'll see about rent. Now, in the meanwhile, I wouldna be so heathen as to send ye away without a bite. Ye'll stay for a wee cup of tea and some of Mrs Peebles' renowned Dundee cake." He went to the door. "Martha!"

Mrs Peebles came hurrying along the passage, carrying a tray laden with tea and cakes. She was beaming as she carefully laid the tray on one of the many small tables.

"I knew you wouldn't wish the young couple to go out into such a night without a little something to warm their insides," she said, twinkling up at the old man. He grunted again.

"Aye, aye, well, that will be all now, Mrs Peebles. I'll see ye tomorrow."

"That you will sir, if we're spared," she said as she went out of the door, wishing Amos and Gertie a 'bonny goodnight' as she went.

The cake was excellent and the tea warming. A wind had got up and there was a threat of snow in the heavy clouds as Gertie and Amos finally said goodnight and thank you to the old man. The cold soon broke the spell of sleepy contentment that had enveloped the little cottage and they hurried back into town and the welcome lights of the house in Beresford Street, Gertie clinging tightly to her new wedding bonnet. Mrs Mabbett welcomed them warmly with yet another cup of tea, this time enhanced with a 'nip of something to warm your innards' as she put it (although Amos had noticed a touch of something in the tea Mrs Peebles had offered them. So Mr Ranwell wasn't averse to a little drop himself at times!) Gertie excitedly told Mrs Mabbett the news while Amos stood before the fire, one foot on the fender, staring down into the flames.

"And there is to be no rent to pay for six months!" Gertie was saying to the widow. But Amos intervened.

"My dear, I cannot think it is right that we should use this hall as though it were given to us in charity. I cannot, I will not take it on such an agreement. No!" he said, holding up his hand as both women opened their mouths to argue, "No, my mind is made up. We will write to the good Mr Ranwell, thanking him for his offer, but explaining that we would not consider such a transaction without payment of at least a small rent. This can be taken from the weekly collection, a part going to renovation and the rest to Mr Ranwell until the building is finished, when any moneys we have left can go towards starting up your Sunday School, Gertie. We will start the way we intend to continue; beholden to no one."

There was a long silence as both women stared at him. This was no longer the carefree and handsome young man that Gertie had fallen in love with so many years ago. It was a prim-mouthed bigot who was mouthing the words of the men who seemed to have so influenced him during his years at college. Something inside Gertie rose up in mutiny. There was no way she was going to let these unworldly bigots and all *men* at that, continue to influence her beloved husband! She and Amos would work together as equals or not at all. She faced him squarely.

"Amos Parker, haw dare you speak to me as though I were...I were..."

"A subordinate?" put in Mrs Mabbett.

"Yes, a subordinate. I am your wife and, I hope, your equal. And I will not," Here she stamped her foot. "I will not see you turn into one of those old fuddy-duddies from your precious academy. If you don't want the hall for nothing, then let us discuss it like sensible adults. I cannot agree that it would be 'charity' as you call it, since the hall is lying idle now and by letting us use it we would be saving souls, which to my mind would be payment enough! But we must talk about it together. Besides," she added lamely. "The hall was my idea, and I should be consulted on any decisions made."

She realized that she had been shouting at her beloved, but with the last comment his face had suddenly relaxed, and he had burst out laughing.

"Why, my little termagant, I had no idea that you would be angry at my suggestion. Of course we are equal, you and I, and you are quite right to say that all decisions must be made together. And you are included, of course, ma'am," he said, turning to Mrs Mabbett with his charming smile. "Now, let the three of us sit and discuss this business sensibly. Gertie, I have explained to you why I am unhappy with Mr Ranwell's offer. You feel that by offering to preach to a congregation we are giving payment enough. Mrs Mabbett, what is your opinion?"

Once more the ugly moment had passed, but Gertie was becoming aware that her adored husband, having been 'got at' as she put it to herself, needed the steadying influence of her own down to earth practical nature to keep him from becoming too dogmatic. She was also aware that she would have to tread very delicately if she were to succeed in holding on to the good-natured young man she had fallen in love with. Once they gained a wife, men seemed to be obsessed with becoming some sort of patriarch! *Her Amos was not going to descend to that level*, she vowed firmly. Mrs Mabbett was voicing her views.

"Well, Amos dear, it seems to me that if this Mr Ranwell thinks it suitable to let you use his hall without a fee, then you should not look a gift horse in the teeth, so to speak, but more think of it as God's will. After all, you are not going to use the hall for immoral purposes, but to spread His Word. Where can be the harm in accepting a gift for that purpose? Now, I think you should write to Mr Ranwell, but merely to express your thanks and urge that if the venture is a success, then he must accept a small rent in gratitude. Now, Gertie, you kiss your husband and make up, both of you, and then we must all go to bed, as it is well past midnight and we shall all be good for nothing in the morning."

And so it was agreed. The letter was sent, the keys obtained, and a small army of helpers was conscripted to sweep and clean and put the little chapel into some semblance of order for Amos to carry out God's work.

Chapter Seven

The snow fell heavily over the next few days, but Gertie and Amos found no lack of helpers from among their workmates in the arsenal. Joe, the great atheist, rallied the men and the very next Monday evening after gaining the keys to Bethel Chapel, a small lamp-lit procession could be seen making its way towards the river and the Ship and Half-moon stairs where the forlorn little wooden building lay, its windows broken, moss growing between the missing slates of the roof and the garden in which it stood a mass of weeks, lying black and dead in the snow. Gertie pushed open the ancient gate and they all trooped up to the door. Amos fumbled for the key and eventually found it in his jacket pocket. He held it up for inspection and then ceremoniously unlocked the rickety door. They all stepped cautiously inside. The light from the lamps cast eerie shadows round the walls, which had originally been painted white, but which now seemed to be growing various unspeakable things on their damp surfaces. Joe took out a notebook, licked the tip of a pencil and then began laboriously to make a note of all the immediate renovations needed. The walls would be serviceable enough for now if they were given a good scrub. Jack, who was the proud possessor of a roof ladder, said he'd have a go at the slates and Tom, the arsenal handyman, fingered the broken chairs with his wise old fingers and reckoned most of them could be repaired with 'a bit of hope and aid from the Good Lord!'

The table which served for an altar was in relatively good condition, although mice seemed to have had a field day with the cloth covering it. They poked about in all the dark corners and it was then that they found the little harmonium. Joshua's eyes lit up. He fancied himself as something of a keyboard specialist and his house, all four rooms of it, was crammed from floor to ceiling with instruments of all shapes and sizes, much to the despair of his good-natured wife. He ran his hands over the instrument lovingly and tried playing it. A noise like a wailing banshee issued forth and everyone exclaimed in alarm, but Joshua, unperturbed, merely said that he'd bring his hand cart over 'first thing Sundy' and take the wretched creature away. "I'll soon set her up, good as new," he assured anyone who was listening. But the rest of the party had moved on to the little room at the back to inspect the pump and the range with its old rusty kettle still perched jauntily on the metal plate. While everyone nosed about in the kitchen Gertie returned to the hall. Joshua had found a music stool and on lifting the lid had discovered a pile of musty, yellowing hymn sheets, complete with musical accompaniments. They both exclaimed over it and Gertie decided to take them home to learn. She vowed to practise so that when the harmonium was mended she would be able to play the hymns for Amos' services.

Little more could be done that evening as it was already very late, the hall was icy cold, and they all had to be up betimes in the morning, but it was agreed that they would meet on the Sunday, after morning service, armed with brushes and mops and ladders and all the hammers, nails and paraphernalia needed to make the chapel hospitable.

On Sunday, good as their word, everyone arrived at the chapel just after midday, Daniel, who worked in the same shed as Amos, bringing his whole family with him ; his wife, as broad as Daniel was thin, saying that 'you can't trust these men to do a proper job of it!' she quickly set five of their six children to work, scrubbing the floors, while she took a bucket and long broom, and, with her sleeves rolled up to her plump white elbows, she proceeded to wash the walls, her last child, a baby of five or six months, strapped to her back. Daniel took himself off to the kitchen where he could be heard pottering happily among the pipes of the old stove, while everyone else set about their various allotted tasks. Will, a glazier, cut his hand slightly on a jagged piece of glass and Gertie hurried him out to the pump which, to her great delight, still spouted clean, sweet water. She carefully bathed Will's hand and wrapped it in a piece of linen torn from her own pinafore. But except for the odd slightly muffled blasphemous exclamation as a hammer hit an unsuspecting thumb and a muffled cry as Jack nearly fell through the roof, there were no real mishaps and after three hours, including a break to eat their packed lunches, the hall was already looking relatively clean and almost cheerful. Joshua had brought jars of surplus Arsenal paint and brushes which had been sitting idle and unused for some years in one of the empty sheds. After being assured by his foreman that he would be doing the place a service by 'finding a good home for them', he had piled them up on his ancient cart and brought them over to the chapel. Once they'd been unloaded, he lovingly lifted the old harmonium up into the now empty space, helped by some of the men, promising that he would make it good as new. Gertie sang as she polished the table and those chairs that were still serviceable and then she produced a tape-measure from her pinafore pocket and began measuring the windows. Amos stopped painting the front door and stared at her in surprise.

"What are you doing, little'un?" he asked her, his face alight with amusement. She answered from the top of the stool where she was perched, her arms stretched out across the top of the window.

"Two foot six inches." She looked down at Amos. "I'm measuring the windows, that's what! Some nice yellow gingham curtains will go a treat up here and make the place look really lived in."

"But, sweetheart, this is a church, not a parlour!"

She climbed down off the stool.

"Yes, I know, Amos, but don't forget that it is going to be a Sunday School and a soup kitchen as well eventually. I don't see why we have to be all miserable just because we are worshipping God. You've said as much yourself, remember, and so did Mr Johnson!"

But Amos was so happy with the progress made in renovating his little chapel that for once he was in no mood to remonstrate with his wife. If she wanted curtains, she should have curtains!

"Very well, darling. Although where the money is to come from to buy yards of gingham, I have no notion."

Rather surprised that Amos had not put on his prim voice and argued with her, she gave him a quick hug and returned to her measuring. She hoped Mrs Mabbett had organised a good dinner that evening to keep her husband in such a mellow mood.

By the time February was well advanced the chapel was transformed. Its white walls were clean and spotless, new windows sparkled behind their merry gingham curtains and several rows of sturdy chairs stood on the scrubbed stone floor. The women had clubbed together to help buy the materials needed for the curtains and new tablecloth and Mrs Mabbett, exhibiting yet another accomplishment, had shown Gertie how to sew hems and match patterns. The wives of all the men involved in the enterprise had taken a keen delight in seeing to it that their husbands spent their spare time usefully in Bethel Chapel and often went with them to make sure that they didn't end up at the Ship instead. But their genuine enthusiasm for the venture seemed to be contagious and much of the talk in the arsenal was about methods of roofing, dovetail joints and ways of keeping fungus at bay. Gradually more men came along to help, or merely to 'inspect the work', as they put it sheepishly, not wishing anyone to think that they had 'got religion'!

But by March, with the little garden dug, spring bulbs already showing through and everything clean and sparkling, Amos decided that it was time to hold his first service. Joshua had done a remarkable job on the harmonium and now, instead of a horrible wail, the little instrument produced a soft and gentle tone. Gertie had practised hard and could now manage a half dozen of the easier hymns with scarcely a wrong note.

"The men won't notice anyway," Amos had commented. "Most of them are probably tone deaf!"

"Well, we'll see. But I want everything to be as good as possible," she had answered, hoping that all her hard work had not been in vain.

She needn't have worried, however. That first Sunday it seemed to Gertie and Amos that almost the whole of the arsenal workforce was crammed into the tiny building, all the seats taken, with people having stand in the aisles, at the back and even squashed into the tiny kitchen. Amos welcomed them all and Gertie struck up the first hymn. It was then that she knew all their prayers, hard work and even quarrels, had been worth every second; for, above the general singing of the congregation, rose a number of rich male voices that filled the room until, to Gertie's ear, the little chapel could as well have been a cathedral for the beauty of the sound heard that day. She played as she had never played before, the tears rolling down her cheeks as her fingers blindly found the right notes and her feet pedalled as fast as they were able. The hymn ended at last and the silence that fell on the congregation that glorious spring morning was as joyful as the singing of a multitude of angels, at least, so Gertie thought as she turned to look at Amos, who was standing at the altar-table, its green cloth fresh and clean as the day. His face was transformed, and his voice shook as he began to speak:

"Dearest brethren, brothers and sisters, let us give thanks to God for this most glorious of days. I know many of you have laboured unceasingly and given all of your precious spare moments to bring about this joyful transformation, and I also know that now you have seen the fruits of your labour you will continue to support and preserve the life of this beautiful house of God. Brethren, let that transformation which we see all about us enter into our souls that we may know the true Word of the Lord and enter at last into His own glorious House, when the day of judgement finally arrives. Let us face God fresh and unsullied, as this little chapel stands today."

As he spoke the congregation listened, spell-bound. There was no doubt that most of the people there felt a proprietorial affection for the building and many of them already held Amos in great regard for his courage and tenacity. Never once, as far as they were aware, had he faltered in his belief that one day he would bring the Word of God to his fellow workers, so fulfilling the words of his Ordination. Gertie knew that they could not expect to fill the chapel to overflowing every Sunday, but she felt certain that they could, from now on, be sure of a respectable number of men who would be happy to accompany their wives at least once each Sunday to hear Amos preach. And she vowed also that, with such singers amongst their company, she and Amos would see to it that by cajoling, wheedling or even threats, they would have a fine choir to add to the glory of their smart new House of Worship!

At the end of the service, she and Amos stood at the door and shook hands with the entire congregation. Everyone praised their work and promised to come along to support them 'as often as is possible, Preacher and Mrs Parker, things being what they are', as most of them said, apologetically.

Finally everyone had gone and Gertie, Amos and their little chapel were alone at last.

"Darling, you were wonderful. How my heart was singing for you. And oh, Amos, did you hear those fine voices? We must set about stating a choir!" Gertie was in turn hugging her husband and dancing down the aisle. Laughingly Amos tried to quiet her, but he was too full of happiness himself to be dismayed at her indecorous behaviour.

"Hush, my love." He laughed. "That is no way for the wife of a successful Minister to behave! I am not sure that a choir is a normal part of Methodist worship, but, oh Gertie, did you see their faces? And you could hear a pin drop when I preached! We have done it! All our hard work has paid off and I only hope we can persuade them to stay. If only half that number attend from now on, we will have achieved something!"

They hurried home arm in arm to tell Mrs Mabbett the news. That good lady, although supportive as ever, felt that she could not desert Mr Johnson, not even for her beloved Gertie and Amos. Besides, this new venture was mainly designed to encourage those heathen factory workers who until now had never set foot inside a chapel, let alone joined in a service. Mr Johnson need have no fears of losing his congregation; those folk were already confirmed in their belief.

So that evening, after they had paid a visit to Mr Johnson and his wife to tell them all about the great success, they all sat round the rickety pianoforte while Gertie played some of their favourite hymns and later, as the port wine took effect, some slightly less solemn songs as well until, tired but very happy, they all went to bed to sleep the sleep of the just.

The next day many of the men came up to Amos to shake his hand, saying little and not quite able to look him in the eye. Amos knew this to be a great compliment, so he himself said little in his turn, but he knew that he had won the first battle. Now, he guessed, it was up to the wives to keep their men-folk on the straight and narrow. He knew that novelty would be the spur for the first few weeks, but after that had worn off, what then? Would the sense of religious fervour be strong enough to keep them coming every Sunday, after a week of back-breaking work and the tavern beckoning as a way of release? Perhaps Gertie was right; the men obviously enjoyed singing and maybe the chance of joining a choir would be an incentive to keep them attending on a regular basis. Even if such a thing was rather unorthodox in his ministry, it was better than losing the men altogether. Amos pondered on this and by that Monday evening he had made up his mind. They would start a choir and he would advertise the very next Sunday. He told Gertie of his plan and she was overjoyed.

"Oh Amos, this is wonderful news," she said, clapping her hands, her little face with its halo of brown curls, radiant and her dark eyes sparkling. "Who shall we employ to train it?"

But this was something he had not thought of in his enthusiasm. He could hardly ask Mr Johnson's advice on this question as that good Minister rather frowned on too much singing, except hymns of a very robust and martial nature, hardly conducive to the more delicate needs of a choir and all the musical training that entailed, at least to begin with. The full-blooded hymns could come later!

"There is Mr Probyn over the road. He teaches the pianoforte to some of the little girls who live near. Perhaps he could do it?"

"Well," said Amos, feeling rather deflated. "We could ask him. But we can't pay a fee. Most of the paint we used to refurbish the chapel was bought on tick, except the bit Joshua managed to bring, and we're going to have to repay that first from the collection money. That in itself is going to take some time! Perhaps he'd be willing to do it for nothing for a while at least, as it is in a good cause."

They decided to wait until the next Sunday to see how many signed up to join the choir before asking Mr Probyn for his services. The weather had turned cold and in the following few days a sleeting, driving rain was being blown by March winds into every corner and crevice and it seemed impossible to keep warm or dry. On the Thursday evening Gertie and Amos decided to pay a visit to Bethel Chapel to make sure it was standing up under the onslaught. They fought their way to Rodney Street, nearly bent double against the wind. Amos had brought a box of vestas and a good supply of candles as well as two lamps and as soon as they were inside the building they lit as many of the candles as they could, their frozen fingers fumbling and clumsy. But as the flickering light passed over the interior of the little building they cried out in disbelief. The floor was awash! Rain was pouring in from gaping holes in the roof and one of the windows was swinging loose on its rusty hinges, banging against the wall, rain spraying over the chairs under it. Gertie rushed over and closed the window, exclaiming in dismay at the sodden material which was leaving mud-spattered marks on the newly painted wall. Her lovely curtains! As they looked about them their hearts sank. It was as though God had not wanted them to offer a fine new building to Him for His worship! Or was He just testing them? Had it all been too easy? Gertie splashed her way across the floor to the harmonium. She tried it anxiously, but it still seemed to be in good order, as were the table and altar cloth. Most of the leaks seemed to be at the front part of the roof. They peered quickly into the kitchen, but all was well in there as far as they could see. They collected two buckets which had been left after the cleaning was finished, and a bowl used for the pump water. They put them under the worst of the leaks, mopped up as much of the water as possible with a mot and cloths thoughtfully provided by 'Mrs Joe', as she was known and then, after checking that all the windows were securely locked, they left the chapel and battled their way home. The wind was behind them now and it nearly blew them back to Beresford Street, Gertie carefully carrying the muddy curtains under her shawl.

Once back home, with Mrs Mabbett fussing round them, clucking and tutting, they put their wet clothes in front of the fire, while she plied them with hot tea and insisted that Gertie take some evil tasting mixture for her troublesome cough. Then they all sat down and discussed what could be done to save the chapel.

"We'll have to get Jack down there as soon as maybe on Sunday morning to mend the roof. Some more slates must have blown off in the gale. We'll go down each evening and empty the buckets while the weather is like this and let us hope it clears up a bit before the next service."

But although the wind dropped, the rain showed no signs of letting up and by Sunday, exhausted and defeated after battling with the flooded floor, Gertie and Amos let Jack into the chapel early in order to try to get it into some semblance of order before the service began. He had brought some oilcloth with him which he laid over the worst area of the roof and nailed down as many tiles as he could before becoming completely soaked. Gertie had managed to light the old stove and she draped his overcoat on a chair in front of it as she hovered about him, fussing and worrying.

"Oh, jack, you're soaked! You look like a drowned rat. Here, let me take your boots off and put them on the stove to dry. You can't sit all morning in those!"

Jack remonstrated with her, but she would have none of it, so he sheepishly pattered about helping to clean up in socks that he commented were 'more holy than righteous', and his boots steaming gently in the kitchen.

Gertie hung the newly laundered curtain back at the window, the floor was once again mopped and dried, the buckets hidden away beside the pump and everything was spruced up and made as ready as possible for the service. The oilcloth seemed to serve its function satisfactorily as far as they could tell.

As eleven o'clock neared Gertie and Amos became apprehensive. Would anyone turn up today? The weather was dismal, and enthusiasm would almost certainly have waned now that the chapel was completed and no longer a novelty. Amos stood at the open door, glancing anxiously down the lane that led to the main road. Would they come? Gertie shouted to him to close the door as he was letting all the warmth out and the stack of wood, thoughtfully provided by Tom and with which she was feeding the stove, was dwindling rapidly. Jack put his boots back on before the smell of cooking leather 'knocked them all sideways', as he put it, and then busied himself straightening up the chairs and placing the hymn books along the rows. Amos nervously checked his sermon yet again and Gertie practised the more tricky bits of the day's hymns. Eleven o'clock. Five minute past. Ten minutes. And then, at a nearly quarter past eleven, just as the three of them were beginning to give up hope, the door burst open and a number of wet and bedraggled towns folk trouped into the chapel, shaking their wet clothes as they sat themselves down in the rows of chairs, chattering and dripping as they went.

"Sorry we're so late, Minister, but the road is flooded, and it took us an age to get acrost!" said Mrs Joe, beaming and wiping her face on her shawl as she spoke. "But we're all here now, so you can get started!"

And here they certainly were! Not the numbers of the first Sunday, but every chair was taken, and a few were standing in a little crowd at the back. His heart full, Amos welcomed them once again, thanking them for their devotion in answering the call of the Lord during such adverse weather.

The service proved to be as boisterous as ever, the little stove doing its proud duty, the ancient and creaking pipes which ran round the floors, warming the little chapel and causing steam to rise from the damp and aromatic garments, camphor being the predominant perfume. The singing was as rich and enthusiastic as on the previous occasion and so, at the end of the service, Amos announced his plan to start up a choir.

"...so, if any of you fine singers wish to stay behind after the service, we will take your names and organise a day and time for rehearsals. My wife and I feel that such God-given talent should not be wasted and what more fitting way of using those gifts than in His praise?"

It was settled. Fifteen men, caps in hand, shuffled up to the table when the service was over, pushed by their determined wives, and four rather elderly ladies, all spinsters and sisters to the various factory men, also offered their services. Gertie was delighted as she took their names.

"Next Sunday, when we have completed all the arrangements," she said, praying silently that Mr Probyn would comply, "we will announce all the details of choir practice, days to meet and so on. Thank you all for your support. My husband and I look forward to seeing you all next Sunday."

"Well, at least we are sure of nineteen in the congregation!" she said smilingly to Amos as they cleared away the hymn books and locked up for the day. Amos laughed.

"So my sermons aren't enough to keep their interest," he said, taking her in his arms and kissing the tip of her turned-up nose. "Oh ye of little faith!" and they walked happily back through the stinging rain to their warm and welcoming home, love in their steps and hope in their hearts.

Chapter Eight

They had no need to fear, however. Mr Probyn almost kissed them in his excitement at being asked to train a choir.

"We have no funds, Mr Probyn, so for the present it will all have to be voluntary. Perhaps later..."

"My dear, good lady," broke in the impecunious little pianoforte teacher, taking Gertie's hand and holding it tight in both of his. "Dear lady, it will be my delight and joy to aid you in this most reverent of tasks! I have to admit to neglecting my duty for some time now in terms of worshipping the 'Good Lord', as it were, my enthusiasm having somewhat waned as I survey my position teaching music to the less than earnest! But this, *this*, dear lady, will spur me on, God willing, to greater things! Pecuniary arrangements are the least of my thoughts as I accept such a great compliment. You shall have your choir, that I can promise you and no better voices shall be raised to Him on High! On this I give you my word."

Amos and Gertie, dazed by such eloquence, thanked him profusely and arranged that he should meet the members of the new choir the very next Sunday.

So, after the service, the hall packed as ever, the choir members all stayed behind to be introduced to Mr Probyn and a day and time arranged for them to practise. Everything was set up, a small corner of the chapel, by the harmonium, was cleared for the choristers and by the following Sunday, Bethel Chapel was the proud possessor of one of the finest choirs in the town.

During the next few weeks the congregation settled down to a respectable number of regulars. Amos held only the one service a day, not wishing to antagonise the men whose support he most needed. The choir flourished, Mr Probyn's pale cheeks began to gain a rosy glow and Gertie's fingers loosened as they roamed with greater confidence over the keyboard. Mr Probyn might have a rather odd way of speaking, but once in front of the singers his musical knowledge and gentle ways soon won them over and the men began to take a pride in the voices which, he told them were of the greatest gifts from God.

"For what do angels do, but sing His praises throughout eternity? What greater glory can there be for we poor mortals than to join that Heavenly Host and raise our voices in harmony with theirs?"

Thus did Mr Probyn encourage the men from the arsenal, who felt privileged to be part of such an enterprise. They were happy, Mr Probyn was truly fulfilled for the first time in his life and Amos thanked the Lord constantly for the realisation of all his dreams. Only Gertie was troubled. She still desperately wanted to help the poorest of the town but had no idea how she was to set about such a daunting task. She tried broaching the subject to Amos, but he was so busy dividing his time between working and running the chapel that he had little thought for anything else. In fact Gertie was feeling not a little neglected. She was working hard as well. Mrs Mabbett, no longer as young as she was, relied heavily on Gertie's experience and understanding in helping the little girls who were constantly being sent from the orphanage and workhouse to work in the cartridge shed. Yet Amos expected Gertie to keep up her hymn practice, provide cakes and tea for the choir, keep his clothes clean and in good condition and provide all the other services expected of a dutiful wife. Exhausted, lonely and with a cough constantly troubling her, she began to feel that she was nothing more than a skivvy to this husband of hers, who, in her eyes, thought more of his chapel than he did of his wife. She decided to pay a visit to Mrs Johnson. That kind lady would be sure to know the answers to Gertie's many questions.

As Amos only held a morning service, Gertie was still able to help out at the Johnson's Sunday School whenever she was able, and so, one Sunday afternoon, on a glorious spring day in late April, Gertie made her way down the little alleyway beside the Joseph Street Chapel to the Johnson's house. Mrs Johnson was shocked to see how thin and pale Gertie had become and led her straight into the parlour, instructing her little maid to bring tea and cakes and then firmly closing the parlour door.

"Do sit down, Gertie dear and tell me all about that husband of yours."

Gertie sat down, rather surprised at Mrs Johnson's words. She had imagined that it would be difficult to broach the subject of Amos' neglect of her to this gracious lady, but with a comforting cup of tea in one hand and a fairy cake in the other, she began to pour her heart out to an apparently willing ear. She explained how she supported and approved of everything that Amos did, that his entire thought was for God and the men of the arsenal, and that he never even looked at another woman. He was kind, gently and fervent in his love of 'God'. "But..."

"But he expects you to do the work of six, is absent more than he is at home, and neglects to offer you even the simplest recognition for all your support and hard work?"

Mrs Johnson was smiling gently as she spoke. She leaned forward and took Gertie's hands in her own as Gertie tried to choke back the tears. It was true! She was feeling neglected. Mrs Johnson patted the cold little hands as she went on in her warm, encouraging tones.

"Gertie, do you not realise that you are experiencing all the tribulations of the wife of a true minister of God? I felt exactly as you do when I first married Will. But over the years I have realised that it has been my privilege to support such a man, secure in the knowledge that he could not have managed the half of his activities without my help, advice and, yes, to be honest, my secret martyrdom. And Amos has not yet got a stipend, so he has to work twice as hard to prove that he can do what he has set his heart on. I can assure you, my dear, that although young Amos might have omitted to tell you how he feels about you, he has spoken to Will and myself in such glowing terms that it appears he has married a veritable angel! Now, I cannot pretend that life will change for you, in fact the more successful he is the less you will see of him. But he will still need all the support you can give, from listening to his sermon to darning his socks, but remember that if our menfolk are to succeed then they are lost without a helpmeet, lover and nursemaid all rolled into one! You are very young my dear, and at sixteen such a task must seem formidable indeed. But I was little more than your age when Will and I were wed, and I soon realised that it was truly my place to ensure that our marriage worked. I also realised that I needed to have an area of interest which was entirely my own. I suggest that you do the same. And always remember, it is far better to be a little neglected by a husband who is devoting himself to God rather than one who is a philanderer!"

Gertie, listening forlornly to this picture of her rather bleak and back-breaking future, jumped at the chance of explaining her desire to help the poorest in the town.

"You see, Ma'am, I have always cherished the hope that I could start up a soup kitchen and a Sunday School for orphans and the children of the workhouse, just as you have done. The chapel is quite suitable now; it has a little kitchen and I have put pretty curtains at the windows. It is bright and cheerful, and I know how to teach reading and writing to those sort of children. After all, I was one myself, so I know what it is like! But Amos is so busy with his congregation and I have to practise really hard to keep up with all the hymns Mr Probyn wants the choir to sing, and Mrs Mabbett's maid Sarah is leaving to get married herself in two weeks. There are so many things I want to do, but apart from not having any time, I just don't know how to set about it all!"

There was a silence for a while as the two women sat, staring into the flames of the comforting fire. Mrs Johnson spoke at last.

"I think, first of all my dear, that you must sort out your domestic arrangements. I am sure that there are any number of girls from the orphanage who would give anything to come to work for Mrs Mabbett as a maidservant. And here is the secret of being prudent with all your arrangements. Ensure that the good lady engages one who is sufficiently capable in reading and writing so that she is able to aid you in the Sunday School. Share the household tasks between you as much as you are confident you can both manage and concentrate to begin with on the smooth running of your home. Once the girl is sufficiently trained she will be able to take over all the tasks that are at present so irksome and time consuming to you, and it will leave you free to undertake those interests which are so dear to your heart. When that time comes, return to me and I will endeavour to help you to begin your ministering in earnest. I visit the prison, the infirmary and the poorest quarters of the town quite frequently. It would be both a help and a great pleasure to have company to my work which, I must tell you, is often of a most harrowing nature. Now, think about these things, take your time, for, as Christ says, 'the poor will be with us always', and I shall expect to see you when you feel ready and able to extend your work in the way you so ardently desire."

Warmed by the fire and by the fact that someone had taken the time and trouble to listen to her at last, Gertie thanked Mrs Johnson, allowing herself to be enveloped in a tight hug and went off home with hope in her heart and a vow that she would follow the advice of the good Minister's wife to the letter. The idea of engaging a maidservant who could help with the Sunday School was an excellent one and she determined to press Mrs Mabbett into letting her choose from among the girls at the orphanage. Mrs Mabbett agreed, happy to be able to relinquish yet another arduous task to the seemingly indefatigable Gertie.

The letter of request which Gertie wrote was addressed simply to 'The Matron' at the workhouse. She had no idea whether Mrs Pritchett was still holding sway over all those poor souls, but she hoped fervently that another and more kindly presence was now in residence. Times were changing, the terrible austerity created by the New Poor Law of 1834 was gradually being set aside and a more generous attitude towards the poor and hapless was slowly gaining ground. Gertie knew that it was people like the Johnsons and even women from the 'upper classes', as she put it, who were spreading these new ideas and she hoped that such attitudes were reaching those forlorn folk cooped up in the workhouse. Since there was no distinction between the orphans and the children of the poorest inmates, the term 'orphanage' was rather an overstatement for the actual establishment, so Gertie directed her letter to the workhouse, but stated her preference for an orphan girl, knowing just how cold and friendless life could be for a frightened child alone in such a place. Even if they could give only one girl a home and a little hope, then they would have done something, especially since Gertie and Amos' marriage had made it even more difficult for Mrs Mabbett to take in any more factory girls. "It wouldn't be suitable!" she had said, somewhat enigmatically.

As she walked to the post, Gertie set to thinking of that other letter she had written so many years ago and of how Amos had helped her. He had been so kind and had such a swashbuckling spirit. She hoped, with a little sadness, that his religion was not damping the fires of his naturally warm nature. Religious zeal was all very well, but she had read enough to know how easy it was for even the sweetest nature to become entrenched and dogmatic. Well, he was very young, younger than she was in some ways, and so she would have to watch him very carefully. By gently laughing at him when he became too pompous and teasing him when he put on his patronising airs she found she could usually bring back the old Amos, but it was tiring and at times irritating. She knew that she herself was no saint, and must often do things that annoyed him, but he never said a word in anger. If only he would argue or remonstrate with her like normal couples do, but instead he would put on his most prim face and merely say, 'Gertie, my dear', in a prosy and disapproving voice. She sighed. Mrs Johnsons' advice was excellent, but oh, how difficult it was to act the demure little wife when she wanted to shout and argue and laugh at him and with him like two normal mortals! She wondered what on earth they had taught him at that wretched college!

It was several days before a reply to her letter appeared in her postal box. Permission was granted to her to use her lunch break to go down to the post-office, but it cost her three trips before the precious letter arrived. It was addressed to Mrs Parker, and as this was the first time that she had seen her name written like that on a letter, or even received a letter other than the one from the Queen, as she always thought of it, she flushed and laughed out loud, much to the consternation of the good folk going quietly about their business in the post-office. Taking no notice of the curious and disapproving glances of the honest customers she hurried back to the arsenal, where she excitedly showed Mrs Mabbett and her friends the direction written in careful copperplate on the sealed paper. Everyone admired the writing and exclaimed over the beautiful black stamp graciously adorning the thick paper.

"It is certainly a very splendid letter, Gertie. But what does it say?" asked Mrs Mabbett, amused but somewhat impatient. The girls had all left their tables and were crowding round, and it took several minutes to get them back to their cartridges, on the promise that Gertie would read the contents out loud. Everyone trouped back to their work as Gertie carefully unsealed the letter and read it out to the expectant girls.

'My dear Mrs Parker,

It is very good of you to offer a situation in your establishment to one of our orphan girls. If agreeable to your good self, we can offer three young damsels for your inspection...'

Here Gertie broke off. "They make it sound like a cattle market," she said, looking up. Everyone giggled, but urged her to continue:

'...for your inspection. They are Sarah, Mary and Susan.

'As the Sabbath is the day of rest, when these girls will be at leisure during the afternoon, between services, it would seem a good opportunity to keep them out of mischief by commending them to your scrutiny for an hour or so. Unless I hear further from you, shall we say the Sunday after this one, at two-thirty sharp?

'I look forward to our future meeting Ma'am.

Your most obedient servant,
Jeremiah Smith, Warden'

There was a moment's silence and then Maud, not known for her finesse, let out a long breath.

"Cor blimey! What did all that mean?"

Everyone giggled again but Gertie said:

"I think it means I am to go to the workhouse on Sunday week and choose from one of those three girls."

"Well, why didn't he say so, instead of prosing on so?" asked Maud indignantly. "No wonder it takes such an age to get anything done for the inmates if that's the way the bosses all go on!"

But Mrs Mabbett decided it was time to back to concentrating on the cartridges, so she shushed Maud, ordered Gertie back to her place and went back to helping some of the newer intake who were still a little clumsy and unsure.

Amos and Mrs Johnson were consulted, and both agreed that it was perfectly in order for Gertie to visit the workhouse on the Sabbath, and so, on the first Sunday in May, after playing for the service at Bethel Chapel and rushing back to Beresford Street for a quick luncheon, Gertie walked up the steep hill and across the common to Cage Lane and the workhouse. Her heart was thumping, and all kinds of thoughts were crowding into her mind. Memories of being always cold, miserable, hungry and frightened, mingled with the excitement of her first day at school and those early days of her meeting with Amos She approached the large and forbidding doors with trepidation, feeling so small and insignificant confronted by such a fortress, but she gathered up every bit of her courage and pulled the iron bell-pull. An eerie jangling was set up inside and then she heard heavy footsteps approaching, and finally the sound of several bolts being drawn back. Gertie swallowed. This reminded her of the tales of ogre's castles that she had been told as a child when she had helped the women to sew or prepare vegetables as an orphan herself. But this was no ogre. As the doors were opened a little, thin man peered out. He wore brown trousers and a red waistcoat and with his bright and twinkling eyes and chirping voice he reminded Gertie of nothing so much as a robin.

"Mrs Parker? Ah, come in, my dear ma'am, do. I see you have been so kind as to bring the fine weather with you! My parlour is just here. Pray be seated and I will fetch the young ladies to you. If you are agreeable, I suggest you see them one at a time, commencing with Sarah? And in the meanwhile, perhaps I can coax you into accepting a small glass of port wine?"

Gertie, her eyes wide with wonder at the changed situation in this once so gloomy prison, said it was perfectly agreeable to meet the girls one at a time, but declined the port wine. As the little man hurried out fussily, she looked round at the white walls, the fire burning in the huge hearth and the glistening brass ornaments on the various cabinets. The last time she had been in this apartment had been under the baleful eye of Mrs Pritchett. But the room had not been comfortable then. *Dark and menacing*, the though made Gertie shiver. What had happened to change all this? Surely it could not have been brought about by this one little man?

She sat down in a remarkably comfortable chair and waited, but before long 'Mr Robin' as she called him to herself, reappeared, pushing a little girl of about ten years old into the room.

"Now then, Sarah, curtsey to Mrs Parker and answer her questions sensibly. You have nothing to fear."

"Yes sir," the girl said, staring sullenly at Gertie. She looked clean and well-fed, but Gertie sensed a rebellious spirit that would not be easy to tame. Certainly she felt unequal to yet another struggle, but out of politeness she spoke gently to the girl.

"Come, Sarah, sit by me and tell me about yourself," she said, patting the couch.

The girl stared but didn't move or speak. Mr Smith prompted her.

"Do as the kind lady says, Sarah."

"There ain't nothing to tell. Me mum and dad are dead and me and me little bruvver live 'ere."

"I see," said Gertie quietly. "Well, Sarah, how would you like to come and live in my house and help Mrs Mabbett and me to cook and clean? You would have your own little room and two shillings a week wages!"

There was another silence. Gertie felt slightly unnerved by the unwavering stare from those dark, unfathomable eyes. Mr Smith prompted again.

"You'd like that, wouldn't you, Sarah?"

"No, miss. I don't want to be no maidservant." And then, before the stunned couple could say anything more, Sarah burst out passionately, "Please, Miss, I want to be an actress. I don't want to cook and clean and keep house. I want to act on the stage and travel round with a company and…and…oh please, miss, say you'll 'elp me to do this!"

She had fallen on her knees and was clutching at Gertie's dress. Mr smith stood up in confusion.

"Yes, well, that will do, Sarah! Do get up, there's a good girl. Mrs Parker has not come here to put you on the stage!" He turned to Gertie, "This is the result of allowing a travelling troupe to present dramatics to our young people! I had no idea…did not realise…the impact on romantic young minds…"

He was literally wringing his hands in his concern, but Gertie, releasing the clutching fingers from her well-worn dress, raised the girl to her feet. She held the desperate little hands in her own and looked steadily into the dark, turbulent eyes.

"I understand how you feel, Sarah, and would not dream of imposing servitude on such a free spirit. I was an orphan here myself, you know, so I know the need you feel for independence and not be just one of the crowd. I do not know how I can help you in your desire, but I will certainly do my best and will not forget you. In the meantime, however, have patience and be a good girl. Do as Mr Smith says and learn your tasks diligently. You cannot be a fine artist without education."

She gave the girl a quick hug and Sarah, breathless, her eyes shining, said,

"Yes, ma'am, thank you ma'am. I shall do exactly as you say, ma'am," and she went off, hopeful for the first time in her young life. Gertie sighed. She turned to Mr Smith with her gentle smile.

"Perhaps Mary will be more suitable for my needs?"

But Mary proved to be small and thin. She looked about nine-year-old, though Mr Smith assured Gertie that she was in fact 'twelve this very Whitsuntide.' But although the child was sweet and submissive, Gertie doubted whether she would have the strength to undertake the tasks which would be her lot in their busy household.

"Would you like to cook and clean for me, Mary?" she asked. The child looked rather frightened.

"If you please, ma'am, I would rather read to you or sew."

"Is that what you like doing?"

"Oh, yes, ma'am. Mrs Pullchett says I should be 'prenticed to a seamstress. I should like that. It would be quiet and not tire me so."

Gertie looked questioningly at the warden.

"Can that be arranged?" she asked him.

"In time, certainly, ma'am. Mary is a little young as yet to be 'prenticed to a trade!"

"I was only nine when I was put to cartridge making," said Gertie, smiling again, "but you are quite right, Mr Smith. Mary should continue her education here a little longer before she thinks of joining a profession." She turned to Mary,

"I am sure that you will one day make a very fine seamstress, Mary. But now you must be a good girl and do everything Mr Smith says."

She took the little girl in her arms and gave her a gentle hug, almost afraid of breaking the frail little thing, and then let her go. Mr Smith told her to inform Susan that Mrs Parker was ready for her now. Mary whispered a 'yes, sir, thank you, ma'am,' and gave a slight curtsey as she went in search of Susan.

Gertie sat down again. She'd had no idea that choosing an orphan to be her maid would be so fraught with dangers and pitfalls! She wondered what on earth she would encounter with Susan. But the girl that came confidently into the warden's parlour was tall, bright-eyed, strong and glowing with health. She walked straight up to Gertie and held out her hand. Before Gertie could speak she said,

"My name is Susan, ma'am. I am thirteen years old, I can cook real nice dinners and am considered a dab 'and at washing and cleaning. I'm strong and I don't mind 'ard work! Mrs Pullchett says that I would be a godsend to any 'ouse."

Mr Smith, hovering distractedly in the background, was signalling to her to be silent, but Gertie only laughed and patted the seat beside her.

"Well, Susan, you are certainly not lost for words. Come and sit here and I shall ask you a few questions. I shall expect honest, straight answers, mind, but by the looks of you, that's what I shall get! Now then, can you bake bread?"

"Yes, ma'am."

"Good! When you roast potatoes, what must you do?"

"Why, parboil 'em, ma'am, then put them in the 'ot fat round the joint, with a bit of salt to make 'am all crispy. Then baste 'em, regler."

"Quite right. But we don't have a joint very often. Can you make a decent meal out of scraps and bits of vegetables?"

"I know how to do a really lovely stew, ma'am. My mum come from Liverpool and she said they call it Scouse up there, and she said you put everything in it."

"Is your mother here?"

"No. She died, Miss. They 'ad cholera 'ere a few years ago and there was a meeting of all the toffs and then the old matron was thrown out and Mrs Pullchett and Mr Smiff was put in charge. It's a lot better now, ma'am, but me mum was one of the last to die of the cholera."

"I am so sorry, Susan. Tell me about your life here now."

Gertie and the girl chatted on for some time like old friends until Mr Smith, fingering his watch and looking anxiously at the clock on the mantle shelf started coughing and hovering by the window. Gertie looked up at last.

"Why, Mr Smith, whatever must you think of me? But Susan has so much to tell me, and I got quite carried away! If she is agreeable, Susan will suit us very well. Would you like that, Susan, to come and live with us, and help with the household duties? You will have your own room and two shillings a week."

Susan stood up and once again shook Gertie's hand.

"I should like it very much, ma'am. You won't be sorry, that's a promise."

"Then we have a bargain." She turned to Mr Smith. "When can Susan start? Our present maid leaves us this Friday."

"Then let us say the Monday following? That will give Susan time to arrange the work that she is at present engaged in here to be undertaken by another inmate." He held out his hand. "We are most grateful to you, Mrs Parker and I am sure you will be very pleased with Susan, who is a lucky girl. Now Susan, you go back to your duties and I will show Mrs Parker out. This way, ma'am."

He escorted Gertie to the door, his robin eyes twinkling happily, and his chest puffed out with pleasure. Gertie thanked him and shook his hand once more. Details were agreed on the chaperoning of Susan to Beresford Street on Monday and then the great doors closed behind Gertie for the second time in her life, but in what strangely altered circumstances!

Chapter Nine

Susan proved to be worth every penny of the two shillings a week she was paid. With her own room, all meals found (even though she cooked them herself), and the little white apron and cap, she was 'as 'appy as a pig in clover', as she rather graphically put it. Mrs Mabbett decided that, hard working or not, this young lady needed to be taught a few refinements, and set about the task with more zeal than was always acceptable to the down to earth Susan, who stated in no uncertain terms that she was ''ere to cook and clean and scrub', but had no intention of aping 'one of them toffs'!

Mrs Mabbett soon gave up, and things settled down to a relatively constant routine, with Susan, for all her coarse speech, turning the house into a new pin. Meals were hot, regular and very tasty, socks were darned, and clothes mended and everything at last ran like clockwork. Gertie was delighted. Now that she had a little time to spare she decided to broach the subject of the soup kitchen once more to Amos. It was a few days after his twentieth birthday, and he had received a small raise. Between them they were now bringing home twelve shillings a week, and, in spite of what they paid towards Susan's keep and their rent to Mrs Mabbett, Gertie felt that she could finally put a tiny amount of their hard-earned wealth towards helping the poorest in the town. It was, after all, one of the reasons why they had taken on the Bethel Chapel. What was the point of her putting pretty gingham curtains up at the window if it was to be used only one hour a week! But Amos, tired from having to work an extra shift, and irritated by such a trite argument, put on his prim face and said he didn't want to talk about it at present.

"There will be time enough to think about such things when we can afford to pay Mr Ranwell the rent we will owe once the six months are up. Until then we must save every penny, as I have no intention of either being in debt or beholden to the Presbyterians! We already owe them our thanks and that is enough. No!" as Gertie began to remonstrate with him, "No, Gertie, my mind is made up . Your soup kitchen must wait, my dear. You are a good, kind-hearted girl, but you do not always see the practicalities of the situation. Like all women, you follow your emotions and while that is a very fine trait in a person, it can blind them to what are the realistic possibilities…"

"*What?* Blind them to *what?* What on earth are you talking about, Amos? First of all, yes, I *do* follow my heart, my 'emotions' as you put it. And what's wrong with that, I should like to know. I'd rather that than be like some prosy old bore you seem to be turning into. And second," Gertie's voice was beginning to rise angrily, "I can see no reason why a soup kitchen should cost us a great deal! At least we can try! Let's look at how much we've got in the collection box and make a start. I helped you to get the Chapel! Now you should help me to set up the soup kitchen, like you promised you would."

Tears of anger were pouring down her cheeks as she stood facing him, her hands pulling at a linen kerchief and her eyes dark and fierce. Pale and with an expression of infinite sadness in his own eyes, Amos led her gently to the settle. He took her hands in his and sat beside her. She looked into his face and suddenly all her wrath left her. With a great sob, she clasped her arms round him, crying and disclaiming into his collar.

"Oh, Amos, Amos, I didn't mean it. You are not a prosy bore, and I don't know what made me say such a terrible thing! Darling, I love you, can you ever forgive me? Say you will, say you are not angry!" she sobbed, clutching at his coat and almost shaking him as she cried.

Amos hushed her and stroked her hair and spoke gentle words to her until she became calm again. Then he took her face in his hands and looked hard into her eyes.

"You are right, my love. I *am* becoming a prosy old bore. It is not my intention to do so, but my vocation seems at times to colour my actions. I see the world in a different light from how it was when we were young and innocent. Then we had no responsibilities and were free to dream, but now, now, to make those dreams a reality we must take actions and follow paths that may at times seem slow and irksome. I care just as much as you do about the poor and hopeless, but think for one moment, darling. You are not yet seventeen, a vital, beautiful young woman, planning to work among some of the roughest people in the town. Even you, brought up as you were in the workhouse, have not seen how some of those poor creatures live; the squalor; the filth and…yes, the immorality that such degradation brings. *I* would think twice before going to such places; how much more dangerous would it be for you? No, my love, I cannot allow you to put yourself in such danger."

Gertie listened quietly to this speech, the sad realisation dawning on her that they were worlds apart in many things, she and Amos. She loved him too dearly to listen to any little warning signals that might be sounding in her head, but she knew that if she wanted to accomplish anything for herself then it was not to Amos that she could turn from now on. How she was to keep his love while disobeying his commands she did not know, but she knew that she must try, for if she became not more than his little wife, the obedient follower of his orders, then his love for her would surely die. He had fallen in love with her as she was, and she had no intention of being moulded into something else, something that he would learn to despise. So began Gertie's plan for the gentle deception of her beloved husband.

++++++++++

The months that followed were filled with working longer hours at the arsenal, writing and giving sermons to the steady numbers that filled the little Chapel on Sundays and counting the pennies that were mounting in the collection box. Although no amount had been stated for renting the Chapel, Amos felt that at last they had enough to pay off at least some of the debt. It was therefore on a fine, sunny evening in august that the young couple, hand in hand, all arguments forgotten for the moment walked across the common to the little cottage belonging to Mr Ranwell, the Scottish Minister. Mrs Peebles opened the door, a broad smile of welcome on her face, but she motioned them to keep quiet as she whispered that the Minister was not full pleased with the stories he had heard that a harmonium was defiling his Chapel.

"You will need to pacify the Old Gentleman," she said behind her hand. "For the Scottish Presbyterians are not permitting such profane things!" But she smiled slightly as she spoke, and her eyes twinkled merrily. Having been primed, Gertie and Amos entered the stifling little room in some trepidation but determined to stand up to the Minister.

"After all, if he is letting us worship there and we are paying him rent, we have a right to follow the ways of the Methodists. There can be nothing wrong in that. Besides, the harmonium was already there," whispered Gertie, as Mrs Peebles stood in the doorway and announced them. The old man was standing looking into the flames of a crackling fire, but at their entrance he turned round, his expression dark and his eyes like glittering black diamonds under his bushy brows.

"So the two of you would defile my Chapel, would ye?" he shot at them before they could say a word of greeting. "I'll no have the devil's prattle under God's roof, and that's final!"

Gertie moved swiftly forward and took hold of the thin, bony hands, looking innocently up into his stern countenance.

"No, indeed, Sir, there is no devil's prattle, of that I can assure you. But in order to encourage the men and gain their enthusiasm, we have put them all to work, mending the roof, painting and cleaning the walls and keeping the chairs in good order. When Joshua found the old harmonium, his heart sank, and he took it all the way home with him to mend it. Oh, Mr Ranwell, you would have rejoiced with us if you could have seen his face when he made it work again. I don't know how it was that the instrument was in your Chapel in the first place if you do not allow such things, but surely you cannot thin k ill of us to put the lovely sounds to good use in the praise of God? And it seems such a pity to waste so much hard work and…and *love*!"

Mr Ranwell looked down at the vibrant young face and cleared his throat.

"Aye, aye, well, you're a cunning little vixen, young woman, but I do believe there's no harm in ye, and I'll take it kindly meant. If your intention is to pay a rent for the building, then we'll say no more about it, it being no longer my province, as it were. But I don't approve, mind, I most certainly do *not* approve! As for the wretched thing being in the Chapel in the first place, I have no idea how it got there, unless the poor wee building has been used as a dumping ground for Godless things."

The two young people thanked the old minister profusely and agreed that the grand sum of one shilling a month would be very suitable. A deed was drawn up, Mrs Peebles was called in to witness the signing of the Documents, the fee for the last six months was waived, much to Gertie's relief, and then they sat down to tea and yet another delicious cake. At last, as the sun set in brilliant fiery red across the common, lighting up the furze in its glow, Gertie and Amos walked home, tired but satisfied.

Now that everything was in order and Amos no longer felt beholden to Mr Ranwell, Gertie decided it was time to pay another visit to Mrs Johnson and discuss plans for the long-awaited soup kitchen. So one evening in early

September, while Amos was out supervising the training of the choir, or 'getting under Mr Probyn's feet,' as Gertie rather more prosaically put it, she set out for the little house behind the Johnson's Chapel, where she was welcomed warmly by the ever-patient preacher's wife. They went into the parlour where Gertie slowly stripped off her gloves and unpinned her bonnet, trying to think of what she was to say as she laid them on a chair. She had no idea how she was to explain her plan to deceive her husband, but once again the older woman seemed to read her thoughts.

"Sit down, my dear, and tell me your plans, for I am sure that is why you are here."

The door opened and a maid, about the same age as Susan, came in, carefully carrying a rather laden tray. She put it on a small table, gave a slight curtsy and left, but not before Gertie had seen the expression of curiosity on her face. She turned enquiringly to Mrs Johnson, but that lady only laughed.

"You must realise, Gertie, that my Emily and your Susan are of an age. They both come from the workhouse and have been friends for most of their lives. There is nothing in your establishment or mine that they do not know of intimately! How do you suppose I seem to know all your business almost before you do yourself?"

Gertie was aghast. So all their quarrels, all the most intimate details of their life were passed around for all to know. Mrs Johnson laughed gently again and patted Gertie's hand.

"You mustn't mind, my dear. There is no harm in the girls and their intimacy shows how much they care for us all. The gossip goes no further than between Emily and myself, for Susan is very fond of you, you know, and wishes to champion your causes. She feels sometimes you are – held back. So I rather gather that is why you have come to me this evening?"

Gertie relaxed and sighed. How did one become such an understanding person? She knew she would never have the wisdom of Mrs Johnson, if she lived to be a hundred, but somehow that was made not to matter. Gertie had a role in God's scheme of things and Mrs Johnson was there to help her to realise that goal and put it into practice. She sipped at the cup of tea which the preacher's wife had offered her and said hesitantly,

"You know that it is my heart's desire to open a soup kitchen for the poorest in our community. Amos is against this at present, even though he agreed that it was a good idea when we first took over the Bethel Chapel. But now he is, he seems –"

"He is prevaricating. 'You are too young; the danger is too great; you do not understand the ways of the world' – you, who were born and bred in the workhouse and who have spent half your life helping to make dangerous armaments! But as the wife of a minister you are of far more help now knowing how to pour a cup of tea and perhaps make some jam to be sold at the next Christmas fair, knowing that you have done your part by ensuring that the proceeds go to the 'deserving poor'. That is it, is it not? And inside you are seething with anger and frustration and racked with guilt. With your help your husband is pursuing his dream, while you must stay in the background and be the submissive wire. What has happened to the wonderful buccaneering spirit that so endeared him to you, the fun, the freedom? These are the things that pass through your mind and are sowing the seeds of bitterness and guilt in your soul, aren't they, Gertie?"

Tears poured down Gertie's cheeks and she burst out, "I *do* love him Mrs Johnson, oh I do, so *much.* But he seems not to care anymore for the things that mattered to us both at first. Even his sermons have changed!" She choked on a sob as she said the last words and Mrs Johnson swiftly left her chair and cradled Gertie in her arms.

"There," she soothed, stroking the wayward hair from the girl's forehead. "There, I know. I understand it all. But you love him and that is all that matters. And if you believe his love for you has died, then you are not the sensible girl I take you for. He relies entirely on you, on your support, your admiration and your love. He would not be so confident, so sure of himself if this were no so. Nor would he fill the Bethel Chapel with the good honest folk of the arsenal, if you were not his constant support and companion. I told you once before, and I tell you again, being a minister's wife is one of the most difficult tasks any woman can undertake, but it can also be one of the most rewarding. You do not imagine that Mr Johnson and I have lived an idyll all our married lives do you?"

Gertie gradually stopped crying as the gentle voice soothed her, and now she looked up into the older woman's face.

"But I am sure you did not have horrible quarrels and call him dreadful names, as I have done," she whispered on a sob.

Mrs Johnson got up from her knees where she had been holding Gertie and went over to the door. She pointed to a mark on the wall:

"That, my dear, is the remains of a cup of tea that I threw at my beloved husband just as he went out of the room in one of his more than usually pompous departures. I am ashamed to say that I ranted at him like the proverbial fishwife and threw the full cup straight at the door. Luckily my aim is not what it might be, and I missed him and the door, and the result is what you see there! That, Gertie, was but one month ago! So you see, my dear," she said, sitting down and pouring them both out another cup of tea, " all is not lost between you and your dearest Amos. I leave the mark to remind myself of my unbridled temper and also to remember that my own poor, dear, bewildered Will was kindness itself in listening to my complaints later that day. He still does not quite understand what so angered me, but he *does* listen, as I am sure your Amos will, if you explain your feelings to him each time your anger tries to get the better of you. And it will happen again many times, I can assure you. No, let us put all our anger and silly frustrations behind us and set about the business of helping you to realise your dream. First, in order not to deceive your husband, I suggest that you accompany me when I go on my visits, ministering to the poor women and widows of the town. You go home and tell Amos, *tell him,* mind, what you intend to do and that I will feel happier having someone to help me as I am not as young as I was and find carrying the baskets is becoming too tiring. Tell him also that I have discussed the idea of having help with Mr Johnson and that he approves and will be happier in his own mind if I am no longer alone on such occasions. As this is all true, I am sure Amos will not find fault with this plan and we can decide how to set about the next stage once this idea is established. Now, what do you say? Will this do for now?"

Gertie was thrilled. She thanked the Minister's wife profusely and went on her way, her heart lighter once more. She thought back to that letter she had written to the Queen so long ago and realised that it was not the people in high places that were the best ones to help the poorest, but people like herself and Mrs Johnson, who had knowledge of such things, and understood the problems. Whoever heard of Queen Victoria taking a basket of cast-off clothing down into the dirtiest parts of London and giving them to widows who were always hungry and often the worse for drinking gin! Gertie giggled at the idea and tripped lightly home; her head full of plans for the future. She guessed that she would find it necessary to do a good bit of persuading before Amos would agree to her accompanying Mrs Johnson, but she was also confident that she would succeed

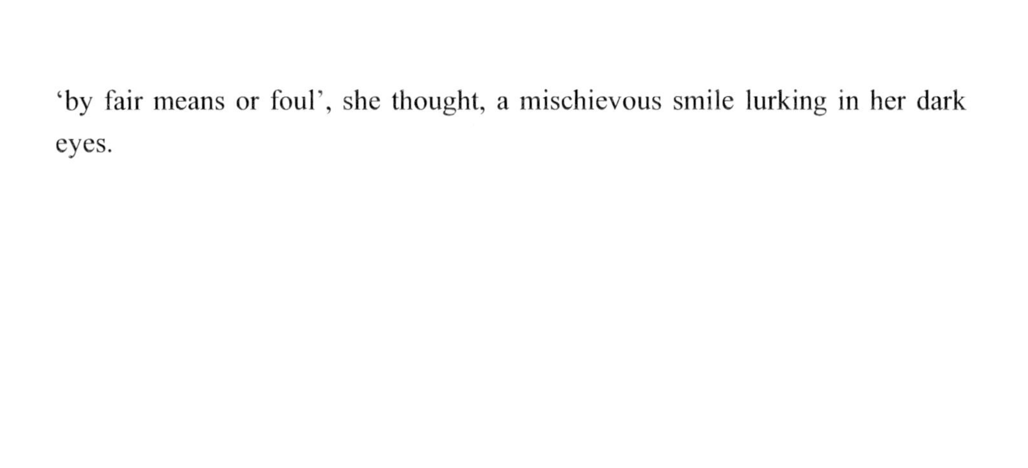

'by fair means or foul', she thought, a mischievous smile lurking in her dark eyes.

Chapter Ten

It was on a wet September day, in 1851, just two months after her seventeenth birthday, that Gertie, having been granted a free afternoon from the arsenal, accompanied Mrs Johnson in an ancient coach she had procured from somewhere that took them down into the poorest parts of the docklands, to begin her lessons in 'ministering', as the Minister's wife put it. There had been some rather fraught scenes between Gertie and Amos before he finally crumbled under the combined onslaught of Gertie's tears and Mr Johnson's assurances that nothing had yet happened to deter his beloved Anabelle. In any case, he was certain that nothing but the devil incarnate would stop her from continuing with her work.

"And I will be much happier in my mind if she has a companion, someone upon whom she can rely and who has youth on her side," he said. "After all, we are none of us getting any younger, but your little Gertie seems to have boundless energy. Put it to good use, my boy, before she is taken up with other responsibilities!"

There was a twinkle in the older Minister's eye as he spoke, and Amos, momentarily mystified, suddenly flushed and laughed.

"Oh, we neither of us have time nor can afford family ties at present," he said, turning his cap in his hand rather wistfully as he spoke. He had gone to see Mr Johnson in the hopes that the Minister would support him in dissuading Gertie from her intentions, but he soon realised that instead of being appalled by the plan, the older man was delighted. And so it was that Gertie and Anabelle, a heavy basket on each arm, alighted from the coach on this wet and stormy day to bring succour to the poor and needy.

The streets were narrow and grimy, the gutters running with filthy water and the few folk standing aimlessly on the street corners or peering out of doorways were thin and seemed to be dressed in nothing but rags. Although Gertie had been brought up in a workhouse, it had been up on the common in the fresh, clean air, and, for all its strict and dreary routine, had been thought something of an 'advanced' experiment as poor houses go, causing some eyebrows to lift amongst the more conventional pillars of the community. So nothing had prepared Gertie for the sights that met her eyes as she and Mrs Johnson journeyed further into the misery and degradation that was the lot of the many hundreds packed into the tiny, squalid dwellings down by the docks. The smell was dreadful and Gertie wretched as she ran to keep up with the indefatigable Mrs Johnson. She put a kerchief to her nose, and they hurried on in silence until they came to a particularly horrendous street, full of dwellings that looked as though they were little more than ancient ruins from some earlier primitive settlement. Mrs Johnson stopped.

"Gertie, my dear, if you are to accompany me into any of these hovels, you must learn to accept the aromas. You will get used to them in time, as have the poor wretches who live in them without hope of escape. You have to remember that there are no toiletry facilities *whatsoever!"*

Guiltily Gertie put away her kerchief, and together the two women walked through the gurgling channels of filthy water to the nearest dwelling. A child who looked about three years old, as filthy as the mud with which it was playing, looked solemnly up at them as they passed him and pushed open the broken-down door, Mrs Johnson calling out as they entered the squalid, freezing room. Gertie nearly passed out at the sight that met her eyes. The room contained one broken down chair, bundles of rags in the corners and a large, cracked chamber pot. The smell was indescribable. And amongst all this the room seemed to be full of people. A woman, who looked to be about sixty, was sitting in the chair, nursing a wailing infant, a man was lying on one of the bundles of rags, smoking something evil-smelling, and four other children, ranging from about six to ten, were huddled together in a corner of the room, fighting over a jug which appeared to contain some liquid. The mud floor was soaking wet, there was no heating of any kind in the room and Gertie could see daylight through the holes in the roof. She stood, turned to stone, as the older woman stepped over something unspeakable in the doorway and walked swiftly into the room, a merry greeting on her lips. The children all rose and ran to her, silently holding out their hands, their huge eyes in their sunken faces wide with expectation. The Minister's wife put her basket down on a relatively clean-looking parch of floor and carefully removed the linen cover. The inside was overflowing with food; bread, cheeses, cold meats and milk. She handed a wedge of cheese, some slices of ham and a small canister of milk to the oldest child, while the younger ones were each given a hunk of bread. While all this was going on, neither the man lying on the rages, nor the woman in the chair moved. It was as though Gertie and Mrs Johnson were invisible. Once the children had returned to their corner, the Minister's wife spread some paper on the floor and set down upon it the remainder of the loaf of bread and some more slices of meat, along with a thick, warm blanket. Then, without a word, she went back out into the street. Gertie followed her in a bemused state.

"There, Gertie," said Mrs Johnson, gently. "That is your first experience of ministering. Nobody said it would be easy."

Gertie swallowed and managed to say,

"No, ma'am, it was not easy. I never…I mean…I never thought…"

"You never thought that humanity could sink so low? No, my dear, few do realize and the majority of those who do merely condemn. It seems never to have occurred to them to ask why someone falls into such conditions of squalor. How old do you think the mother is?"

Gertie gave a start. "Why I am sure not as old as she looks. Perhaps about thirty something?"

"She is twenty-four. Six children living, two dead and her man a hopeless addict."

"Is he the father?" Gertie asked, tentatively.

"Of the last five. The first was by the girl's own father. I don't know about the other two. Oh, don't look so shocked," as Gertie gasped in horror. "That's nothing new here. Things are looked at differently when there is simply no hope. What does it matter who fathered the children? They'll most of them never see maturity anyway. Average life expectancy here is twenty-eight, much as it was generally three hundred years ago."

The Minister's wife was no longer speaking in her usual gentle tones. Her voice had grown harsh and angry, and she strode through the slush and grime without heed to the twigs and muck sticking to the hem of her skirts. Several women seemed to be waiting expectantly outside the next hovel and, as Gertie approached, they made coarse remarks, many of which Gertie was unable to understand. Mrs Johnson whisked her past them, whispering to her to take no notice and admonishing the women in sharp accents to 'keep such language to yourselves' Catcalls and whistles followed them into the next building and Gertie pressed close against the older woman, an unknown fear making her throat feel dry and constricted. She only hoped that Mrs Johnson knew what she was doing.

Conditions in this hovel were, if anything, worse than in the first one they had visited. They descended some slimy steps into what seemed to Gertie to be an underground cavern, where several families appeared to be huddled together in carious corners. The only light came from a cracked barred window at street level, water ran down the walls, filth and slime were everywhere and in one of the corners lay what looked like a shrouded body. Gertie stood aghast, but Mrs Johnson went on into the room and straight over to the group of people round the still form.

"Not buried him yet, Maggie," she said bluntly, more of a statement than a question. "I'll get the undertaker down here immediately."

"You'll be lucky," said a voice from a small bundle of rags in the far corner. "'E won't come down 'ere, not for nuffink. It's me wot's got to drag the old devil up them steps, that's wot. I ain't got the strength and none of them's goin' to 'elp. You tell me what I'm, to do, Mrs 'igh an' mighty! Will you carry 'im up there?"

Mrs Johnson put down her basket with a thud and shouted in a voice more like that of a sergeant major than a well-bred minister's wife,

"Joe, you and that no-good lazy son of yours, come here and give me a hand," and with that she went over to the figure in the shroud, lifted one end and began to drag it towards the door. Two men, weaving from side to side, took hold of the other end of the corpse and between them and the older woman they dragged the gruesome remains up the steps, along the passage and out into the street. Gertie swiftly laid out some of the food and clothing from the basket onto a piece of clean paper, then hurried up the steps as fast as the slime would allow. Slipping and half crying, her gloves filthy from the grime as she tried to cling to the walls, she arrived at last in the welcome light of the street. Mrs Johnson had chased the curious girls out of the way, ordering one to run to the undertakers, "This very minute, Fanny and I'll give you twopence."

Fanny ran off and the corpse was laid in the mud as the rain gurgled and ran in streams round the filthy shroud. Gertie was beginning to feel faint. Never in her worst dreams had she imagined she would encounter such horrendous sights as had met her eyes that day. *Is this really what happens every day among the poor, or is this simply a terrible exception?* she thought, as she tried not to listen to the suggestive comments from the smirking girls, who had surrounded both women.

"I know the very gent for you, miss brown curls," said one. "'E'd pay 'andsome for that neat figure, all white and clean!"

Someone else said something in an undertone which Gertie couldn't hear, and there was raucous laughter.

"That's enough, Mabel, we don't want to hear about your 'protectors'. There's some food downstairs and I suggest you go down and get some before it all goes. Here's a penny for each of you. Don't spend it all on gin, mind."

And with that Mrs Johnson gave each grubby hand a penny and the girls ran off to what looked like a dingy shop at the far end of the street. She sighed.

"I don't know why I bother!" she said, as Fanny returned, leading an ancient horse and cart bearing what looked to be an even more ancient man sitting amongst a muddle of old sacks and pieces of wood.

"'Ere's 'arry, Mrs J, come to bury me dad. They've 'eld a place in the pauper's pit, so he can go there right now, and good riddance."

The two men who had helped to carry the corpse up the steps and who all this time had been leaning against a wall swigging from evil-looking bottles, came forward at a word from Mrs Johnson and helped 'arry to fling the pitiful thing into the cart. They climbed in and set off down the road, the horse looking as if it was unlikely to make it to the graveside before itself keeling over and dying. Mrs Johnson gave Fanny the promised twopence and turned back to Gertie.

"Well, my dear, I think we have done quite enough for one day, and you look as though you could do with a stiff drink yourself! Come along." And with that she swept off up the street towards where they had left the coach, Gertie following as best she could while trying to overcome the feelings of nausea and faintness that were threatening to suffocate her senses. They reached the coach at last, Jim, the coachman, muttering under his breath as he walked the disgruntled horses up and down in the rain, and chased off curious passers-by not used to seeing such a fine vehicle in their part of the town. Shaking the worst of the wet from their soaking garments, the two women sat down thankfully at last in the relative comfort of the old coach. Gertie heaved a sigh of relief and turned her pale face to her companion.

"I think Amos is right, my dear Mrs Johnson," she said in a quavering voice, her hands clenching and unclenching on the linen kerchief, "I am really not the right person to do this kind of ministering. Perhaps I should keep to jam-making and playing the harmonium on Sundays, after all!"

The older woman sniffed and took Gertie's hands firmly in her own.

"Nonsense, Gertie! No one is the 'right person', as you put it, for doing such work. Do you think I relish going into those stinking hovels, risking life and limb for a collection of seemingly thankless lay-abouts? Of course I do not. But neither can I lay my head on my pillow at night knowing that babies are being reared in that filth and squalor, children being abused and raped and all finally succumbing to the inevitable evil solace of drink and opium. Hunger, disease, hopelessness, these are the only bedfellows that truly embrace those poor hapless souls and since no one else seems concerned, then people such as ourselves, rich beyond the dreams of avarice comparatively speaking, must bring them comfort, at least to their bodies. Whether God will redeem their souls is not my concern. I leave that to the ministry of my dearest husband. Now, believe me," she said, looking hard into Gertie's frightened eyes. "Unbelievable though it might seem, you will become accustomed to such sights if you hold on to your faith and stick the course. I will be always at your side, but it is the only way that you can learn how to respond to these people. If you want your soup kitchen to be a success, then you must win the trust of the most unlikely of customers! There, that is better," as Gertie managed a watery smile. "We will make a harridan of you yet. Now you go indoors, and I will inform you of the next time I intend to go into the town. I generally go once a week, and although for you it means a half day's loss of wages, it is what is expected of a minister's wife, truly it is. Goodbye, my dear, and God Bless you." And with a hug and a gentle kiss, she handed Gertie down from the carriage into the arms of the coachman. Then the steps were put up and the coach swung off down the road, much to the interest of the wide-eyed locals. Gertie blew her nose decisively, straightened her gown and walked up the steps to her front door. She rang the bell, Susan insisting that it was not 'the done thing' for ladies in Gertie's position to have to unlock the door for themselves. Gertie smiled to herself as she entered into the little maid's dreams of serving in a grand house, and soon she was sitting in dry, clean clothes in front of a blazing fire in the parlour, sipping tea and eating fairy cakes. Although the day was beginning to get dark Mrs Babbett was not yet returned from the arsenal, so, warm and sleepy after her ordeal, Gertie fell into a deep sleep, herself dreaming of performing great deeds for the Parish poor and at last gaining the ear of the Queen. She awoke with a start to hear the front door slam and voices in the hall. Quickly neatening her hair and brushing cake crumbs from her dress she hurried out to greet her long-suffering husband. He and the widow had arrived together and there was a great to-do as everybody told everybody else about how wet it was and how their day had gone. But soon peace was restored, and they all sat round the dinner table while Gertie told them of her experiences ministering to the poor. She kept the descriptions of the scenes she had witnessed as simple and unemotional as possible, but even so much of the squalor and degradation still crept into the telling. Amos listened in silence as Mrs Babbett blessed herself and tut-tutted, but when the account came to an end Gertie turned rebelliously to Amos;

"I know what you are thinking, darling, and at first I said as much to Mrs Johnson, that I am not the person for such work, but she assured me that I was talking nonsense, that no one is the right person, but that with perseverance we can make a difference at least to the conditions these poor souls live in. Believe me, Amos, she is right and, as you can see, I came to no harm. Why, I have not even coughed once," she added brightly, her usually pale face rosy and her bright eyes sparkling. Amos shifted slightly in his chair and looked down at his empty plate. Gertie could sense that he was struggling with his emotions, but wisely said nothing. The old clock in the corner ticked away the seconds until at last Amos spoke. Gertie knew that they had passed a milestone in their relationship and that they were both growing up at last. She listened to her husband's speech with a slight twinge of sadness. The old, almost carefree days were gone forever, but something rich and worthwhile was already being sown in their place.

"Mrs Johnson is, as ever, a very wise woman, my dear," Amos began. "And I know that my little firedragon will never be happy unless she is trying to put right all the ills of the world. Well, Gertie, that is a very ambitious undertaking, but in the meanwhile I am sure that between you, you and the good minister's wife will make a small dent in the conditions of our own Parish! One half day a week is not too much to ask, and you go with my blessing. But remember, a moment of danger and you end your ministering for ever! Is that understood? I love you too much to allow you to submit yourself to possible physical harm!"

His voice had risen and, as his fist hit the table, Gertie noticed with awe that his eyes glittered with a sudden hard determination. He looked magnificent! She breathed in sharply;

"Oh, yes, Amos, of course I understand. I would never want to do anything that could make you angry!" and to the widow's secret amusement, Gertie skirted the table and threw herself into her somewhat startled husband's arms. They embraced for a moment and then, unclasping her hands from round his neck, Amos said,

"Yes, well, see to it that you keep to your side of the bargain. And when you have been out with the minister's wife a few times, we will think about the soup kitchen."

Although that outing was the first of many that Gertie and Mrs Johnson undertook in their ministering, they rarely went as far afield again as the London docks. Generally they contented themselves with visiting the poor of Woolwich itself and although poverty was rife there, it was in no way as appalling as the lot of those poor wretches that Gertie had seen on her first visit. Cold, hungry and dressed in little more than rags the resident might be, but they seemed in general to retain a certain dignity that kept them in general from succumbing to the pitfalls of alcohol and drugs that was the lot of the 'London poor' as Mrs Johnson called them. It may have been that there was some chance of work, even though it was only on a piece-meal basis, or perhaps the Guardians of the workhouse unions were a kindlier lot, but whatever the case, Gertie felt that there was less hopelessness and more optimism amongst these people. Nevertheless, to get them to come along to the Chapel even with the enticement of a bowl of soup, let alone to attend a service there, was going to be enormously difficult and Gertie could see that she was going to have her work cut out! Apart from anything else, many of them insisted that they didn't want to be beholden to 'some high and might lady's charity,' and they could 'get along very nicely thank you without them poking their bossy noses in.' When Mrs Johnson pointed out to one harassed mother that her little girl could do with some nourishing food on a more permanent basis rather than when it was possible for the minister's wife to get down into town, the woman shouted abuse at them both and pushed them out of the door, uttering obscene oaths and screaming at them not to bother coming back. Gertie noticed that the basket of food remained behind, however.

"Don't worry, my dear, when she has sobered up she will be full of remorse and even return the basket when next we visit! We have just three more visits to make and then I think we should return home as it is almost dark already."

As they walked back to the welcome lights of Gertie's house they discussed the possibilities of setting up a soup kitchen in the next few weeks. Gertie suggested that it might be a good idea to make Christmas the reason for encouraging people to come along and enjoy the hospitality of the little Chapel without feeling that they were accepting charity. Then, when they saw how nice it was and that they could send their children to Sunday School there without any charge, they might think again about visiting it more often. Perhaps it was wrong to call it a soup kitchen? They must think of a more enticing name for the building when it was not being a Chapel.

The two women had arrived at Gertie's doorstep by this time and Mrs Johnson accepted an invitation to join the family for a cup of tea. The weather had turned very cold, and heavy flakes of snow were beginning to fall as they stomped into the hall, shaking their pelisses and bonnets as they handed them over to Susan. A roaring fire was alight in the parlour and Amos was already sitting before it reading the local newspaper. He rose as the two women entered, scolding and placing Mrs Johnson in the chair nearest the fire then chafing Gertie's cold hands.

"I don't know what Mr Johnson will think of me, allowing my wife to insist on your taking her ministering on such a day as this! You really must forgive her, ma'am, but she is very foolish and headstrong and there is no denying her once she has got a bee in her bonnet!"

Amos spoke quickly as he warmed Gertie's hands, not looking at the older woman, but she only laughed softly and laid a gentle hand on his arm.

" I am suitably scolded, Amos, for it is most certainly I, not your 'headstrong' wife, as you put it, who insisted on going ministering today. While I appreciate the concern you feel for us both, I can assure you that we are both very strong and it is in weather like this that those poor creatures need us most. Surely as a ministering Christian yourself you would not have us be only fair-weather friends? I am certain that a little snow has not put you off your course in the past and will never do so in the future! Now, Gertie has some very exciting ideas for her soup kitchen, and I think we should discuss them."

All this was said in the softest and sweetest of voices, but Amos was beginning to realise how difficult was Mr Johnson's lot in remaining master in his house! How long would it be before his own little Gertie learned the tricks of womanhood herself? And by the time she had finished outlining her splendid plan he knew that she had already taken many strides down that road. He also knew that he must do all in his power to retain mastery over his own household but realised how slippery that slope was going to be. He listened to the vibrant voice and looked into the sparkling eyes and for the moment at least, his grip loosened, and he found himself tumbling headlong into this gentle, all-engulfing trap.

Chapter Eleven

As Christmas drew near, Gertie decided that the little Chapel must be decorated with holly and a pretty tree. Instead of calling it the soup kitchen, she and Mrs Johnson agreed that 'Gertie's Soup Bowl' would be a rather more encouraging name to entice the local poor and down and outs into its welcoming warmth. Gradually, with her winning smile and pleasant manner, Gertie had won the hearts of some of the women at least, and had even had a promise from a few that they would send their children to the Sunday school 'only to get them out from under my feet, mind, I don't want none of your Jesusing getting into their 'eads. Education's no good for them – they're goin' on the stall like their dad. 'E never 'ad no schooling and 'e does alright. But I'll give you an 'and evenins when I can.'

And so it was that for two whole weeks before Christmas, every evening saw Susan, Gertie and even Mrs Babbett, stirring the great boiler in the scullery, a smell of various delicious soups making everyone ravenous even after a large and satisfying dinner. After work each day Gertie ventured to the market where she bought up all the day's old vegetables at give-away prices and collected those that had been saved specially for her by the wives who appeared delighted that they were to get their offspring off their hands for an hour on Sundays. By the end of a week two cauldrons of soup were carefully carried in Joshua's ancient cart down to the Chapel and lovingly put on the stove in the little 'kitchen'. The weather was so cold that there was no chance of the soup going bad by the next day, although Gertie made sure that the lids were on properly before she left. 'We may be as poor as the church mice, but they are not going to get my soup!' she said firmly.

The next day, Sunday, the little Chapel was full as usual for the service in the morning and since Gertie was staying behind in order to prepare the afternoon Sunday school, she had put a light under one of the cauldrons in order to have soup ready for the thin and hungry children she hoped would be attending. But she soon realised that this was something of a mistake. Fidgeting and rustling began to interrupt the normal flow of the service as a glorious smell of vegetable soup wafted through the Chapel, tickling the noses of the hungry folk who knew that had nothing to go back home to but some boiled mutton and sad vegetables if they were lucky. And when the service came to an end Gertie was surprised to see that most of the congregation was staying behind, chatting to one another, congratulating Amos on his specially fine sermon and some even vaguely fingering the keys of the old harmonium, while all were casting surreptitious glances back at the kitchen. Every bowl and spoon that they could 'beg, borrow or steal', as Gertie irreverently put it, was piled up on the rickety enamel-topped table in the kitchen, but even so there would never be enough to serve an entire congregation that morning. But she knew that she could not send these folk back to their cold homes without some comfort to show her thanks for their unwavering loyalty over these many months. So she stood bravely in the middle of the floor and clapped her hands. The talking gradually died down and against much shushing and foot shuffling she managed to gain their attention at last.

"If you would care to line up, those of you who have a moment, I would just like your opinion on our soup, most of the contents of which have been supplied by the good people of this Parish. However, as I am not the best of cooks, and Susan has a great deal to do in our household, I wish to ensure that I have not managed to poison anyone! There are not enough bowls for you all at once, so as soon as you have finished, would you hand yours back to me and I will wash it for the next person. Mrs Daniel, I know I can call on your good nature to help." And in this way each member of the congregation went away that morning with some warm and delicious soup inside them, assuring Gertie and Amos that they would most certainly spread the word that Gertie's Soup Bowl' was very well worth visiting.

Mr Bratskill, baker for the Artillery, had promised that any loaves left unused by the officers would be dropped off at the Chapel every Sunday afternoon, 'them only being thrown away else, Miss. Captain Jones, 'e's a proper gent 'e is, ma'am; 'e says as 'ow it's awlright for me to bring 'em. No sense in wastin' food if there's them as is goin' 'ungry for want of a crust, Captain Jones says'. And sure enough, at two o'clock prompt, Mr Bratskill's van stopped at the door of Bethel Chapel and he came down the aisle carrying two baskets full of loaves and rolls, which he unloaded on to the table beside the bowls and spoons. He was a short, jolly man, and his constant cheerful chatter was well known throughout the Parish.

'There we are, Miss, good as me word. Made this mornin', but that lot up there, they don't need it! It's all roast beef and brandy with them so you get your lot to tuck in and there'll be more where that come from.'

With that he trotted off, scarcely waiting for Gertie's profuse thanks. Mr Bratskill had never set foot inside the Chapel until now, and Gertie doubted that he would ever do so again except to deliver the bread, but as far as she was concerned he was an angel sent from On High.

At three o'clock sharp Gertie opened the door of the Chapel, over which was the brightly coloured sign 'Gertie's soup bowl', lighted up with one small lamp. She waited expectantly for the onrush of children she was optimistically hoping would fill the little space she had set aside on either side of the altar table, one side for girls, the other for boys as she had remembered from her school days. Everything was ready; two pretty screens had been covered with any pictures she could find of animals and holy scenes, mostly donated generously by Mrs Babbett and all the chairs had a letter on them for every letter of the alphabet. On the altar table stood Gertie's greatest joy – a scene of the nativity, complete with wise men, shepherds, animals, Joseph, Mary and Jesus, all made from paper and coloured in lovingly by Susan and herself. They had made paste from a little flour and water and every figure was carefully stuck into place against a background of night sky and stars, with one particularly large star shining over the crib. On the floor, beside the harmonium, stood a Christmas tree covered in pretty pieces of paper and cloth. Gertie was sure the children would never have seen anything so beautiful, for Prince Albert's idea of Christmas decorations was still a novelty to English children and she had hunted in every corner of the market before she had found a stallholder brave enough to sell such outlandish things. It had cost her six whole pence but was worth every penny. How beautiful Balmoral must look, with all the candles and the gorgeous clothes worn by the ladies, and, Gertie was sure, a huge tree hung with presents of every kind. So she waited and she waited and soon she had to light the lamps and the candles on the harmonium as the day darkened and snow began to fall once more. Amos had promised to return at the end of the hour to conduct the prayers, but the little Chapel was still as silent and empty as the tomb when he finally stomped in, his collar turned up against the cold and his shoulders covered in snow. He looked round the hall, then, without a word he took his young wife in his arms and cradled her, muttering soothingly as she began to sob into the melting flakes on his chest.

"Oh, Amos, they don't care! Their children can starve for all they care, and they can't even walk the few yards to our Chapel to give them nourishment."

"There, there, my darling, my precious. And after all your hard work and dreams too. Perhaps the snow has put them off. After all, they have few rags to wear and little defence against this cold. Perhaps, when the weather is milder..."

But Gertie had lifted her face from his coat.

"No, Amos, they only said they will come to get me to go away. They never had any intention of bringing their children here, even if it was a warm sunny day. Our only hope now is the down and outs and I am not even sure that they will bother. They would rather have gin than good food to warm their insides! I am beginning to believe that these people are not worth bothering about. They will never help themselves and any help we give them is thrown back in our faces. You should hear some of the language that Mrs Johnson and I have shouted at us when we go ministering to them! Why will they do nothing? Why, even as a small child in the workhouse, I tried to better my lot. And I have done, haven't I, Amos? We have both come from the workhouse and yet we are comfortable and happy and are even able to spare a little time and money to help others. If we can do it, why can't they?"

Amos had led Gertie to a chair by this time and was holding her hands in his, facing her, the large letter L staring jauntily back at him from behind her as she leant forward in her earnestness to understand this strange world of poverty and oppression. He remained silent for a moment, considering how best to dispel her gloom. He had guessed how it would be, certainly, but had never had the heart to tell her, and besides, she would have scorned any negative arguments he might have put to her. He sighed. Amos loved Gertie dearly, but life with her was never to be a tranquil bed of roses! He chaffed her cold hands gently and kissed her damp cheeks. Against his better judgement he must try to raise her hopes over her precious soup kitchen, even though in his heart of hearts he had never desired her to take up such a dangerous enterprise. But Gertie was Gertie, and he was more proud of her spirit than he could say. On no account must he let that brave heart be dashed. So he chided her for her lack of faith, talking more perhaps to satisfy his own concerns than to encourage her along her chosen course.

"My darling, you must never give up hope. Only think how Christ Himself was derided and treated for His belief in the people; why, He even died for us, and still we sin! But without Him and all He fought for, we would stand no hope at all. Because of Him, because He never gave in to depression or lost faith, we now have the opportunity to stand before our Maker on the great day of Judgment and, if we repent all our sins, we will live in His Kingdom forever. It is not for us to criticise others or wonder at their lack of honesty and loyalty. It is for us to bring the word of God to them and to give them the chance to join Him in that Kingdom. And by showing kindness, tolerance and compassion, even in such small things as giving succour to the needy, we are showing them the way. But what you are doing and what you have planned is no small thing," he added hurriedly, as he felt her bridle. "But a great sacrifice on your part. On no account must you give up now, at the first attempt! Why, if they want you to 'go away', as you put it, then the only way for them to do that is to bring their children here, where your wonderful soup will turn them into plump, rosy little pilgrims! Come, Gertie, let me see that wilful smile of yours and hear your word of admonishment for preaching you such a sermon."

Amos was at last beginning to understand his little wife, for, with these last words, the spark of anger that was starting to light her eyes suddenly turned to laughter and she almost tipped off her chair as she hugged him tightly.

"Oh, Amos, what am I to do with you? You preach to me with a sermon which would have done Mr Pidmore proud, and then you laugh at me for being angry! You are, of course, quite right, as ever, but I had no idea that you felt about my soup kitchen as ardently as I do. Oh, thank you, Amos, you have given me such hope! We will go straight away to the arches where the down and outs live and bring them here and not listen to their arguments. We will suffer no resistance. Come, darling, there is no time to spare." She was standing now, her eyes sparkling once more and the old, determined look on her firm little face. Amos stood up laughing and shaking his head.

"But sweetheart, it is snowing hard. I did not mean right this minute. I am sure God would not mean us to catch our deaths at our first attempt!"

But she would hear nothing of his remonstrances, and so, sighing and gathering up his hat and gloves, he helped Gertie on with her pelisse and blowing out the candles for safety's sake, after assuring themselves that the soup was still hot but not burning, they went out into the darkness of the night. And there, standing covered in snow, their thin, pinched faces apologetic their feet shuffling with embarrassment, was a small group of men and women, each one little more than a bundle of rags, staring up at Gertie's sign. Whether it was the not very expert picture of a bowl of steaming soup, or the smell wafting out of the chapel, or because word had finally got round, nobody knew, but it was certain that here was a group of people in need of help. And Gertie intended to help them, whether they liked it or not. She turned and opened the door. Light and warmth glowed merrily from the lamps inside and a murmur went up from the crowd.

"Come along in, please, everyone is welcome, and no one is turned away from Gertie's Soup Bowl. There is soup and bread enough for all and a warm fire to dry your clothes. This way, that's right, right down to the kitchen." And with that, everyone began to shuffle sheepishly through the little Chapel towards the warmth and smell of food. Gertie's cup overflowed.

Chapter Twelve

As the clothes of her 'visitors' dried out, various aromas filled the steamy air of the little kitchen, not least among them the smell of gin and other more unmentionable things. Apart from the slurping of soup, the ragged band ate in silence, thanking Gertie in embarrassed mumbles as she put a bowl and hunk of bread into each grimy hand. The stove roared away, Amos having doubts about the strength of its iron chimney pipe, but Gertie, blithely unaware of any danger which might overtake the Chapel, was chatting away to the silent recipients, as she filled and refilled the proffered bowls.

"Forgive me, ladies and gents, but I don't know your names. Charlie? You are Charlie? Oh, sorry, Charles, well, Charles, there is more and to spare. Do let me refill your bowl. And let me see, you are? Why, yes of course, you are Ada. Eat up, Ada, I want nothing left. That's right. Now, you all know my name – it is Gertie. I want to introduce my dear husband, the preacher, to you. His name is Amos and none of this could have come about without his help. So I am sure you will not object to his thanking God on our behalf for His providing us such abundance this night. No, you need not stop eating. Amos, dear, come and give thanks to God for His gifts!"

There was a stunned silence as Charles, his spoon halfway to his mouth, stared at Amos, who had been keeping himself busy up until now in tidying up the music on the harmonium. Not sure who was the most embarrassed, himself or the guests, Amos squeezed into the tiny kitchen and looked round at the sad and ragged little group. He groaned inwardly. Why had he allowed himself to talk his beloved into continuing with her plans? He cleared his throat and began, while the slurping and appreciative noises resumed.

"Dearly beloved..." No, that was wrong. He tried again. "We are gathered here to give thanks to the Lord..."

"No, we ain't, guv, we're 'ere to cop on to this 'ere beano. The Lord never give us nuffin'."

There were a few grunts of agreement from among the group and eating continued. Amos sighed again and tried once more.

"For what we have received, may the Lord make us truly thankful," and, catching sight of his wife's amused smile, he hurried back to the relative safety of the harmonium corner. Ashamed, be busied himself once more with the music stool. For what we have received, indeed! Is that all he had the courage to manage, a simple Grace. How could he call himself a Preacher of the Word, if that was all he could manage when faced with the indifference of the needy multitude? Well, perhaps not the multitude, but the needy poor of his Parish at any rate. He would have to do better than that if he were to save their souls. And it was their souls that was his part of the bargain. Gertie fed their bodies; he fed their souls. But what with? What do you say to people who have had every ounce of humanity beaten out of them? He cast his mind back to his own days before he was sent to the workhouse, the time when his own father struggled to feed the two of them after his sweet mother had died of the fever. Always hungry, usually on the run from the 'Peelers' , his life had been barren of anything but harshness and cold brutality. His father had not really been a bad man and had tried to do his best for Amos and the little sister who had died a few months after their mother, but trying to survive in the misery of London's hopeless poverty had led to a life of constant crime and finally gaol, where he too had succumbed to a fever. What kind of words and actions would have been the instrument to turn his father back to God, Amos wondered. But fine words wouldn't do it on their own. And praying certainly wouldn't! What good was the promise of a life here-after when you are cold and hungry in this one? No, what Gertie was doing was the way to these people's hearts, he admitted glumly. Feed their bodies first, then work on their souls, if it is not too late. Remember Christ and the five thousand! Ashamedly he crept back into the tiny kitchen, crammed with grimed and smelly humanity, and began to help Gertie pump water over the bowls, licked almost clean as they were handed back with grunts and noises of apparent gratitude. Warmed, fed and not bothered with any 'Jesus preachin', as one thin bundle kindly put it, the little group finally took itself off to the tunnels and arches that were considered home, each person jealously guarding a bundle of precious bits garnered in the struggle through life. The bowls were carefully washed and stacked, the spoons put away in a drawer of the rickety table which had been rescued from an outhouse and scrubbed clean, and the empty soup pans carried to the front door. Gertie and Amos worked in silence, neither wishing to voice their thoughts; Gertie bitter that the children had been denied the succour they needed and Amos ashamed that he could do nothing for these lost souls, at least at present.

But word must have spread among the poor and oppressed of the town for the next Sunday afternoon, just a few days before Christmas, with the soup once more hopefully simmering on the stove and the bowls and spoons sparkling on a clean cloth covering the patchwork paint of the little table, a loud chatter was to he heard outside the door of the Chapel. Gertie rushed to open the door and was nearly knocked to the ground as what seemed like a tide of children of all ages and sizes pushed past her and sat themselves noisily on the chairs ranged round the Christmas tree. Harassed women, scolding and chiding without effect, followed reluctantly, telling the unregarding mob to 'be'ave and speak when you're spoken to or you'll get a clip round the ear', and other such reprimands, while some of the less timid children had already started poking and pulling at the Nativity scene.

"'Ere, look, it's a little baby. 'E's got a thing round 'is 'ead! What's that, Ma, what's that thing?"

"It's the baby Jesus, you dafty, that's 'is 'alo. It shows 'e's 'oly!"

"Oh, that's good! A 'oly 'alo!"

"'Oly 'alo, 'oly 'alo." They all started to sing in chorus, laughing and falling off their chairs, one particularly large lad falling into the Christmas tree and knocking it over into the harmonium. Before Gertie could get her breath back a sudden shout surprised everyone into silence.

"Be quiet!" Amos was standing at the altar table and he seemed to have grown about two feet as he glared at the silent but defiant faces. "I will not have such behaviour in the house of God. Now, you will each sit quietly, and a bowl of soup will be handed to you. You will not grab or argue but wait your turn patiently. Your turn will come, never fear. My name is Amos, and I am the Preacher, and this is my wife Mrs Parker." Here he held out his arm to Gertie, who went and stood by his side, her face glowing with pride and happiness. "You will treat Mrs Parker with the greatest respect, as it is she who has brought all this soup for you and made the Chapel so nice. In return you will leave the pictures and tree alone and start to learn your letters. Now, ladies," he said, turning to the stunned mothers. "Would you be so kind as to help in serving the soup to your little ones?"

The 'little ones' were by now pinching each other or slyly trying to pull the bows off the tree without being observed. Arguments started and were stopped by mothers, mainly with a sharp slap round the head and two or three large lads were finally extricated from a pile on the floor and made to stand in a corner behind the harmonium, where they contented themselves by mouthing obscenities at the nearest girls, the shyer ones being reduced to tears. After much noise, snatching and arguing, everyone, including the mothers, finally had a bowl of soup and a fresh bread roll. The children seemed incapable of doing anything quietly, but surprisingly little of the precious soup got spilt and after a few minutes, during which could be heard many satisfied noises of appreciation, all the food had disappeared and the children, in an even grubbier and stickier state than before, were seated on their relevant chairs, the sexes separated, while the mothers made a great to-do or clearing up in the tiny scullery. Finally the business of trying to teach the children their lessons began, Amos standing in front and Gertie sitting behind the altar table.

Although Gertie had prepared a set of tracts and lessons for several weeks to come, it had never occurred to her that the children would be so unruly. Having been brought up in workhouse conditions, where even a whisper could result in a beating or being locked in a dark room for hours on end, she had imagined that all children would sit quietly and obey their teacher. Never in her wildest nightmares had she imagined anything like the behaviour of these little barbarians, who seemed incapable of sitting still for a moment, let alone listening to anything she or even Amos had to say. They had obviously got what they had come for, free food, and as far as they were concerned it was now time to raise havoc. After several attempts to persuade the lads to return to their side of the hall, comforting the little girls who were being bullied by the boys and putting to one side the two chairs whose legs had got broken in a scuffle, Amos, his anger mounting and his face grim with fury, took hold of two of the biggest lads by an ear each and dragged them to the front, beside the altar table. He stood for a moment, while the boys struggled and swore, but he held on with grim determination until the rabble quieted and an expectant hush descended on the hall. What would the preacher do? Would he send for the Peelers? Some of the children began to stand up with an idea of making their escape before they were 'nabbed', but Amos' voice, thundering out in the silence, pushed them back into their seats, turned to stone in their terror.

'Cor, this is a turn up' was the main thought running through the little group.

"Sit down and be quiet! How dare you behave like little savages in the house of God." He paused to make the words seem more awesome, both boys still struggling in his grasp. "Never." Looking around with his piercing glance at each child in turn. "Never have I seen such behaviour, no, not even in the workhouse where both Mrs Parker and I were brought up! We were taught manners then, and you will learn them now, if you know what's good for you. Go and sit down," letting go of the boys and pointing to two empty chairs in the front row of lads. "If I have any more of that behaviour from you, or from anyone else," again looking round at each petrified face, "there will be trouble. Very great trouble. Now, we will begin by saying a prayer asking the Lord to forgive us our sins and to teach us the right path. Put your hands together and close your eyes. Repeat after me: 'Lord, forgive us for being so rude and for misbehaving in your house,' Say it, all of you," he ordered, as some of the boys mumbled unintelligibly into their hands, giggling and pulling faces as the terror wore off. "You, William, isn't it? Repeat those words to the rest of us!"

Sheepishly William stood silent, his mocking smile gradually turning to sullen anger, but he finally managed to repeat the words in the correct order and at last the rest of the prayer had been spoken and repeated by the subdued children to Amos' satisfaction.

"Good, now you have promised God that you will behave, so if you break that promise you will have the fires of hell to deal with as well as me. Do you understand that?"

There were muffled yeses and one or two little girls started sobbing again, but after a while their fears were forgotten as Amos began to tell them stories from the texts that Gertie had prepared. Gertie knew that he was a good preacher, but she had never heard him telling such tales before. Everyone, including herself and even the mothers who had crept in from the scullery, sat spellbound as Amos brought to life people and places that had long since gone. When he had stopped talking, Gertie broke the silence by standing up and smiling round sweetly at the grubby, upturned faces. Savages or not, her heart went out to these waifs, who knew little more than cold, hunger and a swift clip round the ear, unless it was from their father's belt. No wonder they were little rebels when they were given half a chance! She turned to Amos.

"Thank you, Amos, we really enjoyed those stories, didn't we, children?"

There were some muffled grunts and foot shuffling, but she went on undaunted, still smiling her warm, generous smile and speaking in gentle accents,

"Now, your first Sunday school is nearly at an end, but first." She had to raise her voice slightly, as chairs were pushed back, and the bolder ones began to leave. "First I want you all to look at the chair you are sitting on. Yes, stand up and look at what is drawn on the back. Each chair has a letter, and I want you to remember the shape of that letter so that you choose the same chair to sit in each time you come. That will be your chair. Now you may go, but quietly and without rushing!"

Her last words were drowned out as the children made for the door as fast as they could, their mothers chasing after them with coats and scraps of rags, shouting and threatening as the door finally closed and the hall was quiet at last. Gertie sat down with a plop on to her chair and put her head in her hands. Amos went over to her and started to speak to her in soothing words of encouragement, but he suddenly realised that her shoulders were shaking not with sobs but with laughter. Gertie was laughing, the tears rolling down her cheeks.

"Oh, Amos, Amos," she gasped, between gulps. "Oh, if only you could have seen yourself, holding those two boys by the ear and threatening hell fire on them all. Did you see their faces? Oh, poor little things, they'll have nightmares for weeks. Oh, what a monster you are!" She continued giggling into her kerchief.

"Monster am I; I'll give them monster! If I had my way, I'd flay the lot of them! Monster indeed!"

Her giggling subsided, and Gertie took him in her arms, kissing him gently.

"You do not mean that, darling. Why, you were wonderful, telling them stories and showing them a world they had never before dreamed of! Giving them food is one thing, but what they really need is love and understanding and I believe today you gave them both. They will be back."

"Certainly they will, they can't resist your soup!"

"No, Amos, it is not just the soup, although that is a pull, stories and I am sure that once we have taught them a little self-discipline..."

"A little! That lot wouldn't know discipline if they were all conscripted into the Artillery!"

But he was wrong. The children did come back the next Sunday and more besides and once the original group had fought sufficiently over which chair was theirs and everybody had been found a seat, the few mothers who could find the time from their hectic routine of dealing with numerous children and noisy, drunken husbands, helped again with the soup, and once more everyone listened to Amos weaving Bible stories. Gertie had managed to beg an old blackboard and easel from the workhouse school, and she began to teach the children their letters. Within weeks news of the new Sunday school had spread and Susan was added to the 'staff' to help with the little ones and keep reasonable order among the children as a whole. She seemed to 'have a way with her' as Mrs Mabbett put. Children automatically obeyed her, and the now well-ordered and disciplined school began to flourish as winter turned into spring. What with playing for the morning service, teaching at the Sunday school and keeping the soup kitchen open in the evenings, Sundays were becoming even more exhausting than weekdays for Gertie, who still insisted on accompanying Mrs Johnson on her visits to the poor. Soon her cough became more than merely troublesome. One morning in early March, with the sun shining into their bedroom window and sparrows cheeping on the ledge, Gertie knew that she couldn't get up. Exhausted from coughing all night and trying not to wake Amos, she lay for some time after Susan had knocked on their door whispering urgently that it was 'gone six, Mrs, and time you was up'. Gertie turned to give Amos a shake and then realised that his side of the bed was empty. She had a moment's panic, until, seeing him with lather all over his face as he managed to shave in the tiny mirror by the window, she lay back on the bolster once more. Amos turned.

"Why, you are awake, darling. I tried not to disturb you as you were asleep at last. Now listen to me and don't argue," he said, walking over to her as he wiped the soap off with a towel. "You are not well enough to get out of bed, let alone go to the arsenal today, so I am going to call on Dr Craig on my way to work and he will come to see you. Susan can be relied upon to run the house today, and tomorrow we will see. No, I will brook no arguments," as she tried to sit up and remonstrate with him. "You are unwell now, but if we are sensible it will get no worse, and you will be back at your bench before you can say 'knife'! Now, lie down and Susan shall bring you some warm milk and bread and butter. That's right, sweetheart, keep warm and I will come back at lunchtime to see how you progress." He soothed her forehead, and surprisingly, for once Gertie did not feel like arguing. In fact she snuggled down thankfully in the bed and gave Amos a rather wan smile.

"Oh, Amos, you are so good to me. I am sorry to be so stupid. I can't think how I got this silly cold!"

Amos hushed her and then gave her a kiss on her flushed cheek before going gently from the room and hurrying downstairs to the dining room. Mrs Mabbett was there, looking anxious.

"How is she? I heard her coughing in the night and thought we might have to call the doctor there and then."

"She is very poorly, Mrs Mabbett. I shall go for the doctor directly and will return at lunchtime. In the meanwhile, perhaps you would be so good as to ask Susan to attend to Gertie and see to the household arrangements. I have no time for breakfast but will take this slice of bread with me to eat later."

While Mrs Mabbett clucked and fussed over him he wrapped a large chunk of bread in his clean kerchief, managed a few sips of tea and was off before the good lady could do no more than wish him good luck. She found Susan, who was expertly polishing the stove in the kitchen and explained the situation. Susan stood up and wiped a blackened hand across her forehead, leaving a line of blacklead mingling with the wayward auburn locks that always managed to escape from her cap.

"Don't you worry, Mrs M. I'll soon sort everything out and see to the Mrs. That little thing needs caring for and no mistake, especially in her condition!"

"Why, you don't mean…"

"Lor, yes. Haven't you noticed? Sick as a pig she was last Thursday morning, then she goes off to that there arsenal as if nothing 'ad 'appened. 'Is nibs needs to take more care of 'er, and that's for sure!"

"Now then, Susan, I will have none of that talk. Mr Parker is all goodness, but he has a great deal to worry about, what with the chapel and everything and now this."

And Mrs Mabbett sailed out of the kitchen before Susan could argue. But the widow wasn't really angry with the little maid. It was true that Amos had a lot to cope with, but she did feel that he neglected Gertie, who, in spite of being occupied with her work and the poor, often seemed lonely and in want of a little comfort from that man of hers. Perhaps motherhood would change all that, though how they were all going to cope with Gertie leaving her work and another mouth to feed she couldn't say. Still, it would be lovely to have a baby in the house, she thought wistfully. She brushed the thought aside and hurried off to the arsenal, after checking that Gertie was comfortable. She was fast asleep, her breath coming in rasps and her cheeks still flushed. Mrs Mabbett looked grim as she left the house, but she refused to consider the worst. Gertie was strong; she was a workhouse child, used to combating all the ills to be found in a place of that sort. No, she would come through this as she had come through all her other trials. She would. She *must*!

Mrs Mabbett was so intent on her thoughts that she failed to notice the doctor until she almost bumped into him.

"Why, there you are, Mrs Mabbett, I understand little Mrs Parker is ill. I am on my way to your house now to attend her. What is your diagnosis?"

"Oh, Doctor Craig, I don't know where we are at, really I don't. Little Gertie is that ill with the fever and her cough, and now I believe her to be in the family way! Susan will let you in; I must get on as I am late already, and we cannot afford to have my wages docked as well. I will call on you this evening if that is acceptable and you can tell me what must be done with my poor little girl then."

And before the good doctor could gather breath to reply the widow was gone. He hurried on to the house, where Susan met him on the doorstep, her usually placid features twisted into fear and distress.

"Come in, Doctor, do. The little Mrs is that bad and won't take nothing, even though she is coughing fit to bust. She'll lose the baby if she goes on like this and that will kill her sir, I know it will. This way, sir, if you please," and she led the way upstairs.

"Dr Craig, ma'am." And she hurried out of the room, shutting the door swiftly behind her. The doctor sat down on the bed and took Gertie's wrist in his strong, dependable hand.

"Well, well, Mrs Parker, ma'am, so you are not feeling yourself today?" he said in his soft, Scottish tones.

"No, doctor, it is this silly cough. I cannot seem to find relief from it, and I worry that it keeps Amos awake. You see, he works so hard and needs all the sleep he can get."

"And you do not work hard, I suppose? It is a regular picnic working on the cartridges all day long, not to mention being a preacher's wife, running a Sunday school and a soup kitchen. You're running yourself into the ground, young lady and no amount of physic will get you right unless you slow down a little. Now, I am going to give you a thorough examination and then we will see what we shall see. Susan!" he shouted, going to the door. The maid came running up the stairs, breathless and panting.

"Yes, sir, you called sir?"

"Yes, I am going to examine your mistress and I desire you to be present."

At the end of the examination, during which he hummed and ha'ad and said uh ha, he took from his bag a bottle of black, evil-looking liquid and then snapped the clasp shut.

"See that your mistress takes this dreadful stuff three times a day in hot water, Susan. It will ease the cough and bring down the fever. Brook no arguments and force it down her throat if necessary," he said, his eyes twinkling. "For I believe it to have been a concoction of the devil if it did not have such beneficial effects." He turned to Gertie, his face gentle. "You must stay here until you are strong enough to venture downstairs, Mrs Parker and that will not be for a week at least. You have the bairn to think of now, as well as yourself and that hell-raising husband of yours! Now, Susan shall prepare some of this monstrous elixir for you and I shall return this evening to see how you go on. Goodbye and do as you are bid!" and he followed Susan down the stairs.

"You may tell Mr Parker that his wife has nothing life-threatening, thank the good Lord, but she must rest for a good long while. She is nothing but a wee bit of a thing and thinks she can labour like a Hercules. You are a good girl, Susan, and I know that the household couldn't run without your level headed and practical help. But you are strong and hard work doesn't frighten you. I rely on you absolutely. I will return this evening." And with that he was gone, leaving Susan in a turmoil of emotions, proud that he had such confidence in her, and daunted by the responsibility he seemed to be placing on her shoulders. She turned and went back into the house, which suddenly seemed for the first time since she had come to live there to be dark and forbidding.

++++++++++

Gertie remained confined to her room for two weeks, the cough sometimes seeming to recede, only to come back again with a force that frightened Amos. But after finishing off two bottles of the horrible linctus and being given the best food that Susan could find with the dwindling finances, Gertie began to rally. Her fever subsided, the cough grew less and less frequent and no longer racked her whole body, and she began to get some strength back into her limbs. She was aware that there had been some secret discussions going on between Amos and Mrs Mabbett, but she had no idea what they had been concocting between them, so on the day that she finally ventured downstairs, Gertie vowed that she would find out what they had been planning while she was confined so conveniently to the bed. With Susan helping her, she managed the two flights of stairs down to the parlour, where a fire had been lit even though it was a warm spring day, and she sank thankfully on to the rather hard settle. Susan fussed round her, tucking in blankets and bringing her a cup of strong, sweet tea, and then, after seeing that she had something to read, took herself off to the scullery to prepare the vegetables for dinner. Gertie lay back, the trembling in her legs slowly subsiding, and she shut her eyes, listening to the comforting lick of the flames in the hearth and the tick of the clock on the mantel shelf. It was all very well being told that she must not worry or stress herself in any way. But how were they to manage, if she was unable to return to the arsenal and with a baby as well? Of course she would worry. Amos himself was beginning to look pale now, and she was sure that Mrs Mabbett had lost quite a stone in weight! Tears began to trickle down her cheeks as she felt the hopelessness of their situation. After all, there was no soup kitchen to help *them.* This made her smile, and she guiltily brushed the tears away. She mustn't let Amos see her like this! He was always reassuring her that God would provide, and she must believe in his assurances now more than ever. Though *how* He was to provide she had no idea!

At last she heard voices in the hall and the reassuring firm tread of her beloved. Her depression lifted immediately. Now all would be well, and they would discuss how they could manage for the future. Amos rushed over to her, his arms open and an expression of delighted relief on his face. Her heart jumped as he gathered her into his arms, murmuring gentle words as he kissed her eyes and her cheeks and finally her lips.

"Oh, my darling, it is so good to see you on the mend at last. I have been out of my mind with worry. Gertie I have been a cruel and thoughtless husband and promise that from now on I will take the greatest care of you. For you are more precious to me than rubies!"

Delighted though she was to be hugged by her adored Amos, Gertie couldn't help but be a little amused that even at this moment of such heightened passion he found expression for his relief in Biblical quotations. Rubies, indeed! But she said nothing, only hugging him back, laughing up into his fine dark eyes and saying that if he treated her like one of those silly, helpless, fashionable females he would be sorry. Mrs Mabbett hovered in the background, her kindly face beaming through her tears, and there was general mayhem until Susan announced that dinner was ready. Exhausted by so much emotion, Gertie was helped to sit up on her couch and a tray was laid across her knees. Left in peace at last, while the others went into the dining room, Gertie ate the delicious food ravenously. She was certainly feeling better, but she would have to rally soon, before her fears, which she had joked about to Amos, became a reality. There was no way that she was going to be treated like the little china doll that was the lot of so many females. She might not be strong, and she would certainly be hampered in her plans by motherhood, but other women with strength of mind coped, and so would she!

Chapter Thirteen

While Gertie had been safely tucked away in bed, Amos and Mrs Babbett had not been idle. It was agreed that Gertie could not continue with the soup kitchen and the Sunday School without more help than she was getting at present, so Amos decided to follow up a plan that had been forming n his mind for some time. First, he needed to get a proper Ministry so that the little Bethel Chapel could become a recognised Church and he could earn a living. Then the Sunday School would become part of the Church and, hopefully, would accrue a little income, enough to release Gertie from her onerous work at the arsenal. Amos knew he could not organise all this on his own; the church would need deacons and all manner of recognised bodies. He had approached the kindly Mr Johnson about how to set all these ideas in motion, but the long-suffering preacher was too busy to give more than fleeting advice about how to begin. It seemed that the best person to go to was the Congregational preacher Thomas Richardson, who had founded the Sunday School Union only four years preciously, had established the Building Society and who seemed the most appropriate person to approach both for advice and possible financial aid.

So one evening, only a few days after Gertie had made her first appearance downstairs, cap in hand and with no little trepidation, Amos climbed the steps of the imposing building close to Upper Market Street where Mr Richardson lived with his large family. Amos remembered in the Spring of last year this clever but kindly man had come to talk to the men of the arsenal about the wonders and value of the Great Exhibition, describing the works of industry of all nations, and how he had received such a hearty reception. He was obviously a popular man as well as a good businessman, but would Amos being a Methodist make a difference? He hoped not. He pulled the great black bellpull at the side of the imposing front doors and soon a neat little maid was ushering Amos into a large but cluttered study. She announced him as 'Mr Parker, sir', and then slid silently from the room, closing the door gently behind her. The man rising from a huge leather chair behind the mahogany desk was much younger than Amos remembered, ad as he held out his hand in greeting Amos was relieved by the gentle kindness in his eyes. All awkwardness left him as he sat opposite this great man, who smiled his beaming smile and offered Amos a cigar.

"No, thank you, sir, I don't smoke," Amos stuttered, feeling rather ungrateful.

"Very wise, very wise, Mr Parker. A nasty, smelly habit, but one I've dropped myself into since I've gone up in the world! Silly thing to do really. Now, how can I help you?"

Amos cleared his throat. Then his mind went blank, and he shifted awkwardly in his chair. Why was he here? It was really to raise money for Gertie's Sunday School, but he couldn't say that outright. No, he would have to start with the Ministry. He cleared his throat again as Mr Richardson waited patiently, taking long puffs on his cigar and blowing the smoke up to the ceiling. Then, as he leant forward to flick the ash into a crystal ashtray, he looked up at Amos.

"You are wondering how you can ask me for money and clothe the request in respectability. Is that it?"

The words were said quite gently, and without any malice, but Amos realized that, benevolent though he was, this man was no fool and wouldn't take kindly to fancy talk. He took a deep breath and waded in.

"You are quite right, sir, financial help is part of what I seek. But, as I explained to you in my letter, I have re-opened the little Bethel Chapel by the Ship and Half-Moon stairs, and my wife and I hold Methodist meetings there every Sunday morning. We have also started a Sunday School and my wife runs a soup kitchen for the poor of the Parish. Until now I had hoped for an existing Ministry to become vacant, but my wife has been poorly and is due to be confined in September. She can no longer carry on all her duties, working in the cartridge factory and running a home, and so we must forego her income. As you can imagine, there is little enough to spare in our present situation and with Gertie not working and another mouth to feed…"

Amos had been speaking so earnestly that he broke off, suddenly aware that he must have sounded like one of his sermons. But the other man was listening and watching him intently, and as Amos stopped speaking he leant forward once more and stubbed out his cigar. There was silence for a moment, then Mr Richardson grunted and neatened up some papers on the desk. At last he looked up and there was genuine concern in his face.

"I was aware that your wife had started a soup kitchen. There isn't much that passes me by in this town. But I hadn't realized the extent of it. Sunday school, working at the factory, preacher's wife. And she goes off with Mrs Johnson into the moth of Hades, I'll be bound, to do their 'ministering'! They come from a special mould, these women. And how old is this paragon? Twenty, twenty-one?"

"Not yet eighteen, sir."

"Not yet eighteen! And already she has the whole of Woolwich at her feet! But tell me, young man, what makes you, a Methodist, think that I, a strict Congregational man, would be willing to help you find a Ministry, or funds for this soup kitchen of yours?"

Amos shifted again and tried to put his thoughts in order. He was quite unused to facing an intellect at least as powerful as his own and it unnerved him. He suddenly felt very young, aware that he had not even reached the twenty-one years that would give him the authority of manhood. Still, here he was, an ordained reverend with nowhere to call a ministry, and unable to face Gertie without something coming out of this interview, so he gathered his courage and once more plunged in.

"I understand, sir, that you are a founder of the Woolwich Sunday School Union. It was really Gertie's idea to start up a Sunday school, but, apart from the help given to us by the Reverend Johnson and his wife, we really have no support. Gertie insisted that we look for a disused chapel for me to preach in, to the men of the arsenal and she has been my rock all along, but now..."

"Now this 'rock' is in need of a little support herself. Well, young man, I will see what I can do. The pair of you seem to have done some pretty splendid things between you so far, and it would be a pity for it to fall by the wayside for want of a little cash and help from a higher quarter. Ministries are not two a penny, but from what I hear, you already have a respectable congregation so it shouldn't be too hard to persuade the powers that be to offer you something. Not that it's a fortune, mind. It'll be hand to mouth for some time to come, but, by the looks of you, that won't come as any novelty. Now, I shall make the appropriate arrangements for you to meet the Sunday School Union Committee, and once you have been accepted that will be the time to approach the Methodist hierarchy for a ministry. I know some of them, they use my Building society! Now you go back to that little wife of yours and tell her not to worry. Thomas Richardson will come up trumps, don't you doubt it!"

Stuttering his thanks, Amos left the sumptuous house, full of excitement and a sense of relief. For the first time since their marriage he felt he had really accomplished something on his own. He wanted to make Gertie proud of him and now here was this Mr Richardson, preacher, businessman, someone with standing in society, all ready and willing to help him, Amos Parker, workhouse boy. He ran up the steps to his house with a light heart, but as soon as he reached the top step he realized that something was wrong. The front door was open and the hall empty. Where was Susan, or Mrs Mabbett. He called out but there was no answer. He hung his hat on its hook and rushed upstairs, calling agitatedly for Gertie and as he reached the top landing Mrs Mabbett came out of their room, his and Gertie's, talking solemnly to Dr Craig. They turned as Amos reached them, panting and trying to catch his breath.

"What is it, what is wrong?" he asked frantically. The doctor spoke soothingly, taking him by the arm and leading him into the room and taking him over to the window, explaining in a whisper,

"It is nothing to worry about as yet, Amos, but your wife needs complete rest for some time to come. Her cough has returned and for a while there were fears for the baby, but we have managed to stabilize them both and provided she lies quite still and quiet for two weeks more all should be well. She has the heart of a lion, your Gertie, but her body is frail. Not enough food and proper care when she was little, that is the main problem. I have seen it all too often in workhouse products. Now, she is asleep at last, so do not disturb her. She has a remedy which she is to take four times a day. It might make her drowsy, but I assure you it will not harm the infant. I will return in two days, unless there is a development, in which case you will send for me immediately. Now I must leave you or my wife will think I have run off with one of the Sisters of Mercy!" The two men moved towards the door. The doctor coughed discreetly. "If you will not think it an impertinence, how are you both to manage in your new situation?"

As they walked down the stairs, Amos explained to the good doctor, who had become as much a friend as a physician, about the help that Mr Richardson had promised. Dr Craig was rather amused by Amos' admission.

"So you go to the great man himself. Nothing but the best for your Gertie, eh? But you are quite right to approach Tom. I've known him since he was in leading strings and he is as good a man as you could find in the whole of Kent in my opinion. If anyone can help, young Tom Richardson can. Got a fine head on his shoulders, he has; fine businessman and philanthropist. He'll see you right even if your churches are forever squabbling! Now, good night, Amos, and don't you worry about your lass. She'll be just fine."

But in spite of the doctor's assurances, Amos felt a shadow had fallen across the house. He looked into the parlour, where Mrs Mabbett was sitting mending some sheets. She put down her work and went over to him, giving him a quick peck on the cheek and leading him to a chair by the fire, for although it was late May, the evenings were still cold.

"Sit down here and I shall get Susan to bring you a nice hot toddy," said the widow, sailing out of the room before he could argue. He could hear the clinking of crockery in the scullery, and leaned back in the chair, closing his eyes and enjoying the heat of the fire as it warmed his chilled feet. In spite of his anxiety he must have dozed off, for suddenly there was Mrs Mabbett again, clucking and pulling one of the many occasional tables towards him, where she placed the glass of milk, which had been liberally laced with something.

"There, no you drink that, and no arguing. A little something left over from Christmas for just such an emergency. Purely medicinal, mind, but it'll give you a good night's sleep, though don't you go disturbing your wife with those clomping great boots of yours!" She busied herself putting away her mending, then wished him 'good night', reminding him to 'mind the fire, we don't all want to be burnt in our beds', then she was gone, and he was left to his own reflections and the comforting milk and brandy. He stared into the flames for some while, sipping his drink and wondering how he could face life if God saw fit to take his beloved Gertie. He determined form now on to show her just how much she meant to him and enjoyed a wallow in guilt as he realized how little he had attended to her needs. Well, all that was going to change! She would want for nothing, his little Gertie. He would tend her from now on with the gentlest of care. He drained the glass, checked the coals and, after blowing out the rest of the candles, took the remaining one to light the way upstairs. Yes, he would treat her with the finest kid gloves. Pleased with this resolve, his conscience salved, he undressed and slid quietly into bed beside his beloved, not pausing to consider whether his beloved would take kindly to being treated with kid gloves.

++++++++++

Amos slept like a log, the brandy doing its work and the following morning he was up bright and early, insisting on getting under Susan's feet in the scullery.

"It's quite alright, Mr Amos, sir, I can manage, really I can," said the patient Susan, but he wouldn't hear of her carrying the breakfast tray up to Gertie.

"No, Susan, I must tend my own wife. Why, whatever would she think of me if I were to leave without seeing that she eats up all her breakfast and kissing her goodbye?"

Susan wisely kept her thoughts to herself, but she rightly judged that the last thing 'The Missus' would want right now was a man fussing over her. And Susan's judgement seldom failed. Exhausted, dispirited and worried that she was neglecting her duties to the poor, Gertie found Amos' ministrations irritating. Her pillow was perfectly comfortable without being plumped up, she was quite capable of eating her egg without help and she hated lots of sugar in her tea. But she tried not to let the grumpiness show and managed a wan smile as Amos gave her a little lecture on taking care of 'you both', as he put it, archly. Oh, dear, she wasn't sure which she disliked most, Amos the neglecting husband, or Amos the attentive. She assured him that she would do exactly as she was told, would drink the linctus four times a day and would ring the hand bell, kingly provided by Mrs Mabbett, whenever she wanted the slighted thing. He kissed her and looked anxiously down at her.

"Now, you are sure you will be alright? Shall I come home at lunch time to check? I really don't like leaving you all day like this."

She summoned up all her energy to assure him that she would be very well looked after in Susan's capable hands, that there was absolutely no need for him to spend his precious lunch hour rushing home to her, and she would be as right as ninepence by this evening once she had spent a day lazing in her bed She managed to send him away at last, and then, dispirited and near to tears as she was, she fell at last into a deep but troubled sleep.

Mr Richardson was as good as his word and a few days later Amos received a letter by special delivery requesting him to attend a meeting of the Sunday School Union on 'Thursday evening next'. He rushed upstairs to Gertie, who was still in bed, proudly showing her the wonderful letter and exclaiming at the fine paper and handsome handwriting. She exclaimed over it dutifully and began worrying about what Amos was to wear.

"For you cannot wear your work clothes, they are far too scruffy, but you seem to be growing too large for your suit at all ends. Your hands and feet stick out like turkey legs and the buttons have the very greatest difficulty in doing up.

You will have to leave the coat open. But then Susan must wash your very best shirt. Oh, I am so useless lying here!"

he shushed her, kissing her eyelids and calling her his silly little'un, the way he used to do. She began to calm down and they talked about the great possibilities that this meeting could bring them.

"Once the Sunday school has been recognised, I shall apply to the Council of Methodist Ministers to be put on the circuit and then it will only be a short time before my ministry is also publicly recognised and I shall be a proper reverend!"

" But you are already ordained, from when you were at the College. Why must we wait for public recognition?"

"Well, darling, that is how it is. Supposing they did not think me a fit preacher or found that my past was not suitable for the church! What then?"

"Oh, really, Amos, what could you possibly have in your past that would prevent your suitability for the Ministry?"

"Why, you never know, I might really be a thief like my father, or lure young females to my castle or…"

But Gertie's shrieks of denial brought Mrs Mabbett up to the room in consternation, convinced that a murderer had managed to get into the house and was strangling her precious Gertie. They calmed the poor woman at last, too embarrassed to explain what had caused the uproar, and soon Amos was shooshed downstairs for his dinner, leaving Gertie feeling hopeful for the first time in weeks. Amos was going to get recognition at last; she was feeling a great deal better and he had called her his 'little'un' again. She heaved a sigh and lay back, smiling happily as she felt a small kick in the middle of her stomach.

Chapter Fourteen

Amos' meeting with the Sunday School Committee was a very formal affair. Apart from Mr Richardson, all the other seven teachers looked highly formidable, most of them being a good deal older, with grizzled whiskers and beetling brows. Amos felt quite apprehensive and couldn't imagine how little children would react to all that solemnity. But they were pleasant enough once the introductions had been carried out and they asked only sensible questions, which Amos was able to answer with a certain amount of confidence. He felt it his duty to point out that it was his wife who had instigated the idea and who had put so much effort into making the school a success, and this seemed to impress the men. After a solid hour of questioning Amos was freed at last, with the promise that they would inform him of any outcome within the week. Once back home he amused the two ladies with a description of his interview, his old humour returning, much to Gertie's delight as she lay propped up on her pillows, Mrs Mabbett holding one of her hands and Amos the other. But Gertie was feeling too relieved to mind being fussed. As long as her Amos was happy and there was the chance of some aid forthcoming, they could coddle her as much as they chose.

The letter arrived at last, welcoming Amos provisionally into the Sunday School Union, with the proviso that he fulfilled a three months trial period with full attendance of the children. Mr Richardson added a postscript to say that once this condition was fulfilled he would contact the Methodist Board and organise a meeting with them to try to create a living for the little chapel. By this time Gertie was much improved and downstairs once more. There was no question of her returning to the arsenal, but she insisted that she help Amos with the Sunday morning services and the school and since the children were by now far better behaved under Susan's stern tutelage, the next three months passed without mishap and Amos was at last admitted formally into the Sunday School Union. A further letter arrived summoning Amos to meet the Methodist Board and that was an even more formidable affair than the Sunday School Union meeting, but he came away quite confident, and one Sunday at the beginning of September, two weeks before Gertie's confinement, just as the service was about to begin, a gentleman with the fullest whiskers Gertie had ever seen, and with black, glittering eyes and clothes to match, walked straight down the little aisle and sat down right in front of Amos. The eyes stared out at him unblinking throughout the service and Amos had to keep all his wits about him not to stumble or lose courage. But he managed it, and even gave a truly resounding sermon, and for some reason the singing that morning seemed even finer than usual, the choir being not too prominent with their harmonies. As soon as the service was over the strange gentleman called to the congregation to remain seated and then he walked up to Amos and stared with his terrible gaze straight into Amos' soft brown eyes. He held out his hand and said, in sonorous accents,

"Joshua Marvell, Board of Ministers. Well, young man, you're a mite young to be a fully-fledged minister and I hope that choir of yours doesn't get too fancy, hiding the true Word with its flummery, but you'll do, my boy, you'll do," and he turned to the expectant audience, all eyes gazing anxiously at Amos, who cleared his throat and introduced the Reverend Marvell. There was a hushed silence as this spectacular news sunk in, and then the older man spoke.

"Brothers and sisters, it is my very pleasant duty to announce that this chapel is now formally recognised as a Methodist place of worship and its first Minister is the Reverend Amos Parker." He turned and shook Amos' hand. "Welcome into the Ministry, my boy, you have a fine gift of oratory."

Everyone was overjoyed and there was a great shaking of hands and congratulations as tears of joy poured down Gertie's cheeks. The Reverend Marvell declined an invitation to dinner, saying that it was most kind, but he had to hurry back to London for an afternoon service, but that a contract of employment would be in the post first thing in the morning. Bemused, their heads swimming in disbelief, Gertie and Amos hurried home to tell Mrs Mabbett the wonderful news. Amos was a Minister at last!

++++++++++

Gertie's confinement was a difficult one. She was in labour two days and for some hours the midwife and the doctor feared for the live of both mother and infant, but the tiny creature was born at last, a girl with black hair and a funny little pink, screwed up Face. Amos thought she was the most beautiful thing he had ever seen and couldn't stop telling his wife what a clever Little'un she was. Gertie, exhausted but content, drifted in and out of sleep for the next few hours, only rousing to feed the hungry child, who the doctor pronounced 'as fit as a flea and with the appetite of a horse'! But although the birth had been hard, under the kind ministrations of Mrs Mabbett and the indefatigable Susan, both mother and baby prospered. Susan adored the child and immediately took on the role of nursemaid along with all her other duties, even procuring an old bassinette in which she pushed her proudly through the streets down to the river, insisting that the river air would do the child the world of good. Gertie was convinced that the dampness would get on her lungs, but baby Lucy thrived and grew into a bonny, happy and uncomplicated little girl.

As a fully-fledged Minister, Amos was on the princely sum of £41 per annum and with a wife and daughter to feed, he knew that it would be impossible for him to give up working at the arsenal completely. Luckily Mr Langham, foreman, needed part-time labour and welcomed Amos back with open arms when, after a few arguments with his wife, worried that he would 'work himself into an early grave, and her with an extra mouth to feed!' Amos agreed to work mornings only, on an hourly basis. The agreement suited everybody, and the Parker household flourished in peace and harmony. Until, that is, Gertie, throwing off her worrying cough and getting stronger by the minute, announced that she wished to resume her ministering with Mrs Johnson. Amos exploded.

"What can you possibly be thinking of? Have you no care for our child, our daughter? Entering those dens of disease, heaven knows what horrors you might bring back with which to impregnate out little girl! Your place is here, in the home, and I will brook no disobedience on the subject. Might I remind you, Gertie, that you promised in the sight of God, to obey me, and I intend to keep you to that promise. I will hear no more of such nonsense!" and with that he stomped out of the room, throwing the door wide. Gertie heard the front door slam, and she was left standing in the terrible silence that seemed to fall on her like winter rain. She sat down on the couch, misery once again enveloping her as it had done so often in the past, before Alice was born. But this was different. She was a prisoner now, tied to the house by binding promises that she had not imagined in her wildest dreams Amos would use against her wants, her deepest needs. Certainly she could not argue with the necessity of keeping the child away from sickness and the perils of ministering. But she could leave her with Susan on the odd occasions when she accompanied Mrs Johnson, and surely that lady would not take her into places where such horrors as cholera lurked? Poverty, hunger, these were things that could be remedied and that was all that Gertie expected to confront. After all, Mrs Johnson had been ministering these twenty years or more and she had suffered nothing but a cold and a slight fever in all that time! Gertie decided that it was time to visit that long-suffering lady once more, so, with the pretence of showing Lucy off to the Johnsons, she wrapped the baby up warm against the chill air and hurried down to the house behind the Methodist Church. Thankfully, Mr Johnson was away visiting a sick relative and Mrs Johnson, delighted to have a chance to cosset Lucy without interference, ushered Gertie into the parlour, where a welcome fire was roaring up the chimney.

"Do sit down, my dear, it is good to see you looking so fit and well. Now, let me see this amazing child of yours. Why, she is a little beauty, just like her mother," and the older woman fussed and petted the baby until a tray of tea was brought in. Mrs Johnson carefully laid Lucy in a large leather chair and then turned to Gertie.

"My dear. I can see that you are having yet more problems with that forceful young husband of yours. The 'promise to obey' bit? Yes, I thought that would happen," as Gertie nodded tearfully. "What is he forbidding this time; returning to part-time work, going ministering or letting Susan push the bassinette? Or all three?" she added smiling. Gertie smiled wanly back and swallowed a sob.

"It is the ministering, Mrs Johnson. He says that I will bring back diseases that could be passed on to Lucy and that he utterly forbids me to accompany you. I have not even broached the subject of my returning to work. Sometimes my lovely boy seems a complete stranger to me and I feel as though I am his property rather than his wife. I would rather he beat me than that he behaved in so cold a manner!"

"Oh, no you wouldn't, I am sure. He is cold to you because it is his only form of defence. He is a kind and gentle man, not a drunken bully, but when his temper threatens to get the better of him his only defence is to curb his emotions as completely as possible. He uses quelling words, he slams out of the house, but he does not harm you! This you must respect above all things in him and love him all the more dearly for it, as he loves you. Remember, he is a man of the cloth and that promise you made to God in your wedding ceremony was held by him to be sacred, even if you did not take it quite that way. The important thing for you to decide now is how you are to interpret that promise without breaking it. Let us consider where you both differ on the subject and where you agree."

Throughout this speech Mrs Johnson had once again been holding both Gertie's hands in her own, talking in a gentle voice and gradually steadied Gertie's emotions, the practical examination of the problem seeming to dispel the hopelessness in the girl's mind. Everything the older woman said was right, of course, although once back at home Gertie was not sure that she would be able to keep the sense of what was said in perspective. Why did she always get so emotional when confronted by Amos and his moods? Mrs Johnson was continuing,

"First of all, my dear, you must agree with your husband that the needs of the baby come first. There is no question about that, and if that means that you cannot go ministering without harming her, then you do not accompany me. You have seen the terrible conditions that some of those poor creatures live in, and that is where outbreaks of cholera and other diseases usually begin. It is only three years since that last dreadful epidemic and who knows when it will strike again! But visiting the worst areas of poverty is not the only method of ministering open to us females! Why, you already run a soup kitchen and I am sure Amos will not forbid that. But I am inclined to agree with him that you should not, at least for some while to come, subject either Lucy or yourself to any danger. This means you cannot accompany me on my ministering, but hush," as she felt Gertie stiffen, "I have another plan for you. You are a workhouse girl and therefore I am sure that you know how to help those young people who are about to leave and who need situations. You have already spoken to me of two such girls. Suppose you approach the authorities and offer your services as a kind of agent, placing young women in respectable work. How does this sound to you?"

At first Gertie felt aghast at the thought of so much responsibility, not knowing how or where she would begin. But as Mrs Johnson outlined the plan further she began to get excited at the idea. Why, Mrs Johnson was correct in saying that she already knew of two young girls who needed placing, little Mary, who wishes to be a seamstress and Sarah, longing to go on the stage. The plan as Mrs Johnson saw it, was to find out which employers locally needed female staff and then to go to Mr Smith and interview likely girls. Gertie had no idea whether employers would welcome such intervention, or whether she would be able to pick out suitable girls for their needs, but Mrs Johnson pointed out that since there were few posts that females could engage to undertake, there could be little difficulty in fitting the girl for the vacancy.

"Let us list the posts of which you know something; cartridge making, maidservant, nanny. Now those which you probably understand well enough; seamstress, teacher, actress, although I suggest you do not encourage such activity in the future! There, that is a beginning, it is not? I suggest that you begin by aiding Mrs Mabbett in her search for suitable girls to work at the cartridge tables. Make a note of all the girls you interview, listing their abilities and then you already have a ready-made set of females to be placed. Why, the plan is fool-proof! Now, you go back to poor dear Amos and tell him that of course he is right and what could you have been thinking of, expecting to go ministering with that Mrs Johnson! Wait a few days and then suggest that you help Mrs Mabbett in choosing girls for the factory. Let the rest take its course."

Gertie was delighted. But she was a little puzzled. How had Mrs Johnson managed to persuade her own husband to let her continue ministering for all those years?

"Why, you see, my dear, neither of our little ones survived and we were not blessed further. I desperately needed something to fill my life after our second loss, and dearest Will respected my wishes in those circumstances. But I would not have continued if we had managed to raise a family. So, you see, I understand both points of view, but I am sure that you agree with me that to cherish your child is the most important work in the world. She is beyond price!"

Gertie was appalled. She had no idea that the Johnsons had ever had children, let alone lost them both. She sat in shocked silence until Mrs Johnson smilingly hugged her and said that it had been long ago and that both she and Mr Johnson had learnt to live with the sadness in their hearts.

"We know that they are with God and never knew the miseries of this world. Their innocence has been preserved forever and one day we will see them again. Until that blessed time we must work to improve the lot of those less fortunate than ourselves, and there are many of them, I can assure you. Now, you go back to Susan, and between you make a fine meal for that hard-working man of yours, for you can be sure that he wants a loving wife, not a slave, and remember that was another of those promises you made." Mrs Johnson picked up the sleeping baby.

"Come along, sweetheart, go to your mother. There. She is perfect. Goodbye, my dear, and remember, you promised to love and honour each other, and keep that as your covenant with God. If you do, you will not go very far wrong!"

Chapter Fifteen

The scheme worked! Feeling a little guilty and telling herself that she was not letting Mrs Johnson down by being in any way devious, Gertie first outlined the idea to Mrs Mabbett, who jumped at the thought that she would no longer have to waste time going to 'that wretched home' as she put it, to interview stupid, recalcitrant girls. Mrs Mabbett was getting a little tetchy as she went on in years and had far less patience with the new recruits to the cartridge factory than when she had first taken Gertie in.

"There's no denying it, Gertie," she admitted one day, "I am not as young as I was and their silly tittle-tattle fair wears me down. If I had the chance, I would retire, but there..."

So she and Gertie cornered Amos one evening in October, just one month after Lucy was born, (and after a particularly fine dinner), and presented Amos with the fully completed plan. To the surprise of both ladies Amos did not quibble. In fact he said he thought it a splendid idea and had been thinking along similar lines himself to occupy his Little'un! Secretly slightly vexed, Gertie ran and put her arms round her husband's neck, hugging him and saying how clever he was to have thought of such an idea just to please her. Mrs Mabbett folded her hands quietly in her lap and kept her peace, pleased with Mrs Johnson's schooling of the little bride. She'd go far, that young lady! And so the plan was hatched.

The first thing to do, Gertie decided, was to write a letter to Mr Smith at the workhouse, explaining that she was to take over from Mrs Mabbett in recruiting young women for the factory. Then, taking Susan with her for safety and the sake of decorum, she would walk round the town peering at the various offices where apprentices were likely to be needed. She would also buy a weekly newspaper and scan the staff-needed columns. Pleased with her brilliant idea, Gertie penned a very neat letter to the Warden and then she and Susan set off with Lucy in the bassinette that afternoon to post the letter and to look in the more hopeful shops in Powis Street, where, amongst others, there was a small tailors and a little drapers store. This last was owned by a Mr Giles, a kindly and benevolent man, who seemed most interested when Gertie approached him in great trepidation, explaining who she was and that she knew of a young lady who was seeking a post as seamstress, and were there any vacancies? Instead of sending her packing, Gertie was surprised to find that Mr Giles was delighted to be able to accommodate the renowned Mrs Parker.

"I do so admire the work you do for our poor, Mrs P! And from what I hear, your husband's a very fine preacher. I would come to chapel if I could, being a lapsed Methodist, so to speak, but what with running the Emporium and Mrs Giles not being too good on her pins now, you know how it is!"

Gertie made all the right noises and she and Susan managed to extricate themselves at last, with promises to produce Mary at the earliest opportunity. Then, against her better judgement, and noisy remonstrations from the prudish Susan, she turned back down to Beresford Street and the new theatre. Gertie had never been in a theatre before in her life and was overcome with wonder and amazement at the sights and smells that met her senses as the two young women were shown backstage to the manager's office. It seems a production of 'A midsummer Night's Dream' was to be performed that very evening and everything seemed very hectic, with people rushing all over the place in a distracted fashion, ladies appearing in the strangest of costumes of the most immodest covering and the orchestral conductor wringing his hands in a frenzy and crying out in a foreign accent,

"They are fools! Idiots! I said two oboes, *two.* And what do they send? One oboe and a bugle! What would I be doing with a *bugle*?"

However, once inside the manager's office, all seemed to be peace and order.

"You must not mind them, my dear Mrs Parker. They are artists. It is incumbent upon them to become distracted on the first night. All will be well once the curtain rises. It always is!" And with that the manager directed the two women to sit down, Susan wedging the bassinette into a small corner of the room , and he heaved himself into a large, winged chair. He opened a box of cigarillos.

"Do you mind if I indulge? It is one of the few things that keep me sane in this profession! Now, in what way can I be of assistance?"

Still a little distressed by all the noise and haste, Gertie had to collect her thoughts for a moment before she could explain her errand to this large and rather overpowering man. But he listened kindly enough when she put Sarah's story to him. The child was now eleven years old, would soon be apprenticed to someone and Gertie felt that it would be far better for everyone to let Sarah follow her desires, at least until she had proved herself or otherwise, than to push her into some work that was irksome to her and consequently which she would not perform to the best of her ability. Gertie wisely omitted to point out that as there was no next of kin to shame apart from a little brother, it hardly mattered if Sarah did go on the stage! But she realised that this might not exactly endear her argument to Mr Savill, so she waited patiently while he puffed the cigarillo, looked up at the ceiling, shuffled some papers and hunted in a drawer of his large mahogany desk for a kerchief. After blowing his nose violently, he pocketed the kerchief and then stubbed out the cigarillo.

"Hm. Eleven years old you say, but small for her years. No family?"

"Only a little brother, a few years younger than herself. Otherwise no one, Sir."

"Hm. Very well, I'll see her. But only to test her out, mind. She could be useful in some of our fairyish sort of scenes and she can help with mending the costumes and the like. Tell Mr Smith to send her along and I'll look her over. If that is all, I'll be saying good day to you, Mrs Parker. Work calls and all that."

And with a shake of his rather large hand, Gertie, Susan and the bassinette were ushered out of the door and back into the chaos. They found their way to the street at last, after a few wrong turnings, rather embarrassingly discovering people in various stages of undress, but once outside they breathed a sigh of relief, and Gertie clapped her hands in excitement.

"We've done it, Susan! We have made an excellent start. Now all we need to do is to go to the workhouse and extricate those two poor children!"

But it was not as simple as that. It seemed that Mr Smith had been poorly, and a Mr Black was acting as temporary Warden. He considered that things had become far too lax at the workhouse and was busy putting the fear of God back into the inmates. His letter in answer to the one Gertie had written to Mr Smith was polite enough, but it was plain that he did not deem it necessary to 'pander to the fancies of those whose place will always be in the lower orders, so to speak.'

"I am sure you would be the first to agree with me, my dear Mrs Parker, that it would an act of the greatest cruelty to raise the hopes of these females when their lot in life is not and never can be anything but the merest drudgery. Sad though it is, it is God's Will, and we must never forget that He 'moves in mysterious ways, His wonders to perform!' And who are we, the weakest of mortals, to question His plans for us?" and so on and so on. Gertie crumpled up the letter in disgust and threw it in the coal scuttle.

"Good heavens, Susan, yet another prosy old bore! Well, I might have been afraid of such a person once, but I can assure you that I will brook no nonsense now," said Gertie, pulling on her ancient but highly serviceable gloves, glad of the patient Mrs Johnson's tuition in such matters. 'The way a lady deals with her gloves is of the utmost importance,' had said that redoubtable lady! Gertie continued, "We shall go and visit this Mr Black immediately and tell him exactly what we think of his precious plans for these poor children." And with that Lucy was once again bundled into the bassinette and the two young women set off with determined strides through the town and up the long hill to Plumstead and the forbidding portals of the workhouse. The bell echoed through the gloomy corridors and eventually the bolts were drawn back, and a small boy looked out at them with a frightened stare.

"Please inform Mr Black that Mrs Parker and maid are without and wish to see him immediately," Gertie said grandly. "It is of the utmost importance," she added loudly, as the boy looked as if he was about to shut the door on them in his fear. He disappeared into the darkness and a voice could be heard calling out who was there disturbing the peace of honest Christians. A thin, gaunt man appeared, looking from Gertie's diminutive height to be about eight feet tall, dressed all in black and looking much like the barge pole that the ferry men used. Covering her amusement as best she could, Gertie held out her elegantly gloved hand and smiled her sweetest and most beguiling smile.

"Mr Black? I am Mrs Parker, and you were so kind as to answer my letter concerning the placing of some of the young ladies in your charge into suitable posts. I do so hope this is not an inconvenient time for us to meet, but I feel it necessary to clarify a few points before we complete our transactions." And with that she swept into the hall and straight on to the Warden's office before anyone had the chance to utter a word. She turned and smiled as the tall man followed her in, hotly trailed by Susan and the bassinette, and, removing her gloves in the most arch manner, sat down on the small couch, patting the space beside her. Speechless, the man sat down while Susan rocked baby Lucy, who had chosen that very moment to wake up and demand feeding.

"Susan, I suggest you walk Lucy up and down the hall and give her some sugar water. I cannot hear myself think, and I am quite sure Mr Black – you *are* Mr Black are you not?" Gertie added, turning to the bemused Warden, who nodded dumbly. “Does not want mulling infants in his office. He already has enough of the poor creatures in his care. Now then, sir, I have your letter here and I wish to go over a few of the issues you were so good as to cover for my edification.” She took the letter out of her reticule, borrowed from Mrs Johnson for just such an occasion, and spread the rather crumpled sheets on her lap. Luckily there were not too many noticeable coal smudges on them, and Gertie was able to keep her composure throughout the interview.

“Now, you use the words ‘merest drudgery’. Is it absolutely essential that a girl, simply through an accident of birth, has to perform mere drudgery? And as to the will of God, why if she has been blessed with a talent, it surely behoves us to put that talent to good use, not to bury it. I myself was born and bred in this very workhouse and look where I am today! Not indulging in drudgery, I can assure you. Now, I know that Mary Parsons will make a good little seamstress, and Mr Giles, who owns the drapery store in Powis Street is looking for just such an apprentice. I have taken the liberty of mentioning Mary to him and he is most eager to take her on provisionally. In addition, I have spoken to Mr Savill, the owner and manager of the theatre and he is also willing to give Sarah a chance. So you see, Mr Black, there is hope for your charges, and I am certain that you will exult in such news.”

Mr Black had sat silent and unbending throughout this onslaught, but as Gertie placed her little hand lightly on his knee he stiffened, and his grey face seemed to turn a deep purple. He gave a rasping cough and stood up suddenly, ringing a bell by the fireplace.

“This is indeed joyful news, Ma’am,” he said faintly, staring at the window above her head. “And we will call the two girls here immediately to assure them of our intentions. However, one swallow, or two in this case, does not make a summer and we should not be too hasty in our rejoicing in case such fortune cannot be repeated. Please send Parsons and Sarah Owen to me at once!” he ordered to a thin face that poked round the door in answer to the bell. The face disappeared and the door closed once more. The Warden walked over to a small table on which were set out a decanter and several glasses. “You will take a small glass of something, Mrs parker, Ma’am?”

“Why, a glass of port wine would be very acceptable, Mr Black. I am so sorry to hear of Mr Smith’s illness. Nothing serious, I hope?”

“Your good health, Ma’am. A touch of overwork, I believe, but the Board feels it is better if he remains away from the worries of the Institution until he is quite recovered. I have recommended at least three month's absolute rest, and in the meantime I am most happy to offer my services. It is to be hoped that he will find everything running smoothly and in good order when he returns. I apportion no blame, of course, but I feel that Mr Smith's deteriorating health allowed things to get a little – shall we say lax – over the past few months. I am sure that once in full vigour he will continue to run our little house in the manner in which he will find it on his return."

'He speaks just the way he writes,' thought Gertie, sipping her rather excellent wine. But she merely nodded and, placing the delicate glass on a small table, once more pulled on her gloves. Just at that moment the door opened again, and two girls entered the room, the first, Mary, looking pale and frightened, the second entering with a confident stride, a dull head taller than the other. Mary stood meekly by the door, but Sarah walked into the centre of the room and stood her ground, looking Mr Black straight in the eye. The Warden beckoned to the smaller girl.

"Come and stand here, beside Sarah, Mary, and address your answers to Mrs Parker, who is kindly come to question you on your suitability for the vacancies which she has most kindly secured for you. Curtsy when you speak and stand up straight! Do not pluck at your skirts, Mary, it gives quite the wrong impression. You do not want Mrs Parker to fancy you a moron. Mrs Parker, Ma'am," and he stood menacingly by the fireplace, while Gertie arranged her thoughts. Now it came down to it, she realised that she had never conducted an interview before for work other than domestic and was not sure what questions she should ask. Oh, well, she would start with the obvious and work on from there. She turned to Mary.

"It's Mary Parsons, isn't it?"

The girl curtsied and answered faintly, "Yes, Ma'am."

"And you would like to become a seamstress, is that not so?"

"Oh, yes, Ma'am, above all things," she said, her face brightening.

"Well, Mary, I have spoken to Mr Giles, who owns the drapers shop in Powis Street, and he says that if he finds you suitable he will take you on as an apprentice, where you will learn the trade in addition to becoming a seamstress, your heart's desire! Now, the work will be hard, and you will earn little more than two shillings a week, with board and lodging, which will be a small attic room above the shop. Do you think you will like such a plan?"

Mary's thin little face had turned a rosy red and she seemed almost unable to whisper in her joy. "Yes, if you please, ma'am."

"Very well, if it is agreeable to Mr Black, I can take you with me this very day to meet Mr Giles. Do you have any relatives at all who may question the scheme?"

"Mary has no one but those of us here who have cared for her wellbeing since her infancy, her mother dying at her birth, and, as with so many of our inmates, no father to be found. I am perfectly agreeable to letting Mary have an interview with Mr Giles and consider it most good of you, Mrs Parker, to put yourself to such trouble. Thank Mrs Parker, young lady, and be grateful that there are people who go out of their way to help lowly orphans such as yourself. Go and stand outside the door until Mrs Parker is ready for you. Now then, Sarah," he said, turning to the waiting girl. Mary left the room while Sarah stood her ground, unabashed by Mr Black's haughty manner.

Gertie explained her plan for Sarah's entry into the theatre world, for which she got a hug, much to the abhorrence of the Warden and the amusement of Gertie. It seemed that Sarah's little brother, now nine years of age, was as sturdy as his sister and was soon to be apprenticed to become a butcher's boy, which seemed to please both him and his sister, so once again there was no one to stand in the path of Sarah's ambition.

"I was brung up dahn the docks, Miss, till me dad got strung up and me mum died in the cholera. That's 'ow we come to be 'ere."

The interview came to an end at last and Gertie, slightly flushed from the wine and her success with the intimidating Warden, ushered both girls out into the sunlight, after extricating Susan from a mob of little girls who were ogling Lucy and fighting to be the next to look in the bassinette. They all made their way across the common and down the hill to the town, Mary, unused to so much exertion in the fresh air, coughing and dragging her feet a little, but they arrived in Beresford Street at last, and Sarah was deposited at the door of the theatre, where she was to be conducted to Mr Savill for the agreed interview. Gertie said she would return to take her back in one hour exactly. It was now eleven o'clock, so she would be back promptly on the stroke of twelve. Then the little group carried on up Powis Street to Mr Giles' drapers store. His wife welcomed the little girl with open arms, professing that she would be the 'child we never had, Mrs P,' and disappearing up the stairs with her. Mr Giles was busy serving customers, but the shop emptied at last, and he put a notice on the front door;

‘closed, back in five minutes’ and, after offering chairs to Gertie and Susan, went upstairs to join his wife. A large clock ticked the minutes away on a wall at the far end of the shop, where rolls of brightly coloured linens were stacked neatly on shelves and Gertie, feeling exhausted from her labours, realised that poor little Lucy was starving. Hoping that the interview would take a little time, she hastily fed the infant and rocked her back to sleep. At last footsteps were heard on the stairs and the three people, Mr and Mrs Giles with Mary looking starry-eyed, came swiftly down into the shop.

“Mrs Parker, Mrs Parker, we cannot thank you enough,” said Mr Giles, shaking Gertie’s hand vigorously. “Mary will fit our needs exactly. Is that not so, me dear?” he added, turning to his wife, who beamed in her turn.

“Oh, indeed, Mr Giles, she will suit us perfectly.”

Happy to have been of help, but realising that time was slipping by, Gertie thanked the Giles’ for giving Mary her chance and explained that she would be able to start work on the following Monday. She gathered everyone together and they all passed out of the shop, Mary walking on air, and hurried back to the theatre, just as twelve struck and Sarah appeared from the players’ entrance, her eyes alight with pleasure.

“’E’s going to take me on, Mum! ’E says I’ve got to learn to talk proper like what you do, and ’elp with the scenery and what not, but I can join the troupe. I said as ’ow you says no later than Mundy, and he says awlright. So I goes on Mundy!”

Chapter Sixteen

The soup kitchen continued to be a success, Gertie managed to find several suitable girls for the cartridge factory, especially to help with the war effort, and Amos' fame as a preacher went on apace. Lucy, as bonny as ever, was, of course, constantly doted on by the three women of the house. Amos, the upright Methodist husband, was well on the way to spoiling the baby outrageously and it became Gertie's task to talk him out of some of his more outlandish plans for Lucy.

"Send her to a private academy for young ladies? What nonsense, Amos. What would she be doing in such a place? She is the daughter of hardworking parents from the lower orders and must not be encouraged to take on grandiose ways. A preacher's daughter she is and a preacher's daughter she must remain, and what is there in that for her to turn up her nose at, I should like to know. I think we should encourage her to be proud of what she is and of her background, not to sneer at such things! Besides, Amos, she is but six months old! There is time and enough to consider her future schooling."

Amos did not argue, for he had learned to hold his tongue when he saw that light in his beloved's eye, but it was plain that he cherished plans for his daughter which did not entirely accord with the ethic of a Methodist preacher. And although he was bringing home a relatively comfortable wage now, Gertie seemed intent on spending much of it on helping the poor, buying better vegetables for the soup kitchen rather than waiting until late Saturday evening, when all the left-overs were being sold off cheap, and handing on the little garments that were now too small for Lucy, rather than putting them away 'for the next one' as Susan put it. Gertie had no intention of falling for a 'next one' for some time to come! She was obedient to her husband in all things, but there were times when tiredness overcame her to such a degree that she would retire for the night soon after dinner and was seemingly fast asleep by the time Amos crept up to the room under the eaves, sighing a little as he undressed carefully and slid under the covers, his wife's warm body so sweet and so unattainable.

Gently, he would put his arms round her and cradle her, but if she was awake she said nothing and gave no sign. And so life went on relatively uneventfully for the little family for some while, Lucy growing into a sturdy toddler, afraid of nothing, her father becoming renowned as a preacher to the working men, and her mother set on emptying the workhouse of all its female inhabitants.

Amos had been angry at first when he learnt that his beloved had not only entered the portals of the playhouse but had dragged along his daughter and maid at the same time. To his surprise Gertie had agreed that it was 'not quite the thing' as she put it, but if he could have seen the light in Sarah's eye when she was accepted into the troupe, then he would have done exactly the same himself. Privately, Amos rather agreed with Mr Black that workhouse girls were generally good for nothing but drudgery and should be taught to expect nothing more, his Gertie being the exception and one in a million, but once again he was wise enough not to argue with her, provided that she promised never to set foot in 'such a den of iniquity' again. Rather guiltily aware that she was not fulfilling her wifely duties as far as her husband was concerned, Gertie agreed readily to any curbs that he might put on her exploits and for the next few months selected only those damsels who were prepared to scrub and sew and cook in households which did not expect abject slavery from their maids, although Gertie suspected that most of them expected not much less!

++++++++++

It was about two years later, with Amos a successful preacher, the Sunday School and Soup Kitchen settled down to a regular intake and Gertie seeming to be completely over her cough that she started feeling sick in the mornings. Another baby! Well, she supposed they could manage this time. Compared with many they were quite comfortable, and it would be a companion for the sunny, hair-brained child who romped her way through life. Lucy was both the darling and the despair of the entire household. Among her many exploits she had fallen from top to bottom down the stairs twice, fallen into the coal cellar once and set fire to the rug after poking at the fire to get at the 'pretty red coal'! anger, a slap on the hand and being shut in her room had no effect on the rumbustious little creature and Susan had her work cut out to keep an eye on her while at the same time continuing to run the home, 'the missus being out and about as much as she is,' she confided proudly to Emily, Mrs Johnson's maid. But Gertie realised that there was no way that Susan could be expected to look after a second child. Unless they could employ a regular nursemaid, she, Gertie, would have to give up all that she had worked so hard for over the years and certainly there was no more money to take on anyone else. Nursemaids were not like servants, either; they expected their own room and meals provided and, oh, all sorts of things that the Parker household would find it impossible to provide. Gertie sighed. Oh, well, she would just have to be patient and see what happened. Something would come along, she was sure. It always did! God would provide!

Amos, of course, was ecstatic at the news. His little Gertie must sit down right now and put her feet up on the settle. No more jaunts to the workhouse and she must only attend to the soup kitchen if she felt *absolutely* well. Older, wiser and rather glad to be looked after for a while, Gertie allowed herself to be cosseted until everyone had got used to the idea that she was not the frail little thing that she had been when carrying Lucy. She eventually persuaded them that she had never felt better and that she could continue her normal rounds provided that she promised to take the greatest care. She had started joining Mrs Johnson on her 'ministering' again, but of course this must stop once more, at least until the new baby was weaned. Susan set about making a new layette of baby clothes, clucking and tutting that the Missus had given away all that good stuff, and little Lucy kept demanding when she could play with the new baba. But a month before the baby was due, during a particularly nasty period of sleety rain and high winds in early May, Gertie had set off on her own, slipping out quietly while Susan was busy with Lucy, to check on the Chapel. Some of the tiles had blown off the roof the previous Sunday, and knowing how busy Amos was now, she decided to see for herself what the damage was and whether it could be easily fixed. Normally it would have been quite a pleasant walk, not too tiring and on this particular morning the sun had made a watery appearance and the wind seemed to have dropped. But she had only got as far as the end of the road when suddenly a great gust lifted the sodden bits of paper and filth from the gutters and let them fall right in the path of the scurrying figures taken by surprise by the strength of the blast. Gertie was blown sideways, tried to keep her balance and slipped on a mess of old cabbages and newspaper. She fell heavily, felt an excruciating pain and passed out.

She woke to find faces peering anxiously down at her. She was being lifted into some sort of coach, but waves of pain and nausea seemed to be tormenting her entire body and in turns fainting and crying out, she lay in agony as the hideous journey back home seemed to take an eternity. Once inside the house pain and blackness enveloped Gertie and she knew nothing more. It was many hours later when, weak, unable to move and suffering unimaginable misery and guilt, she finally opened her eyes, to find Amos sitting grimly in a chair beside her bed. She managed to whisper,

"Oh, Amos, I am so sorry!"

He didn't speak or even look at her, and tears of utter anguish rolled down her cheeks. Oh, what had she done? She wouldn't listen, oh no, not her! She knew best! She must slip away from Susan and go out in this atrocious weather just to satisfy her own pride. And now, her darling, patient husband was to be deprived of the child he so ardently desired. She spoke again,

"The baby, what have they done with it?"

At that Amos turned his head and looked at her. The look pierced her heart. She knew then that she could never sink deeper into the abyss of despair. She had lost the love of this dearest of men, the baby was dead through her own fault and she would be shunned by all her friends. And who could blame them? And her baby, her little one. Oh God! What had she done? Why had she not listened to those whose only concern had been for her safety. She began to sob wearily. Amos had left the room but returned with something in his arms. A bundle which he laid gently on the coverlet. She put her arms out and cradled the sad little bundle, rocking it and crooning gently as it lay still and silent. Suddenly she cried out in amazement. It was alive. The baby was alive! She hugged the tiny creature and great sobs burst from her, her tears falling on to the baby's face as it yawned and began to cry. A harsh voice interrupted her joy.

"Your son needs feeding," and Amos left the room once more.

A son! So Amos' dearest wish had been granted. In spite of everything, of her stupidity and headstrong behaviour, she had given him a son. The misery began to lift a little. Gently she unwrapped the shawl and looked at the little boy. He looked strong and perfect. He was indeed a miracle. As she tried to sit up Susan came into the room and hurried over to the bed.

"Law, Missus, what a fright you give us," she said in her forthright way. "Don't you never go runnin' off again without notice, or I'll quit, honest to God I will!"

Susan's down to earth voice and plain, honest face began to dispel some of the misery that had surrounded Gertie since she had returned to consciousness and, with the help of the maid's strong arms and encouragement, she was able to sit up sufficiently to feed the baby, whose lungs showed no signs of weakness. His little face was bright red and there was no gainsaying his demands. But once held close to Gertie, all sounds ceased except for contented sucking noises and little grunts as both women laughed in relief. The baby was strong, and Gertie was quite certain she would soon be on the mend herself. A visit by the doctor half an hour later assured her that she would soon be up and about again, although the gravity in his face brought on her guilt once again. She felt she must say something to atone for her behaviour; for risking her own life and that of the child.

"Dr Craig, I know how stupid and self-willed I have been and should never have ventured out in this weather, but I was truly trying to help Amos. He is so busy, and the Chapel means so much to him! I only wanted to make sure it was not being flooded or washed away. It was foolish, so foolish, but I really did do it for him."

She was trying to convince herself as much as the doctor, but he only said,

"Have you told him that?"

"No, I don't believe he will speak to me ever again."

"Yes, well, that is a little dramatic, my dear, and must be put down to your post-natal weakness, very natural after such a difficult birth, but you are going to have to show that you are truly repentant to that long-suffering husband of yours. You see, my dear." His voice softened and he took Gertie's hand and patted it gently. "There will be no more children. I did what I could, but the circumstances..."

Gertie was aghast. It wasn't the fact that she could have no more children, but that she was glad that she couldn't have any more. Poor Amos, imagining himself at the head of a table full of his offspring, and here was his wife wanting nothing more than to be recognised as the 'lady bountiful', bringing succour and solace to the under classes. She looked searchingly into the doctor's face:

"It is definite? I really can't have any more, or would it simply be dangerous to try?"

"You really can't have any more. Certain – er – areas had to be removed, Mrs Parker."

"Yes, yes I understand. Does Amos know this?"

"I explained everything to him after the birth. He will learn to overcome his disappointment and he has, after all, two fine, healthy children. But it is up to you now to make amends as best you can. I cannot promise that it will be easy, or speedily remedied, but if you show true remorse and prove to him how much his love and understanding mean to you, I am sure you will win him round. However, the main thing at present is to get you well and strong. You are lucky to have Susan ministering to your needs; she is a gem! She would make a first-class nurse. Now you must rest, and I will be in to see how you go on tomorrow."

And with that the good doctor was gone. His little homily had hardly lifted Gertie's spirits. Her sense of guilt returned, along with a slight and rather surprising anger that all sympathy was with Amos. After all, she really had only been trying to help. Perhaps it was silly of her to go out alone in that weather, but that's all it had been really, just silliness. She had not purposely tried to kill herself or the baby. Bitterness began to take the place of guilt. Once again it was the men who had all the sympathy, who had to be constantly cosseted and appeased, while it was the women who went through the trying nine months of sickness, of being a virtual prisoner due to her 'condition', not to mention the agonies of the birth itself. And then the doctor, another man, lecturing her on how to behave towards her husband. She had supposed that the man she married would be a soul-mate, not a jailor. Gertie sighed. How much more of herself would she have to give to this man whom she adored, but who was not, she determined, going to take away her very need for the freedom to be *herself*, not merely an adjunct to his life, his ministry and his paternal mastery.

Emotionally and physically exhausted, Gertie slept until it was time once more to feed her lusty son.

++++++++++

She didn't see Amos again for several days. Gertie supposed he was punishing her for what she had done and wondered if she would ever again break through that wall of anger and petulance that had culminated in his present hatred of her. For she was sure that he *did* hate her. She would never forget the look he had directed at her when she had first woken up after the baby was born. He had not even discussed the child's name with her but had informed her by way of Mrs Mabbett that his name was to be Jonathan and he was baptised without her presence. She knew she could never have been as cruel, no matter what he had done, but this was the way with such zealous men – all else must take second place to their great works and woe-betide anyone who got in the way of such zeal.

Mrs Mabbett had been as kind and understanding as Amos had been cruel. She and Susan cosseted Gertie, cooed and crooned over the baby and even allowed little Lucy to hold him and gloat over him with all the innate motherhood at her command. Even Mrs Johnson had visited Gertie and consoled her with some sensible words of wisdom.

"It was a foolish thing you did, my dear, and now you have to reap the consequences, but to punish you in this way is, quite frankly, not what a woman of your spirit should be expected to endure. I will say no more on the matter, except to say that I never told you the reason why I was unable to have any more children. I had done much the same as you. Instead of asking the maid, I went out to buy a few items for the baby. I was so excited by the prospect of at last being a mother again and thought that there could be no harm in doing a little quiet shopping. I was set upon by footpads and sadly was not as lucky as you and Amos. I lost our second baby and all chance of having any more. Mr Johnson came round in the end, but it took all my patience and courage in those early years. As I told you, he respected my wish to continue with my ministering once we were reconciled and now we have a happy marriage, but it still takes its toll when I am tired and have to endure certain temperamental outbursts. Women have to endure many things, not least of which are being in some ways still one of our husband's *possessions*, even with the very best of men such as Amos and Charles. So, my dear, no matter how you feel, show your love to him, care for him and be solicitous to his well-being. But, and this is most important – do not show contrition! If you do, he will trample your spirit and you will lose his love and his respect. You will learn to hate one another, instead of learning to accept the little weaknesses and acts of thoughtlessness that make us all human. Agree with him in all things, keep your own counsel and gradually he will see you in a different light. Now, that is enough of my lecturing! I wish you the best of luck with that man of yours, but remember this, Gertie, he is but a man, and cannot be expected to live up to the knight in shining armour that we expect of the poor creatures!"

And with a kiss, the kind woman was gone. Gertie pondered all that she had heard and determined to show Amos how much his love meant to her. From now on she would be the perfect wife and mother and nothing, *nothing* would be allowed to get in the way of that, not the soup kitchen or even Sunday School, although she thought with a wry smile that Amos would not expect her to give that up.

The first few days after Gertie had been well enough to come downstairs and take part in domestic life again had been harrowing for her and for everyone in the household. Amos continued to speak to her as little as possible and then only in the severest terms, mealtimes were strained, with Mrs Mabbett doing her best to keep up a string of cheerful small talk, and Susan almost throwing the dishes down for the Master of the house. But Gertie's naturally sunny temperament and Amos' naturally kindly nature soon began to melt the icy atmosphere and, one evening, after a burst of inspiration on the part of Mrs Mabbett, they all sat in the little parlour, the fire alight, for even though it was May the evenings were still cold. A small bottle of sherry had been surreptitiously unearthed by the good lady and, in spite of a frowning refusal by Amos, she filled a glass for each of them and gradually, Amos unconsciously sipping the pale gold liquid, a warm glow spread through the room. Mrs Mabbett moved to the pianoforte. She began to play a few favourite airs and Gertie quietly joined her, her sweet voice singing the words softly. Soon Mrs Mabbett went on to a duet and, gently, without anyone making any sign that they had noticed, Amos joined them, his fine tenor giving strength and courage to his wife's soprano. Soon they were all three singing with gusto, and it was eleven o'clock before any of them realized the time. Mrs Mabbett exclaimed and folded up the music. She bade the pair a quick goodnight and hurriedly left the room before the atmosphere could be dispelled. Gertie and Amos looked at one another. Suddenly they were in each other's arms, weeping and laughing and telling each other how cruel they had been and how they each felt overcome with guilt and remorse. Gertie, forgetting all the wise advice from Mrs Johnson, promised never to argue about her safety again, and Amos said that from now on he would not act like a tyrant. They went up to their room finally, arm in arm and the house settled down once more to harmony and peace. At least, a peace shattered only by the healthy lungs of master Jonathan, who promised to be a fine baritone to complements his parent's voices.

Chapter Seventeen

It was shortly after this that Mrs Mabbett, tireless and kindly as ever, developed an inflammation of the lungs. In spite of all the doctor could do, and all the care and attention lavished on her by the anxious household, on the 20th of June 1855, the good lady died.

Despair filled the hearts of the Parker family and Susan went silently about her work, her eyes red from sobbing into her pillow each night. The funeral came and went and then came the reading of the Will. Mrs Mabbett had wisely put everything into the hands of a solicitor and this gentleman, a little thin wisp of a man, bewhiskered and bespectacled, sat at the dining room table where the entire household, along with Mr George Gregs, Mrs Mabbett's brother and his good lady, Maud, were assembled.

Apart from a few small items to go to Susan and the Gregs, Mrs Mabbett had left the house and all its contents to Gertie and Amos. While those two sat stunned, Mr Gregs began to rant and rave. What was his sister thinking of, leaving her property to these two, who were not even relatives! The house was his by rights, as her only living male relative! Oh, he wouldn't leave it there; he would contest the Will. He wouldn't sleep until justice had be done! In vain did Mr Meeks, the solicitor, try to hush him, pointing out that Mrs Mabbett could leave her property as she chose. The little man merely got shouted down for his pains. Finally, pushing back his chair and saying, "Come along, Maud," in his most tyrannical voice, the irate brother bustled his wife out of the house, her harsh accents adding agreement to his warning, "You haven't heard the last of this. I will see to it that that pair of scheming workhouse urchins get their just deserts."

Susan closed the front door, her face pale and frightened, as the elderly carriage trundled off into the distance. She returned to the dining room, where Amos and Gertie were still sitting in appalled silence. Muttering that it was all nonsense, and that Mr Gregs could fulminate all he liked, Mr Meeks assured them nevertheless that the house belonged to the Parkers and that was all there was to it. He gathered up his papers, hurriedly downed the last dregs of the coffee so thoughtfully provided by Susan and left the house, assuring Amos in his precise way that there was no need to worry and that there was no cause to suppose that Mr Gregs, already comfortably off himself, could lay any claim to the house in Beresford Street.

Still stunned from the news and sick with horror at Mr Gregs' behaviour, Gertie and Amos clung to each other, while tears of anguish for poor Mrs Mabbett poured down their faces. How dare that man behave in such a way. Apart from very occasionally lending her his carriage, what had he ever done for her? He was very comfortably off, with his business activities, it was whispered, not being entirely above board, and he wanted for nothing. He neither wanted nor needed the house and in all probability would will it over the heads of Gertie and Amos if he ever managed to get his hands on the deeds. Gertie was sure he would throw them out on the street with nothing but the clothes they stood up in, and made Amos promise that nothing would induce him to give in to any threats meted out by 'that dreadful man' as she put it. But Amos' spirit was already roused by such injustice and he assured her angrily that no thieving sinner was going to put his family on the streets!

A few days later, while Amos was working at the arsenal and Susan had taken Lucy to feed the ducks by the river, there came a loud rap on the front door. Gertie had just finished feeding the baby and he was lying gurgling happily in his cradle, where his fond mother was making the kind of faces and noises that only mothers make over their incredible children. She jumped with alarm at the urgent hammering and hurried downstairs to see who on earth was setting up such a din. She opened the door just as George Gregs was about to let fall the knocker once more, and he almost fell into the hall. He pushed past the startled Gertie shouting, "Where is he! Where is that preaching charlatan, the so-called man of the cloth that would take the bread and butter out of the mouths of babes? I know my rights and I will see justice done!"

By this time he had reached the parlour and he stood in front of the fireplace surveying the room. He took in the ancient settle, the threadbare carpet, the pianoforte and finally his eyes alighted on Gertie, standing rigid with anger in the doorway. The high colour left his face, and to Gertie, watching curiously, he seemed to undergo a complete transformation. Removing his tall hat and placing it with care on a chair, he walked slowly forward, his hands held out and a leer which Gertie presumed to be a smile on his thin, pale lips. When he spoke, his voice came soft and wheedling and she shivered, backing away into the hall as he approached.

"Come, my dear, I have no quarrel with you. Perhaps we could come to some arrangement over this. The house certainly should be mine, but if you and your respected husband were to pay a little rent to me, then no more need be said on the matter and you and your family will still have a roof over your heads and no harm done. Let us say the rent you paid my sister plus a little more for the concession I have made should be satisfactory." He drew some papers from the inside of his grubby black coat. "This is an agreement I have drawn up and if you sign it, then it will be all signed, sealed and delivered and your good husband need have no more worries. Let us return to the parlour, where you can peruse the deed if you wish. However, I can assure you there is no need and that you can trust me, who is as near to you as a brother now that our dear Mrs Mabbett has departed."

He had gently pulled Gertie back through the door from the hall and led her to the settle, putting the agreement into her lifeless hands. She looked down at it, but a haze seemed to be before her eyes. He had no right to be there. The house belonged to them, to her and Amos. How dare this horrible man force himself into their home and try to make her sign away her rights, the home which had been bequeathed to them by her dear Mrs Mabbett. Once again anger filled her little frame and, standing up to face him, she screwed the offending papers up into a tight ball and forced them back into his hands saying that she would never sign such a deed. He stepped back, the anger in her face rocking his confidence for a moment. But his self-importance soon returned, and he began to speak gently, in his horrible, wheedling tone as she stood, angry and panting, her fists clenched tightly.

"My dear, you are very young, and a woman and it is well known that females do not understand the refinements of such transactions. I am sure that if Amos were here he would see how fair it is that my sister's property, that of my only living relative, should come to me. After all, I have a large family, a gift which, sadly, you will never be able to offer your husband," here Gertie stiffened and uttered an anguished cry. "And also," he went on, "I have some standing in the world. I am rather more in need of the finances which such a property would bring than is a man of the cloth who should have renounced such riches to follow his calling. Can you not see that by offering you this house at a small rent I am losing a great deal, gaining only the satisfaction that I have not put a destitute family out on the streets. That will be my only reward! I am sure you can see this, now that you are calm once more."

He took Gertie's little fists in his own clumsy hands and drew her towards him, his breath hot and unpleasant on her face. She tried to pull away, but he was strong, and he had his arms round her, crushing her to his dreadful coat before she could escape. Neither of them heard the front door slam through Gertie's cries, but Susan's cool voice, saying,

"Good Heavens, madam, whatever is amiss?" seemed to fall like a thunderbolt on Mr Gregs. He let go of Gertie at once a, grabbing his hat, his breath coming in great rasps, he rushed from the room, shouting that she would hear from him in due course. Gertie, crying uncontrollably, was led to the settle by Susan, who was gently chiding her to be still, all will be well now, and she will send for Amos as soon as she had attended to Lucy. Gertie's sobs gradually subsided and she squeezed Susan's hand.

"Oh, Susan, that dreadful man! He – he was trying to – to *seduce* me. Oh, how could he? How could I let him touch me? I need to bathe; to wash the very smell of him off me. Oh, my dear, dear Susan." She clung to the girl, who soothed her with gentle words, stroking her hair and hushing her. Gradually Gertie relaxed and anger began to take over from the distress and fear that had beset her. Amos must make sure that the dreadful man should never enter their house again! Susan must never let him or his wife in. Was that clear? Susan noted the rising hysteria in Gertie's voice and hushed her all over again, saying that the pair would enter the house over her dead body. She looked so fierce that Gertie managed a watery laugh and insisted that she was feeling better now, so Susan must attend to Lucy who would be getting up to untold trouble if left to herself for much longer. But they both went upstairs together, only to find that Lucy was keeping Jonathan amused with a little toy. The baby was gurgling happily and Lucy, glowing from her walk, was dancing round the cradle, shaking a felt cat in his face. Feeling too emotionally exhausted to do anything else, Gertie sat and watched her two precious children while Susan pottered round tidying up and bringing 'the missus' a nice cup of tea. Gertie wouldn't allow her to fetch Amos from his work, so the household settled down to await the return of its master and to relate to him the terrible happenings of the morning.

++++++++++

When Amos heard the news, Gertie thought he was going to explode with anger. He caught her up in his arms nearly suffocating her as he thought of what might have been. His Gertie in the arms of that brute! She managed to extricate herself at last, while Amos demanded to be told again exactly what that – that – creature had said. In his haste Mr Gregs had dropped the deed he had drawn up when Gertie had thrust it into his hands and it still lay by the settle, a screwed-up ball of yellowish paper. Gertie picked it up, flattening it out as best she could, and handed it to Amos. The writing was scrawled and ill-formed, but the contents were clearly some kind of lease and had the authorisation of a signature from a firm of solicitors. "Jenson, Jenson, Snape and Jenson, Solicitors for Oaths. Hm, I know of them," said Amos. "They are renowned for their shady dealings with fellows on the fringes of society. They would sell a person's grandmother if they could make a penny or two out of it! It is no surprise to me that that rascal has dealings with them. I doubt very much whether his document is legal, but we will send it on to Mr Meeks. In the meantime, my love, I will deal with *Mr* Gregs!"

Gertie begged him not to go, but in vain. Amos was deaf to all the pleading of either woman and finally all they could do was to beg him to be careful. He assured them that they had nothing to fear, and they had to be content with that. The front door slammed and that was the last they saw of him for many hours.

It was in the small hours, long after Gertie had gone to bed, tossing and turning as she wondered what had become of Amos, when she heard the front door gently open and close, and soft footsteps on the stairs. She leapt out of bed, hurriedly putting on her dressing gown and sandals and ran out on to the landing to meet him. But she fell back in horror at the sight that met her. Amos, bruised and bleeding, his second-best jacket torn and blood-spattered, was leaning against the banister, one eye, swollen and blackened, nearly closed and the other gradually turning purple. She shrieked, "Amos, oh Amos, what has he done to you?"

Little caring that she had woken not only the long-suffering Susan, but Lucy and the baby as well, whose cries could probably be heard 'from 'ere to Lands' End' as Susan so graphically put it. She had rushed to the scene, struggling into an apron and boots. 'Or it wouldn't be decent' although the voluminous nightgown she wore covered her entire form in red flannel. She and Gertie helped Amos onto a chair in the bedroom and Susan went to fetch a bowl of hot water and a cloth. Gertie clasped his hands.

"Darling, tell me what happened! What has he done to you? I'll kill him, I'll kill him if he has hurt you! Oh, Amos, oh my love!"

Amos opened his goodish eye.

"If you could stop the children's caterwauling, I might be able to hear myself think," he said, a broad grin on his face. "You think *I* look bad! You should see our Mr Gregs! I don't think you'll be having any more trouble from that gentleman for a long time to come!"

"Oh, Amos, you haven't...you haven't...*really killed* him?" Gertie asked, her face stricken with horror.

"Killed him? No, of course I haven't killed him! But I have certainly put the fear of God into him and his lady wife, and that's the last we'll hear of them. He's met his match at last and he'll think twice before he tries his tricks on innocent people in future! But, oh Gertie, you should have seen his face when I made his nose bleed. I know I should have turned the other cheek, but he began setting about me the moment he opened his door to me and what was I to do? I thought *he* was going to kill *me*!"

Gertie gurgled with laughter and hugged her husband with relief as she washed away the blood from his face, while Susan went to hush the children. At last all was quiet again. Gertie helped Amos out of his ruined jacked and they snuggled down together in the soft, feathery bed, the proud owners of an old, dilapidated but nevertheless their very own, house.

Chapter Eighteen

By 1860 the little family in Beresford Street had grown to include a nursemaid and a scullery maid. The Parkers were considered to be 'comfortable' by their neighbours, who bore them no ill-will, as neither Gertie nor Amos stinted in giving help, advice and even cash, handed over quietly and without a word, when needed. The Sunday School was flourishing, the soup kitchen kept the riff-raff, ragamuffin children and exhausted mothers from the poorest quarter grumblingly content and Mr smith from the Workhouse seemed delighted with the way that he only had to mention that a girl was ready to leave than she was whisked away into some suitable situation by the tireless Gertie.

Gertie had set up a little office above the corner shop at the end of the road, where she worked each morning, Susan and the nursemaid taking it in turns to look after master Jonathan and walking Lucy to the little day school a few streets away. By charging for her services as agent between Mr Smith and prospective employers, Gertie was able to afford the minute rent and the irregular services of Mr Meeks, the solicitor, who drew up the deeds of employment for the workhouse girls. Everyone seemed to be pleased with this arrangement and as Gertie's reputation grew, so did Mr Meeks' business. If Gertie Parker saw fit to trust him, then so could any honest citizen of the town!

Amos had finally left the arsenal, the needs of his parishioners becoming too abundant for him to neglect them even for a short while each week. He went his rounds on the circuit, his sermons were in demand wherever he went, and he seemed apparently fulfilled and happy. Only Gertie knew how much this life had changed him, the once carefree, happy spirit locked forever into this serious and seemingly forbidding figure. And to many people, although they still loved and respected him, Amos *did* seem forbidding. He seldom smiled, his tendency to sermonise instead of to discuss was growing stronger and he kept a remote detachment from his congregation. Even the good helpers from the arsenal, the Daniels, Joshua, Jack and Will, all noticed how apart Amos had grown from them. He did not set himself above them – indeed he always appeared somewhat humble in their company. “But it was this very humble quality which seemed to make him, well distant, if you know what I mean,” said Mrs Daniels. It was most noticeable at poor Tom’s funeral. Tom had been carpenter and handyman at the arsenal for as long as anyone could remember, but a sudden attack of fever had carried him off just before Christmas the winter of ’59. Everyone had rallied round making sure his widow didn’t go without and giving him a funeral with a coffin he would have been proud of; and, of course, Amos officiated at the ceremony. But although he gave a fine sermon and spoke glowingly of Tom’s craftsmanship, kindness and loyalty, he stood well away from the guests at the wake, sipping only a cup of tea and eating next to nothing, while Gertie played hostess, making sure that everyone’s glasses were full, and supporting ‘Mrs Tom’, who seemed scarcely to understand what was happening.

Many people wondered at Gertie’s sprightliness, her happy laughter and obvious contentment. But how could she explain to them that the husband who seemed so forbidding to others was the gentlest, kindest and best of men in the fastness of their own home? He adored his ‘little Gertie’, was immensely proud of her and his two children and seldom spoke a cross word to his family or the servants. Their life was seemingly perfect. But beneath all this perfection Gertie felt a strange spirit of unease and anxiety. Why was Amos so changed? Surely it was not in his nature to be so humourless and stern? Not her charming, delightful, carefree beau who, only a few years before, had stood in the doorway of the drawing room, looking like a surprised penguin! Gertie smiled sadly at the memory. She decided it was long past time that she should seek out her old friend, Mrs Johnson, whom she was unable to meet as often as she had done when they had gone ministering together. With two small children Gertie had given up such dangerous pursuits and the two women saw each other only occasionally these days. So on a fresh April morning, with the birds singing and the few bulbs struggling to keep their heads above the tired earth in the occasional tiny gardens which someone had bothered to till, Gertie trotted off to the Johnson’s house behind the chapel. Mrs Johnson was one of those brave souls who courageously hoped that the bulbs and seeds she had planted with such care would show their faces to the world in due course, and Gertie found her digging a small patch of nut-brown earth. The older woman straightened her back when she saw Gertie and gladly put down the trowel. Any excuse not to have to go on with this back-breaking work, but she was overjoyed to see her young friend after all this time and gave her a great hug, holding Gertie from her and saying how well she looked, and younger than ever.

"Well, my dear, hard work and motherhood certainly suit you. You look positively blooming, which is more than I can say for my poor plants! Do come in and tell me all your news." And she ushered Gertie into the little parlour, calling to Annie to bring some lemonade and cakes.

"Now then, Gertie, you must tell me all the news and gossip. Nothing wrong at home I hope? That husband of yours behaving himself as he should?"

Gertie felt her conscious pricking her. Did she really only visit Mrs Johnson when she wanted advice about Amos? She laughed and said that all was well and that she felt it was such a lovely day, and she hadn't seen her friend for so long, she thought she would just walk round here to find out how she went on. Mrs Johnson smiled but said nothing and Gertie realised that she had been speaking fast to cover her guilt, and felt her cheeks going red.

"There is no need for excuses, my dear. I know what a busy woman you are – we both are – and, believe me, I am touched that you still feel a need to turn to me for advice. Friendship doesn't wain merely because we are unable to visit each other as often as we would like! Now, tell me what is bothering you. Are the children well, not causing you concern?"

Gertie quickly put the good woman's mind at rest regarding the children. No, no, they were happy and healthy, and Lucy was a star pupil at her school. Mrs Johnson was sure this was the case. There was a pause. Then Gertie spoke, trying to put into words the vague unease that she had been feeling for some time. But she was finding it so difficult to explain; to say just what was at the back of her mind.

"You see, Mabel, when I first met Amos he was so jolly and carefree. He was prepared to slay dragons and stare the world in the eye with a grin. Now, outside the home, he is so solemn so serious and even with us laughter is seldom close as it used to be. Why, he is not yet thirty and at times he seems in his mind to be an old man!"

Mrs Johnson listened intently, but the serious look on her face did nothing to allay Gertie's worries. There was a long pause, while both ladies sipped their lemonade and nibbled biscuits. At last Mrs Johnson put down her glass and stood up, walking round the room before sitting down again, absently nibbling another biscuit as she sat in deep thought. At last she turned to Gertie.

"Your husband, my dear, is a very devout man. It seems quite clear to me that simply preaching here, mainly to the converted, is not enough for his great spirit. You must not be surprised if he approaches you soon with the idea of becoming a missionary. Yes, I know this is hard to accept," she went on, as Gertie exclaimed in horror. "But, if you do not want to stifle him forever, you must allow him his freedom to follow the dictates of his heart. Either this, or you will lose him, and what is more important, his own identity will wane, sicken and die. Both you and Amos were born with a mission in life. You are following yours; Amos is not. When he comes to you, don't rail at him, my dear. Let him go. If necessary, let him go alone, or follow him when the children are settled. But take my word for it, he will only be fulfilled when he is taking the Word of God to those poor souls who know nothing of Him."

This time it was Gertie's turn to walk round the room, glancing in the mirror over the fire, looking blindly out of the window at the lowering sky, the day's promise lying as dead as her hopes. Her mind in an incredible whirl, she returned to her chair and looked her friend firmly in the eye.

"You are, as ever, quite right, my dear friend. I shall say nothing, but when he suggests the idea I will support him as in all things. But I could never, *never* join him in such a venture. I have no calling, you see, and certainly no desire to leave these shores for some terrible, disease-ridden land where I do not understand the customs or speak the language. And I am not even sure that it is right for us to interfere in another's way of life. Oh, I am a devout Christian, but even amongst Christians there are many variations and to take one form of it and, well, push it down someone's throat, is not my idea of kindness. I am being crude, I know, but that is how I see it. You must forgive me if you find my attitude unacceptable, but there it is!"

Mrs Johnson, rather than being offended, smiled her gentle smile and waved away the apology.

"I happen to agree with you entirely, Gertie, but we need not tell our menfolk that. It would be better, however, if you were to make it clear from the start, that you have no intention of joining Amos, for you cannot take part in such an undertaking if you do not have a vocation."

Gertie nodded, sunk once more in deep thought, as the two women sat in silent communion, sipping their lemonade and imagining what might have been. Gertie rose at last and, taking leave of her friend, she hurried home feeling less anxious than when she had started out. If this was what Amos wanted, then a missionary he should be! She smiled to herself. Amos knew nothing of their plans for him, herself and Mrs Johnson. Supposing this was the last thing on his mind, and it was something else entirely that was eating away at his soul? But that evening it seemed as though Amos had listened in to her conversation with the Minister's wife, for, standing before the fire, staring into the flames, he suddenly blurted out, without ceremony:

"Gertie, I am going to Africa to become a missionary. It is no use your arguing about it; my mind is made up. You may come with me or stay here as you please. I would rather you came as my wife, but your life is your own to choose to do with as you will."

Gertie sat motionless on the settle. Although she and Mrs Johnson had almost planned this for her husband, she had secretly hoped that it was not so. She knew she could no more join Amos than jump in the river, but how she was to endure months, maybe years of loneliness without him she did not know. He was standing before her now, his face set and a look of anguish in his eyes. His hair, longer now, still stood up in an unruly mass and she had never loved him so much as at this moment. She stood up and put her arms round him, cuddling him against her small body and smoothing the wayward hair.

"If this is what you want, my beloved, then a missionary you shall be. You will make a wonderful one and I know you will take the word of God to the outermost parts of the world. It is your vocation, and you must not deny it. But darling,!" and here she pulled away from him, holding both his hands in hers and looking earnestly up into his face, "I cannot go with you. My heart will be with you always, dearest, but I cannot."

The look of relief on his face turned to misery as she pulled him down on to the settle, still holding tightly to his hands and kissing them with her soft lips.

"Dearest, I love you more than words can say. You are my life. But I would die away from here, from my children and my work and all that I know and understand. I have no vocation. You must know that I would never look at another man and I will wait for you until you return, keeping your home here for you to remember in the long hours when you are far away and perhaps alone."

"I – I have to go. We *could* go together. We could take the children with us. You do not need a vocation. But you are so strong, Gertie, how can I go on without you?"

"Hush, hush, my love. Your inner strength and certain belief will carry you through and you know the children would not survive in such an alien climate. I will still be here! We can write to one another and you will return happy in the knowledge that you have saved so many people! It is as we always said; I look after their bodies and you their souls. We make a fine team still, you and I, Amos. Let us continue to do so in this new, exciting way. And when you return you can regale us all interminably with your stories and anecdotes until we all wish you back in Africa!"

This was said lightly, with a gaiety Gertie was far from feeling. But it managed to lift Amos' gloom and he even managed a laugh at her picture of his sermonising.

So the weeks passed. Mrs Tom and Mrs Daniel agreed to help with the Sunday School, preachers had been allocated to the little Chapel from the circuit and Amos was at last ready to set out on his perilous voyage to what Gertie felt were the far ends of the earth. She knew that others had gone before Amos and that people were people the world over. He main fear was that overwork and the zeal that forced him on had sapped much of Amos' strength and the harsh African climate, added to the various exotic diseases he was bound to come in contact with, not to mention communities who did not wish their life to be disturbed, would weaken him still further. Was he physically strong enough to bear with so much stress and alienation? Gertie doubted it. None of these fears she passed on the Amos, however, and, to make him and herself feel that he was not going so far from them that it may just as well have been the moon, she bought a globe and Amos showed her and the children just where Papa was going to tell people all about Jesus. Lucy and Jonathan thought it all a great adventure and begged to go too.

"Oh, Mama, why cannot we go with Papa and teach all the little children about Jesus? I know they would prefer stories to Papa's great long sermons!" said Lucy, lessening the audacity of her words by tweaking Amos' newly growing and rather wispy beard. Jonathan joined in, leaping round the room shouting, "Go to Africa with Papa," in a rollicking dance that set them all shouting for him to stop. Lucy put her hands over her ears and shouted, "Stop it, Johnno," while Gertie tried catching him and Amos, who had risen to put the globe out of reach of danger, sat plump down again on the settle, shaking his head and saying to whoever would bother to listen, that since he was no longer master in his own house, the sooner he removed to Africa the better! But peace reigned eventually, Gertie saying sternly that no one else was going away, and that's all there was to it, while a rather round-eyed maid and the tight-lipped nanny slipped into the room to take 'the young master and mistress to wash for supper'.

That night Amos tried once more to change Gertie's mind about going with him. He was at last beginning to realize just how much he depended on her down to earth good sense and strength of character. From the little girl who had written to the queen, and whose courage had managed to change conditions in the workhouse, to the vital young woman who ran a home, looked after her husband's every need and managed an employment agency along with caring for all the local poor of the neighbourhood, Gertie was his mainstay on this earth. And now he was going to God Himself only knew where, to slay dragons entirely on his own. Self-doubt and a terrible fear began to fill his whole being. He couldn't do this without Gertie. He needed her; she was his only strength; she was his rod, his staff. So he cried into her hair as they lay in bed, hugging her to him and weeping great, fearful sobs. Once more Gertie hushed him, stroking his hair and whispering words of encouragement and love in the darkness. Had he forgotten why he was going? That it was God Himself that was his rod and staff; that it was His strength and His alone that was all that Amos needed to take the Word to those who knew nothing of the joy of Christ's message. So she spoke gradually stilling and calming the fears of her beloved, until he slept in her arms, her words giving him the final courage to step out into the unknown.

Chapter Nineteen

Amos was gone. Everyone had gathered to see him off and to wish him good luck; a coach had been hired to take him and his luggage to the docks where a small packet boat took him off to the coast and there he was to sail with the head of the Mission in Central Africa. Gertie, a child clinging to each hand, had watched until the coach had rounded the corner and then gone back to the terrible emptiness of the house, where she handed the children over to the nursemaid, then made her way to her bedroom where she sobbed until there were no more tears to shed. Amos had assured her that, the moment they arrived at the mission, he would write with his directions, and until then she must not worry, but pray for him and keep cheerful. She smiled at the memory of how he had gained in strength as she grew more tearful, until it was he who was supporting her. He had waved to all the good folk who wished him well, and stepped into the coach, head held high and a glowing zeal in his eyes that brought back memories of how he had looked when Gertie had first seen him all those years ago, grubby, hair all awry and an intensity in his eyes which had made her heart turn right over. And now this wonderful man, her darling, was gone. She shook herself mentally. What is all this sentimental nonsense? He wasn't gone! Anyone would think he had disappeared from the face of the planet. Why, people had been sailing all over the world for hundreds of years and had still come home to tell the tale. Amos was a good preacher, was loved by all who knew him here, and there was no reason that she could think of why he should not be loved wherever he went.

So Gertie kept reminding herself as those first few, dreadful days passed and she went about her life, responding automatically to the demands of the children and the household, her mind numb and her world in pieces. She wept into her pillow every night in the big, lonely bed, unto all who knew her began to wonder if she were truly ill. Surely it could be not sorrow alone that made her look such a wraith? After all, her husband was treading in the footsteps of many great men that had gone before and he was not alone in his work. He was part of a mission. Nanny expressed these sentiments in her habitual scolding voice and Susan in her more gentle tones, but Gertie seemed unable to lift herself out of the terrible abyss into which she had fallen. Finally, Susan told Mrs Johnson's maid and Mrs Johnson's maid told Mrs Johnson. Mrs Parker was fading away with grief. "And if sunnink wasn't done soon, she would pass away! Thin as a wraith, she looks, and they say she cries sunnink 'orrible awl night. You've got to go to her, ma'am, or she'll die and leave those poor little mites motherless, fatherless little orphings."

Mrs Johnson took the somewhat colourful description of Gertie's plight with the pinch of salt that it deserved, but she was worried, however, that her little friend must be feeling low if even the servants considered it necessary to pass on their gossip to her. So she quickly donned her hat and a light shawl, the weather being unusually clement, even for late May, and hurried round to Beresford street to find out for herself just exactly what the situation was with Gertie. She was ushered into the drawing room, which looked much as it had done ever since Gertie had joined Mrs Mabbett's 'girls' eighteen years ago. The carpets were still threadbare, and the settle looked just as uncomfortable as ever, but Mrs Johnson, ever the stalwart, sat down in its unwelcoming, shiny black surface and spent the moments before Gertie's appearance studying the various rather lurid pictures that were so lovingly framed and put up round the walls, apparently the only additions to the room. She smiled and sighed, once more experiencing the aching lack of children in her own life. But before she herself could become morbid, Gertie appeared, and Mrs Johnson was indeed shocked by the young woman's appearance. She gave a cry and, rising quickly, clasped her friend in her arms. They stood together like this for a long moment, until Gertie gently pulled away and, giving the older woman a watery smile, led her back to the settle.

"It is so good of you to come and see me, my dear friend," she said. "I am being a foolish, silly female, and know that I must lift myself out of this ridiculous humour and rejoice that my husband has been called to preach the Word by God Himself. Only…" she gripped a sodden handkerchief in her hands and her eyes filled with tears again… "Only I miss him *so much.*" And she began sobbing uncontrollable, leaning against her friend's shoulder and giving way to her misery. Mrs Johnson let her cry for a few moments and then began to hush her gently, reminding her of her inner strength which she had shown on so many occasions, and it would only be a few months before her beloved was back in her arms again. The time would pass so swiftly, with the children and her work and the Sunday School and the soup kitchen – "Why, I cannot imagine how you can have had time for a husband at all!" This said with a laugh, pulling Gertie away from her damp shoulder and offering her a fresh, dry kerchief. It had the desired effect and Gertie laughed tremulously, wiping her eyes and jumping up with a guilty cry.

"Oh my dear friend, you are so good to me, but what must you think, taking time to come to me and my not offering you even a crumb. You must have tea and biscuits, for I have eaten enough of yours in my time!" and she rushed to the door, pulling it open in time to cause Susan almost to topple into the room, carrying a tea-tray laden with cups and cakes.

"Oh, my goodness, Susan, how thoughtful of you," she cried as she took the tray from the ever-stolid Susan and placed it on one of the little tables scattered about the room. She helped the preacher's wife to tea and cake and, feeling calmer than she had done for days, she listened while her friend spoke gently and sensibly about the duties of a missionary's wife, and of how special such a woman must be to attract such a man.

"For, you know, your Amos *is* special. Very special. And so are you, my dear. It is a hard burden for you to bear at present, but he will return to you a fulfilled and contented man, and in the meanwhile you must keep reminding yourself what wonderful work he is doing, and how proud of him you must be. We are so lucky with our menfolk, you and I! Would you really have it any other way?"

Gertie began to realise that for all her present loss, she would not want to change a hair on Amos' head. She loved him so much because he was as he was, and secretly acknowledged that, although he had so desperately wanted her to go with him, he had never accused her because of her refusal. Yes, he was a fine man, and she must be a strong woman in return. And so, to the relief of Susan and Nurse, but rather to the vexation of Mrs Johnson's maid, who had relished the idea of a tragedy on a much larger scale, Gertie's eyes remained dry from then on, the fight returned to her spirit and she seemed to grow several inches in height. Gertie was mistress of her situation once again.

++++++++++

And so time passed. It was quite true that once Gertie threw herself into all her duties, being a mother, running the agency and soup kitchen and the Sunday School, not to mention accommodating the various preachers sent to the Chapel to enlighten the dwindling congregation, she had little time to feel lonely. She missed Amos, certainly, with a constant ache, but she also realised that she really did not need him to help in the practical running of her life, not as he needed her! She did not know whether to be pleased or sorry about this, but she had to admit in her innermost heart that it was true. She was not only successful in running all these enterprises, but she was becoming a relatively rich woman. Relative for the area in which she lived, at least, for she had no knowledge of how the 'toffs' as she put it went about things. But when Mrs Johnson, on a friendly visit, suggested that she should look round for a larger house and more help with her domestic duties she was horrified.

"What, leave Beresford Street, after all these years? Why, how would Amos be able to find us? And what would be his thoughts on finding his wife ensconced in a great place with just the seven of us rattling round in it like peas in a pod? And just think of poor Susan and Addie! How would they cope in a bigger house? And as they said, they don't want a whole load of strangers tripping them up and getting under their feet! No, no, I cannot thing of leaving here. And there is no way I would dare even to suggest such an idea to Nurse! She finds her duties hard enough to carry out as it is, what with her knees and her terrible heads!" This last was said with a twinkle in Gertie's eye and Mrs Johnson laughed, saying that Gertie was far too soft on that woman.

"She leads a life of sheer luxury the way you mollycoddle her! It is quite shameful. But really, my dear, if you were able to add one more to your staff, to help Susan if for no other reason, then that would leave you so much more time to attend to all your many commitments. And only think, you could start accompanying me on my ministering again." This time it was Gertie's turn to laugh.

"So all your suggestions for my wellbeing are no more than a selfish desire to see me back again getting covered in filth and fleas simply to make you feel less grimy! Well, I do not need a bigger house in order to do that. I will accompany you and with pleasure, and we can relish the squalor together!"

And with that she hugged her friend, who had to leave to oversee dinner for her little household. At the front door they made plans for the very next day and Gertie returned to her own kitchen, humming happily, much to the amusement of Addie, the kitchen maid, who didn't 'old with ladies of Mrs Parker's situation singin' in front of the servants, nor goin' into the kitchen, neither, for that matter!

++++++++++

A letter came at last. It was the end of July, the weather had been humid and overcast and there were fears of cholera once again, a scourge that hit the town with greater or lesser effect every summer. Gertie had stopped her mercy visits to the poorest quarters and had closed the soup kitchen and Sunday School for a month or so until the danger had passed. After all, as she said to Susan if she got sick and died, what would become of them all? ~this she had written in a long epistle to Amos, not knowing whether he would ever receive any communications from her or whether he himself was safe or even still alive, the directions of his whereabouts having been sent to her some weeks back from a remote mission. So his letter was received with great celebration and delight by the entire household. Everyone had to gather round to hear what the Master had to say about his great adventures, and Gertie commenced reading the letter, with Lucy sitting primly beside her mother on the Horsehair settle, and nurse holding master Jonathan firmly by one hand and Susan holding the other, while Addie hovered shyly in the doorway.

"My dearest Gertrude," Gertie began, while Addie giggled in the background and said, 'Fancy' at the idea of the Missus being called Gertrude! Everyone shushed her and Gertie began again:

My dearest Gertrude,

I hope that you and my little progeny are well.' (More giggles from Addie) 'Words cannot express how much I am missing you all. I pray constantly to God that we may yet be re-united once my work here has been completed. And what work there is to be done! There is so much sickness and poverty, let alone any lack of orthodox religion, that we have to act as doctors, nursemaids, advisors on medication, farming methods and sanitation, as well as being their spiritual advisors! So far we have met only friendliness from the people here, who are quick to learn and grateful for the little help which we are able to give, but conditions in this part of the world are harsh and merciless, with a parched land and little water. If ever a place needed God's help, then this is it.

The journey out was long and several of the party were sick for many days, but I thank God that my internal workings are made of sterner stuff and I was able to help those who were suffering. When we landed at last, we were greeted by the reverend Purdy and his wife and they are the kindest of people. We are the greatest of friends now and I only wish, my beloved wife, that you were here to share in their company and the fortunes of the people native to this country. I know you would make an excellent nurse, but there, I must not indulge in wishful thinking, you did what you thought to be right and a great part of what I love in you is your independent spirit and down-to-earth good sense. However, we could certainly use some of that good sense here at present. I have not the natural patience required for nursing, but I learn!

You say you have closed the Sunday School. Is that wise? We do not want to lose the chance of saving those young souls simply for fear of something which may not materialise! But, as I have already said, I am sure you know best. I suggest you make it plain to all the mothers that the School will open again as soon as the threat of cholera has passed. The soup kitchen is another matter. As you know, I have never been happy knowing that you were mixing with people already suffering from who knows what diseases. Perhaps now is the moment to close it down for good? Still, I leave it to your excellent judgement.

There is so much that is amiss here that I do not know when I can be spared to return home, or even to write often. However, I look forward to your letters and in reading them I hear your gentle voice and can see in my mind your sweet face and laughing eyes...

Here Gertie stopped reading out loud, and, flushing a little, informed the assembled group that the rest of the letter was of a private nature, but that the master sent his love to the children and his regards to everyone in the household. At this nurse hurriedly ushered everyone out into the hall to go about their various tasks, leaving Gertie to read the rest of the letter alone, with moist eyes and a sad heart. Amos loved her so much; if only she had felt able to join him in his mission. So she sat, indulging in a little self-pity for a short while, before giving her mind a little shake, gathering up her skirts and making her way up to the nursery to tell the children how much their father loved them. The rest of the day passed as all other days, except that the little ache in Gertie's heart had grown just that bit larger, and a little less easy to ignore.

Chapter Twenty

The months passed. Sporadic letters came from Amos, and then silence. Gertie threw herself into her various activities, although, since the threat of cholera was still rife in the poorest areas, she kept the soup kitchen and Sunday School closed. Even Mrs Johnson no longer undertook her ministering. But Gertie's agency continued to flourish, and she was gaining a reputation as a first-class businesswoman. Her little office was becoming too small, and she was beginning to wonder what on earth she was to do when, on one momentous day the following June, a letter arrived for her on beautiful, embossed paper. She opened it hurriedly and inside was a short note from Mr Thomas Richardson, founder of the Sunday School Union, asking her if she would be good enough to meet him at his office to discuss a business arrangement, as he understood that she was looking for new premises. If convenient, the first day of July would suit him admirably. Mystified as to how he could have found out such information, she nevertheless wasn't going to 'look a gift 'orse in the teef', as the incorrigible Susan put it, and sent a swift reply agreeing to meet the good man.

The meeting was short and business-like. It seemed Mr Richardson had been following Amos' career as a preacher and after learning that he had become a missionary had enquired after the wellbeing of his wife. Impressed with Gertie's enterprising spirit and learning of her needs, he decided he must meet this paragon, little expecting the slight, girlish figure that walked confidently into his drawing room. He questioned Gertie for what seemed to her an eternity, listened intelligently to her answers and finally offered her a small office at the end of the imposing building on the corner of Powys Street. An affordable rent was agreed, the deal was sealed with a small glass of port wine and Gertie tripped home as happy as any wife could be in the circumstances, clutching the deeds tightly under her pelisse. Mr Meeks soon ratified the agreement and so the business flourished.

Having heard nothing from Amos for several months now, Gertie began to prepare herself for widowhood. Nothing was said and she put on a show of happy expectancy whenever the children talked of 'when Papa comes home', but in her heart she was certain he was dead. Suppose she never found out, never knew what his ending had been? But she was too busy to dwell for long on such dark thoughts; they constantly lay, like something festering, at the back of her mind. Then, on a blustery day in October 1861, another letter arrived for her, this time with all the marks of having journeyed many thousands of miles, judging by its grimy and crumpled appearance. The writing scrawled across the page and in places was almost illegible from damp and a goodly sprinkling of indescribable little creatures, but she deciphered it at last, and, without waiting to explain to the mystified Susan, breathlessly instructed her to fetch a hansom without delay. Then she rushed upstairs, to much clucking at such indecorous behaviour from Addie, who was extremely proper in her ways, kissed the children who were just preparing for school, and rushed down again, gathering pelisse, gloves and reticule as she flew. She climbed into the cab, miraculously produced by the capable Susan, called not to expect her before dark, and was gone. Slowly Susan made her way up the steps to the front door, a worried frown on her brow. Where was her dearest Gertie taking herself off to in such a rush, and without so much as a maidservant to look after her? Had she heard from Amos? Was he dead, or in London, or what? She went into the parlour and picked up the letter which Gertie had dropped in her haste. Susan prided herself on her honesty, but for once she put aside her morals and decided that she must read this letter, for everyone's sake. Bundling the children out of the house with a lame explanation of their mother's sudden exit and exhorting Addie to clean all the vegetables thoroughly – "I don't want my teeth ground down to stumps with all that grit you left on yesterday, my girl." She went back into the parlour and slowly unravelled the spidery script.

"My dear Mrs Parker," she read.

"I am writing to inform you that, while it is not of a terminal nature, your husband, dearest Amos, is subject to fits of the fever and it had been agreed that he is to return to England, once the present bout is ended.

"No one could have been more devout a disciple of the Good Lord, nor worked harder to improve the lot of the poor souls in his care, but his health at last has…" Susan puzzled over the next word for some time, but finally decided it was 'failed'. She read on: "Failed, and the time has come for him to return to the bosom of his family, where I know you will care for him until he is himself again.

"We do not know when he can be got to the coast, nor when a boat will be available, but the shipping company which sails from these shores should be able to furnish you with such details. The directions are," and here an address in London had been written in a slightly clearer hand.

"I remain your most obedient servant,

"Hugh Purdy, Minister."

Susan sat for a long time allowing this information to sink in. So that was where the missus had gone. To London! *Gawd Almighty*, she thought. *I hope she knows what she's doing.*

Gertie arrived at the offices of the shipping company after a long and gruelling journey, the cab depositing her at the new railway station built rather grandly in the Italian style. This was Gertie's first journey by railway, and she found being squashed into the little carriage with a large number of ladies and gentlemen rather strange, but she was too concerned about the reason for her journey to be excited by the new sights and smells. The fare was extortionate, but she hardly cared as she left the terminal and hurried down the street to where the shipping offices were situated, fairly flying into the imposing building. But after hours of frustration speaking to one employee after another and exhausting questions and even arguments, she was no wiser as to her husband's situation than she had been before the letter had arrived. All she knew was that ships had docked at various African ports and ships had sailed from those ports, but where they were bound for and who were the passengers she could not learn.

"But do you not have a passenger list?" she asked one particularly officious young man. He merely replied that they do on the way out, but on the return who knows what landlubber would demand a berth. Gertie drew herself up to her extremely imposing height and told the young man in no uncertain terms that her husband was no 'landlubber' as he called it, but a fine, upstanding Minister of the Cloth, and she would report such insolence. But, although a rather more senior gentleman apologised for his underling's lapse of manners, he was able to give her no more help than any of the others. Frustrated, dispirited and suffering complete exhaustion, she finally gave up the search and arrived home in a state of utter despair. Amos may be on his way home. That is all she was able to tell the breathlessly curious household, and there she left it.

In December the country was cast into terrible gloom by the death of Prince Albert, and although she tried to make Christmas as jolly as possible for the children, Gertie felt the loss of the Queen's husband with a terrible foreboding.

If someone living in such cosseted conditions could die of typhoid, what chance was there for her own beloved husband, prey to all the strange diseases she was sure were rife in those faraway lands? The cholera threat had passed in the town and Gertie had started up the Sunday School and soup kitchen again and with the bad weather the poor began to wander back to drink the soup at least, although the school attendance had become very sparse now that there was no Amos to tell his thrilling stories. Gertie did her best and even little Mr Probyn agreed to teach the children some of the more suitable hymns, which they found they enjoyed singing. But Gertie's heart was no longer in it and the joy which she had once felt seemed to have forsaken her. But among her other gifts, Susan discovered that she, too, was a very able storyteller and took on more and more of the onerous task of teaching the children, while Gertie either took very little part in the service or remained at home to look after her own children on Sundays. And then, on a dreadful day in February, with the wind beating the sleet against the windows and howling like a banshee round the house, every lamp and candle lighted to keep out the dark, there came a loud knocking at the front door. Susan rushed to open it, asking who could be calling at this hour of the evening, and, as Gertie hurried down the stairs, certain that her beloved had succumbed to some unheard-of disease, or fallen prey to a herd of wild animals, Susan set up such a screeching that she got the impression that one of the wild animals had somehow managed to spirit itself from Africa and land in her hallway. But then she stood stock still and felt all the blood drain from her body. Standing framed in the doorway, his black clothed sodden and flecked with sleet, was Amos. Thin, his grey and drawn face covered in a long beard, he looked like a wraith. Gertie stared for what seemed an eternity, and then both women rushed forward, Susan shutting the door against the howling gale, and Gertie crying and hugging the dripping figure, dragging him into the light and warmth of the parlour. They took off his coat and his hat, sat him in the most comfortable chair and pulled off his boots. After Susan's first scream of surprise, neither woman spoke, and, apart from Gertie's occasional sobs, there was silence in the room. The man was exhausted and ill, and both knew instinctively that to rain questions down on him now would be disastrous. The parlour door stood ajar, and two pairs of enormous eyes peered curiously in, both children also sensing that now was no time to get under anyone's feet. Nurse swiftly removed them upstairs again while the two women chafed Amos' feet and hands and Gertie gently laid his head back on a cushion. Without having said a word, he closed his eyes and slept.

It was several hours before Amos at last woke up and was able to accept a little tea and bread and butter. Susan had taken herself off to the scullery to instruct Addie in the art of making gruel and tasty morsels for 'the master's delicate innards' as she graphically put it, while Gertie sat quietly opposite her husband as he slept, questions running round and round in her head, all unable at present to be answered. She could almost shout with frustration at not knowing what had happened but knew that all she must endure at present was patience. Irksome though that was, the realisation that her dearest was at last back in the fastness of their home began to creep over her and the silence was finally broken but her great sobs of joy. Her Amos was home! He had come back to her. Sick, perhaps broken even, but he was home, and she vowed that nothing, nothing would ever separate them again. She would love and cherish this man until her dying day and not all the poor in the world would take her away from ministering to him.

It was while she was indulging in these somewhat melodramatic sentiments that Amos opened his eyes and sat up with a start, looking round wildly and half rising. She hurried quickly to him, hushing him and assuring him that he was indeed in his own home and by his own fireside. He looked up at her and his grey, thin face softened into a wondering smile. Amos took Gertie in his arms and kissed her, long and passionately, then finally lay back on his cushion again and slept once more. Gertie's heart leapt. Her husband was home.

Chapter Twenty-One

Amos was never really quite well after he came home from Africa. His description of his travels and the stories he told of his journeys through such strange and wild places, and of the kindness he met from the people, were enthralling, but he would not dwell on his final journey home. Gertie did not press him, being only thankful that he was back at last. But it had obviously sapped all his strength and aged him to a degree, his wayward hair streaked with grey and his complexion less rosy. Although he returned to his ministry in the Chapel and the congregation began to grow again, bouts of fever often laid him low, and it was at those times that Gertie feared for his future. She felt he would not make old bones and although she herself was still small and slim, she knew she was strong as an ox and unless something like cholera or typhoid struck her down, she would doubtless live to a ripe old age and be a nuisance to all and sundry.

Once he had recovered his strength, Gertie, Susan and Lucy insisted he shave off his beard. Since complaining that, apart from Jonathan, he was beset by a parcel of women made no difference to their remonstrances, he succumbed at last and was led, laughing and declaiming to a chair, where Susan liberally covered his face with lather and removed the offending whiskers. With his face bare and his hair trimmed, the women all pronounced him to be reasonably attractive and at least did not look like something from another planet. With that he had to be satisfied, although secretly he had felt that a beard, a small one at least, gave him stature and confidence. But he need not have worried. His congregation, like Gertie's agency, went from strength to strength, until at last they had to leave the little chapel by the river and rent a larger one further in town. Mr Richardson tried on several occasions to encourage them to move their family to larger premises, but on this Gertie was adamant. She had lived most of her life in the house in Beresford Street, her children had been born there, and, as far as she was concerned, she would die there.

"They'll take me out of here feet first, or I'll know the reason why!"

She had declared, reverting to her workhouse demeanour and since Amos was perfectly happy to remain in the only house he had ever known as home, they continued to live in the cosy old building, surrounded by friendly neighbours and visited often by the wives and sometimes even the men, from the arsenal.

Gertie and Mrs Johnson remained firm friends and as the years passed and many of the dreadful hovels in the worst part of the town were demolished to make way for better housing, the two ladies were able at last to turn their attention to the proper education of the poorer children, opening up first one and then several day schools, Gertie sending some of the more promising girls from the workhouse to study teaching, with a grant from an anonymous benefactor on the proviso that they returned to teach in one of the local new schools. With Gertie's own children growing up fast, Susan left at last to fulfil a coveted ambition to become a nurse, but she and Gertie met as often as their busy lives would allow, meeting in a little tea shop in the High Street and playing the grand ladies of fashion. Jonathan joined the Royal Artillery and on bringing some of his friends home, one poor, hapless young man was ensnared by Lucy, as her father put it, and soon she and her William were married. They shared their married quarters with Jonathan, who rented some rather fine rooms near the barracks, but very soon Gertie discovered to her delight that she and Amos were to become grandparents. Not having had the heart to dismiss Nurse, Lucy was able to employ her to care for her own little ones, and so everyone was happy. Until, that is, that fateful day on the third of September 1878, a day that will stay in the minds of all who experienced the tragedy. For it was on that day that the steamer, the *Princess Alice* had crashed and sunk with the loss of nearly six hundred lives.

The day had been warm and sultry, and Gertie had just finished locking up her little office when she heard a faint commotion coming from the region of the river at the far end of the high street. Weary from a day dealing with rather difficult clients, who were no longer grateful for any place which she could find them and looking forward to the luxury of a hot bath when she got home, she was about to ignore the distant shouting when suddenly one of her neighbours came running up to her, tears streaming down her face.

"Oh, Mrs Parker, oh, it's terrible, terrible. Oh we must go to see what can be done. Come, come quickly." And dragging the astonished Gertie by the sleeve she began running down the high street. Gertie realised that others were running too, and soon it seemed as if the whole of Woolwich was heading for the river. *Like lemmings*, thought Gertie, not yet realising what had happened. But she managed to get her breathless companion to explain to her at last, and then she couldn't run fast enough to get to the scene of the disaster. But the scene, when they did finally arrive, was horrible beyond all description. Crowds had collected on the wharf and the pier, and it seemed that bodies of the dead and dying were being brought in from all directions. Gertie and her companion rushed into the steamboat office and there, filling the floor and the little balcony outside were countless bodies, many of them children. Gertie went from body to body, cries of horror wrenched from her as she recognised neighbours, colleagues and many acquaintances among the dead. As she stood in anguish, helpless as the tide of horror washed over her, a man came up to her. His face was pale and grim as he held out his hand to her.

"William Law, ma'am, second steward. I believe you are Mrs Parker?"

Gertie felt herself go faint and gripped the mantel to keep from falling. Not her Lucy! Not her little ones! Oh, dear God, not those too. She managed to speak, although the words would scarcely come:

'Yes, I am Gertrude Parker. You have some news for me? My family...?'

'I am sorry. Your husband, ma'am. As soon as he heard, he was one of the first to dive into the river and he saved many of the poor souls. But his strength gave out and he went under before we could throw him a line. If you will come with me, ma'am.'

Gertie followed him out, her mind blank and her body moving automatically. Amos? Dead? Surely not! It was all some dreadful mistake. He couldn't be dead. But when she was taken a little further down the wharf, there, still and pale and silent, his clothes sodden and his hair still in the unruly tufts that had so softened her heart, lay the man who had been her lifelong joy. She stood swaying for a moment, and then a great and terrible wail was rent from her lips and she threw herself on her beloved. She was pulling his hair, she was shaking his head and screaming at him, 'Amos! Amos! Don't be dead! Oh, don't leave me like this. Oh, Amos, Amos.' And she broke into great sobs as she lay across his body. Crooning softly to her, Mr Law at last pulled her away and led her, now silent and almost lifeless herself, back to the office. There surrounded by dead bodies and sobbing relatives, a neighbour took Gertie and forced tea down her, chafing her hands and talking gently to her. Kind friends managed to get her back home at last, where Susan, who had been directing the removal of the injured up to the workhouse infirmary, was standing on the steps ready to receive her and tend to her 'dear Missus'.

Gertie remembered little of the following days. The funeral was attended by almost the entire Arsenal, none of them having had time for such luxuries as a river trip. She went through the service as in a dream, Mr Johnson kindly officiating and his wife preparing the funeral meats. Lucy and the family gave what support they could, while Jonathan, who was stationed in India, sent a message of gentle love through the telegraph office. But, for all the kindness, Gertie remained little more than half alive herself. Her beloved was gone; what point was there in going on living? She wanted to die, to dissolve into oblivion, for this misery to end.

Susan returned to the house in Beresford Street whenever she was able to spare time from tending the sick and the survivors from the disaster. But she herself was exhausted and could do little more than try to revive the spirits of her dearest Gertie, the name she had been ordered in no uncertain terms to call the missus once she had taken up nursing.

"For it is a noble profession, Susan, and there can be no social barriers between us, you and me," Gertie had pronounced. But now the only barrier was Gertie's loss of interest in anything. When she did bother to get up she threw on her clothes and skimped her hair back into a knot, but mostly she stayed in bed all day, eating nothing of the dainty morsels the stolid and reliable Addie tried tempting her with. On the occasions of one of Susan's visits, some weeks after Amos' death, Gertie seemed even more morose than usual, sitting in a chair in the parlour, the ashes of yesterday's fire still in the grate and the room covered in a light film of coal dust. Addie was almost wringing her hands in her distress.

'She won't let me in there to tidy up, miss,' she said, 'what's going to become of her I don't know, and that's 'God's truth!'

Susan pushed open the door into the parlour and was shocked at what she saw. Gertie looked like a wraith and neither turned nor spoke as she walked up to her. Suddenly a wave of anger flooded over Susan. This woman wasn't the only one who had lost loved ones, many of them losing whole families. Certainly she had lost her husband, but she had her children and her sturdy and loving grandchildren to care for her, not to mention all the friends and neighbours who were showing her such kindness. She had no business wallowing in this grief, any more than had the Queen herself, who had lost much of the respect of her subjects by shutting herself away as she had done. Susan took hold of Gertie's cold hands and looked down at her. When she spoke, her voice sounded harsh and she shocked even herself by its severity.

'Gertie, indulging in all this misery is not going to bring Amos back. Either you lift yourself out of this state, or you will quickly lose your friends and all of us who are trying to help you. We cannot do that unless you help yourself. Now, come upstairs with me and we will try to make you presentable. No,' as Gertie snatched her hands away and tried to remonstrate, 'I won't listen to no arguments. You will come with me now, and then we shall go and visit Mrs Johnson who will know just how to go on.'

Finally allowing herself to be led upstairs, her face and hands washed, and her hair brushed until it began to shine once more, 'just like it used to, when you was the missus,' said Susan, gently pinning it up into a more becoming style, Gertie began to relax. Dear, kind Susan! She could not lose her as well. She must try, try to live once more, though for what she had no idea. The children? The soup kitchen? The poor? Gertie almost laughed. How could she care for those things, give succour to those people, without Amos? But she allowed Susan to do as she liked with her. What did it matter, after all. She sighed and sat obediently under the nurse's gentle attentions.

'There we are, now turn round and let's 'ave a look at you. That's a lot better. You was beginning to look like tow pennoth of Gawd 'help us.'

This brought a wan smile to the widow's pale lips, as she managed to retort:

'Really, Susan, you're incorrigible. You don't need to lapse into your coarse ways for my sake!'

But this was said with a gentle laugh and Gertie followed Susan downstairs once more, her step a little lighter than it had been for weeks. The waves of misery were receding momentarily and although she knew they would return, she also knew that it was up to herself alone to make them recede to the edge of awareness. Could she find the strength to do it? She didn't know, but for now the clouds were lifting and that was all she cared for at present.

The two women made their way to the Johnson's house, the November day already 'drawing in', as Susan put it and were welcomed by that good lady, now a little stooped, her beautiful black hair streaked with grey. They all went into the parlour, where a welcoming fire was already alight, and Gertie was placed in the fireside chair, Susan and Mrs Johnson sitting on the ancient settle. A young, rosy-faced maid brought in the inevitable laden tray and they all sat round, sipping hot tea and nibbling fairy cakes. Gertie realised how hungry she was and had worked her way through three cakes before she was aware of how greedy she must seem. Guiltily brushing the crumbs from her skirt into the hearth, she tried to concentrate on what the older woman was saying, the warmth and unaccustomed food making her feel relaxed and sleepy at last. Gradually she became aware that Mrs Johnson was addressing some remarks to her. She opened her eyes with a start and begged apology.

'I am so sorry, my dear ma'am, I must have dozed for a moment. The walk in the cold and the warm fire, you understand? You were saying?'

Smiling and gently retrieving Gertie's cup before it fell into the fender, Mrs Johnson said,

'I was merely asking if you would like another cup, Gertie dear. You certainly look as if you need feeding up! What is that Addie about?'

'That's just what I was saying, Mrs Johnson, ma'am. Not that it's Addie's fault! I know for a fact that many's the decent dinner she's had to take down to the new soup kitchens because it was not even touched. I've been telling Gertie, Mrs Parker, that is, if you don't eat you'll turn into a wraith. And we've got our hands full enough up at the infirmary without another mouth to feed!'

'You are quite right, nurse Susan, we must all eat to keep up our strength, whatever our personal suffering.'

Then, turning to Gertie, she took the opportunity to begin her gentle lecture. She had known that it would need some while before she could talk to Gertie in this way, but now she considered that it was time for the widow to stop her public grieving and look to the future.

'You see, my dear,' she began, and then hesitated for a moment. It was not going to be as easy as she thought. Shocked as she had been by Gertie's appearance, she was not prepared for the depth of misery in the widow's eyes. They seemed to be looking into the abyss without hope. It took every ounce of the experience of a Minister's wife to lead Gertie from 'death's dark vale' and back into the light once more. She stared into the fire, wishing she could escape into the magic castles glowing among the flames, and then, shaking herself mentally, she began again. "Your husband, my dear, was a great believer. He had no thought for himself; he suffered pain and disease and even great danger and finally gave his life for others. Do you think he would want you to allow yourself to waste away because he is lost to you on this earth? Have you not understood, after living with him for all those years, that his faith was so great he was certain you would be reunited in Heaven? Gertie, he never doubted for one moment! He gave his all for Christ upon earth, in the blessed belief of life hereafter. How can you fail him now? He would want, expect, know, that you would continue with your good works, uplifted in the knowledge that, soon, in the twinkling of an eye, you will be together again, with no more pain, no more misery. Gertie you must live. For his sake, you must go on living, however hard, no matter how many black moments you suffer, you must go on, as he did, never faltering. I do not know how strong your belief is, but let Amos be your Cross, your Guide, for I am sure you believe, as all good Christians must, in the Resurrection."

A long silence followed this impassioned speech. The room was dark as the candles had guttered out and only the fire drew eerie patterns on the walls. The maid had come in once to renew the candles but had been quickly whisked away by Susan and the two women were left in the silence, each to pursue their own thoughts, Mrs Johnson exhausted by her passion, and not sure if she had done the right thing; Gertie to weigh the older woman's words and gradually to allow the realisation of how selfish she had been to wash over her. She began to cry and apologise effusively, until Mrs Johnson, laughing with relief, handed her a clean kerchief and scolded,

"Come, my dear, you are not now going to indulge in abject guilt to replace your self-pity! You have gone through your mourning, as is only right and proper, now you have to pick up the pieces and begin again. You have a business to run and work to do. After all, do you suppose the poor have miraculously disappeared, just because you have not been there to tend them? No, as our good Lord said, they will be with us always. Now, the good wives of the arsenal have been keeping Gertie's Soup Bowl going, and some of your excellent girls have run the Sunday School, so I shall expect you tomorrow evening to go down with me to ensure that all is running as it should.' She stood up, holding out her hand. 'Goodbye, my dear, until tomorrow, when I shall call for you at seven o'clock sharp."

Gertie took her hand and then threw herself into the proffered arms, her thanks muffled in the good lady's bosom.

And so it was. Whenever the waves of misery threatened to engulf her, Gertie's though turned always to Amos and she found strength in his strength, faith in his faith. In her heart she knew that it was he who had always been her God, but she was a good Christian woman, as Mrs Johnson had said, and if he believed in the afterlife, then so did she. They *would* meet again, because Amos had said so.

The agency flourished and she and Mr Richardson, who had founded the great Woolwich Building Society, became firm friends. Gertie would sometimes be invited to dinner at the big house, and then, after a good but plain meal, they would sit sipping wine, the pleasant smell of his cigar adding to the comfort and peace of their surroundings. They would talk of many things: of Gertie's hopes for the town and of the many books which he had lent her. Together they explored poetry and the great tomes in his library and gradually Gertie realised that, while not always happy, she was content.

Then, one day – it was in the middle of September 1888, just ten years after Amos' death – a letter arrived at the house in Beresford Street. It looked very grand, but something about it was familiar. Gertie's heart turned right over. It was! Yes, she was sure it was! It was identical to the one she had received as a little girl from the Queen. Well, not really the Queen, but…she quickly tore open the cream embossed envelope and spread out the single sheet. Then she sat down plump on the stairs. She read the letter through several times. No, there was no mistake. Rushing through the kitchen, where a delicious smell of baking was wafting from the ovens, she screamed out in the most unladylike manner, "Addie! Addie, the queen wants to meet me. I'm to go to Buckingham Palace and get some sort of honour! Addie, where are you?"

Running from the scullery, wiping her hands on a cloth, her face pale, she cried,

"Why, ma'am, whatever is the to do? Are you hurt? Is the Queen dead? What has happened?"

"No, no, dear Addie, the Queen is alive and well and I am to go to Buckingham Palace to meet her! See, here is the letter, and oh, Addie, she has signed it *herself*!"

Addie took the letter and while she exclaimed over it and blessed herself, Gertie started running round in a demented fashion asking what she should wear, and how should she answer such a command. At last Addie sat her down and brought her a cup of strong, sweet tea, which Gertie hated but drank it all the same, and then, in the kitchen, among all the pots and pans and fresh baked bread, they discussed how they should set about the arrangements for this wonderful visit. First of all, the missus must go to see Mr Richardson, for he was mentioned in the letter as being the one who recommended Gertie for the honour. He would know how to go about things. Then she must purchase a suitable dress and gloves and shoes and…

“Oh, Addie, these things are so expensive, and I have just drawn up new plans for a night hostel for the homeless! How shall I pay for that if I am to spend all this money on myself?”

But Addie, ever practical, shooshed the ‘missus’ and insisted that Gertie could well afford to spend a little of her hard-earned money on herself.

“When did you last spend a penny on your own wardrobe, I should like to know? It all goes on those drunken layabouts and little thanks you get for your labours. You go and indulge yourself for a change, ma’am, for, after all, you can’t meet the Queen looking like a fishwife, now, can you?”

Gertie started to remonstrated that there was nothing wrong with being a fishwife, but she was bundled upstairs to change for dinner, ‘for you must begin as you mean to go on, now that you are to be presented’, explained the glowing Addie, imagining an improved status for the entire household.

The clothes were bought, the letter, with Mr Richardson’s help, was sent and at last the day came for Gertie to set out. Rather than arriving at the Palace smelling of soot and unwashed bodies, Gertie chose to travel to London by coach, not caring much for railway trains. She had her own small little carriage now and this was brought round to the house, neighbours coming out to wish her a safe journey and to send their love to the Queen, ‘Gawd bless ’er’, no rancour in their pleasure at their neighbour’s good fortune. Gertie waved to them until they were no longer visible and then she sat back with a sigh of relief. She pulled the blanket round her, realising that she was cold and, since she had not been able to eat any breakfast in the excitement, she was also hungry. She smiled. Well, it was not the first time! Her thoughts drifted back to her childhood. Oh, wouldn’t Amos be proud of her now! Her dream came true at last. At last she would be able to tell the Queen, face to face, what it was like to be a workhouse child, to be poor and unloved and un-cared for, and how hard her husband had worked in his ministry. And Amos would be there with her, giving her strength as he had always done. She imagined him standing beside her, urging her on, his hair standing on end in its wayward tufts and looking so handsome that her heart still turned over with love for him. She leant back on the squabs and smiled.
Dear Amos.